Her emotions were

Chelsea was concerned about Sam's injury. She was also excited about her feelings for him and that he'd been so open with her. Overwhelmed, she breathed deeply, fighting for control.

Sam nudged her. "Chelsea. Please don't be upset. Whatever it is, it's not a problem. Truth be told…" He took her hand and pulled her close to his chest, resting his head on top of hers once more. "I needed this more than I realized. I missed you and I want to start seeing you again. Are you okay with that?"

Her tears were blurring her vision and clogging her throat. Not ashamed to let him see how she was feeling, she drew back and looked at him and nodded.

"I'm glad," he said softly, before lowering his head to brush his lips across hers.

That kiss was unlike any that Chelsea had shared with Sam before. It left her a little breathless…and more stirred by a kiss than she could remember.

Dear Reader,

The idea for *A Priceless Find* has been around for a while. Chelsea Owens, my heroine, first appeared in my November 2014 release, *A Child's Christmas*, and she's been clamoring for her own story ever since. Once you've read *A Priceless Find*, you'll appreciate that if Chelsea sets her sights on a goal, she goes after it wholeheartedly! In the face of that sort of good-natured determination, I had to give in and write Chelsea's story.

One aspect of writing *A Priceless Find* that I particularly enjoyed was having the famous Isabella Stewart Gardner Museum heist for inspiration. For those readers who are interested in learning about the actual heist, you can do so through the Gardner Museum's website. The crime remains unsolved to date.

If you would like to use *A Priceless Find* for your book club, discussion questions are available on my website at kate-james.com/book-clubs.

I hope you'll enjoy reading Chelsea and Sam's story as much as I did writing it!

As always, I would love to hear from you. You can connect with me through my website (kate-james.com), Facebook page (Facebook.com/katejamesbooks), Twitter (Twitter.com/katejamesbooks) or mail me at PO Box 446, Schomberg, ON, L0G 1T0, Canada.

Thank you for choosing to spend your valuable leisure time with one of my books.

Kate

HEARTWARMING

A Priceless Find

—

Kate James

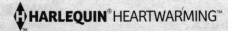

Recycling programs
for this product may
not exist in your area.

ISBN-13: 978-0-373-36858-7

A Priceless Find

This edition published by arrangement with Harlequin Books S.A.

For questions and comments about the quality of this book, please contact us at CustomerService@Harlequin.com.

® and TM are trademarks of Harlequin Enterprises Limited or its corporate affiliates. Trademarks indicated with ® are registered in the United States Patent and Trademark Office, the Canadian Intellectual Property Office and in other countries.

Printed in U.S.A.

Kate James spent much of her childhood abroad before attending university in Canada. She built a successful business career, but her passion has always been literature. As a result, Kate turned her energy to her love of the written word. Kate's goal is to entertain her readers with engaging stories featuring strong, likable characters. Kate has been honored with numerous awards for her writing. She and her husband, Ken, enjoy traveling and the outdoors with their beloved Labrador retrievers.

To all the readers and book reviewers who support my work and make it possible for me to do what I love.

Once again, I would like to recognize the hard work, dedication, professionalism and sheer brilliance of the Harlequin team working behind the scenes to help make each of my books the very best it can be. I would especially like to thank Victoria Curran, Kathryn Lye and Paula Eykelhof for their support and invaluable contributions.

CHAPTER ONE

CHELSEA'S HEART TRIPPED at the sight of the bright yellow Do Not Cross police barricade tape and blue-and-white flashing lights. Peering through her windshield, she couldn't tell for certain this far down Willowbrook Avenue, but it looked as if all the activity was in front of the Sinclair Art Gallery.

It was too early for any of her colleagues to be at work. Whatever was going on, at least none of them would be hurt...*or worse.*

That was her overactive imagination again, she chastised herself. It was probably something as mundane as a malfunction in the gallery's security system.

No. That would explain the police cars but not the barricade tape.

But what else could it be?

Then she thought of the gallery's curator, her friend and mentor, Mr. Hadley, the only person who was occasionally at work before she was.

Chelsea's heart rate kicked up another notch, and she had trouble breathing.

All she could think of was Mr. Hadley.

Pressing down on the accelerator, she sped toward the gallery. As she got closer, she realized the tape wasn't in front of the gallery, after all. Her relief was short-lived, since whatever was going on involved the jewelry store next door. She was very fond of Mr. and Mrs. Rochester, the elderly couple who owned All That Glitters and Shines. She didn't want any harm to befall them, either.

She slowed her ancient Honda Civic to a crawl near the storefront. Judging by the shards of glass strewn across the sidewalk, it had to be a break-in.

How many times had she urged Mr. Rochester to install an enclosed display cabinet on the outside wall—or, at a minimum, security bars—so something like this wouldn't happen? Mr. Rochester always dismissed the idea good-naturedly, saying it wasn't necessary in a friendly place like Camden Falls.

Craning her neck to see inside, she could make out shattered cases and toppled shelving before her view was obstructed by a tall man wearing a Camden Falls Police Department jacket. He was assisting someone across the room. As they turned toward a seating area, she glimpsed the other person.

"Oh, no!" Chelsea quickly pulled over to the curb behind a police cruiser. She slammed her vehicle into Park and jumped out. Ducking under the police tape, she rushed toward the entrance.

"Ma'am!" a police officer who'd been standing by the door called after her. "Ma'am, that's a crime scene. You can't go in there!"

He reached for her, but she evaded his grasp. Her only thought was of Mr. Rochester. "I most certainly can! I'm a friend of the owner's," she stated and pushed her way in through the door.

She couldn't hold back a gasp when she saw Mr. Rochester. He was sitting on a settee, slumped over, his normally ruddy complexion parchment white. A paramedic crouched in front of him and was working to staunch the flow of blood from a wound on his temple.

Ignoring the officer who'd followed her in and dodging another who'd moved to intercept her, she ran over to Mr. Rochester. Dropping to her knees next to where the paramedic was, she touched his knee. "Mr. Roch—"

Before she could finish, a hand clamped around her upper arm and tugged her back up on her feet.

"Hey!" she started to protest, but the words died in her throat as her eyes met the steely blue ones of the cop she'd seen through the window. He was wearing plain clothes under his CFPD jacket and exuded an air of authority.

"Miller!" he called, apparently to the cop who'd been outside. "Who is this and how did she get in here?"

Miller shot Chelsea an exasperated look. "I have no idea who she is, other than that she says she's a friend of his." He pointed at Mr. Rochester. "She ignored the tape and ran past me. I tried to stop her…" He glanced down, but not quickly enough for Chelsea to miss the flush spreading from his neck to his cheeks. "She got by me, Detective," he mumbled. "Sorry."

"You've got to be kidding," the detective retorted. "Well, get her out of here."

"No. Wait!" Chelsea interjected. The detective and Miller both turned to her, but she barely noticed Miller. There was something commanding in the detective's eyes, in his bearing. She supposed he was good-looking, in that tough-and-rugged way, but the frown and obvious exasperation in his eyes didn't do much for his appeal. "It's not the officer's fault," she said. "So there's no point scolding him."

The detective raised a brow, and she thought she saw the corner of his mouth twitch.

"I'm Chelsea Owens," she continued and stuck out her hand with such resolve she didn't give him much choice but to shake it. "I'm a sales associate at the Sinclair Gallery next door. Please, let me stay with Mr. Rochester. He's hurt and…" She motioned around them. "And all this. This store means everything to him and Mrs. Rochester. He could use a friend right now," she said, as the paramedic finished applying a bandage and joined his colleague at a nearby gurney.

The detective held her gaze for several heartbeats. The strong jaw and sharp features seemed to soften—definitely adding to his attractiveness—and he nodded. "All right. But stay with him. Don't move around and don't touch anything. Miller," he called to the other officer. "Don't let her contaminate the scene. If she causes any problems, I'm holding you responsible." Lowering his voice, he murmured something to Miller that Chelsea couldn't hear.

"Understood, Detective Eldridge," Miller responded.

"Just a minute," Chelsea interrupted, drawing Detective Eldridge's attention again. The look in his eyes, not altogether unfriendly but… daunting, made her think better of arguing.

She remained silent and watched him move away. He was tall. At least a couple of inches over six feet. Broad-shouldered, with a confident, efficient gait. Admonishing herself for getting distracted at a time like this, she turned back to Mr. Rochester.

SAM ELDRIDGE WALKED OVER to a couple of crime scene technicians who were taking pictures and dusting for prints.

The older technician, Mike Kincaid, looked up at him. "What's your call on this one?" he asked with a grin. "Prints or no prints?"

It was a game the techs liked to play with Sam. He was right far more often than he was wrong about whether they'd find any evidence. In this case, he didn't want to hazard a guess. Pros tended to leave very little behind. He'd dealt with enough of them in Boston to know that for a fact. But he was getting mixed signals about this incident. There were indications that pros were involved. They hadn't come in through the broken front window. They'd entered from the back without forcing the door open. On the other hand, once they were inside, not only had they broken the large front window, they'd gone to town on the interior. There was too much damage for a pro. Whoever did this would've had time to steal much more if he—or they—had caused less damage. Could it have been personal? "I'm not putting odds on this one," he replied.

"That's a shame," Mike said. "I might've had you this time."

"You've got something for me?" Sam asked hopefully.

"No, but if I was to put money on it…" Mike looked around. "This is sloppy. Amateurish. I'd say we'll find some kind of evidence."

Sam slid his hands into his pants pockets and nodded. "I hope you're right." He glanced over at a display table filled with sparkly diamond engagement rings. He'd done plenty of research when he'd bought Katherine's ring, wanting it to be perfect. The bittersweet memory of the giddy excitement he'd felt back then at the prospect of marrying his high-school sweetheart taunted him. In the years since she'd left, he'd resigned himself to the likelihood that he'd never feel that way again. But despite the passage of time, he remembered enough to know that the display case contained pricey pieces. None appeared to be missing.

It didn't make sense.

Looking around, Sam considered again whether the motivation was something other than theft or if whoever had broken in had lost his temper during the process. But if theft wasn't the point, what was?

He turned back to where Rochester, the owner, was sitting. The guy had to be in his seventies. He'd been injured, which—considering the time of the break-in—probably hadn't been part of the plan. Blunt-force trauma had rendered him unconscious. For how long was undetermined. The paramedics had bandaged his temple and were getting ready to transport him to the hospital to be checked for concussion.

The young woman—Chelsea Owens— was sitting close to Rochester, an arm draped around his shoulders and one of his hands held in her own. She was talking to him so softly that Sam couldn't make out the words, but it was obvious that she cared about the old man.

The way she'd charged into his crime scene was…peculiar. It was extraordinary enough that he'd asked Miller to run her to see if anything popped.

Sam took a moment to study her.

She had enormous green eyes, delicate features and a full mouth painted a strong red. She had short black hair. He figured it took some sort of product to get it all spiky like that on top. She wasn't very tall, five foot four or five at most. She wore a short black dress under a black coat and appeared to have a slim, athletic build. He glanced down and noticed her black stockings. They had a sexy pattern on them. He had to admit there was no faulting her legs.

Not that he'd dated much since Katherine had left him, but when he did, his taste ran to the tall, blonde, leggy type. Chelsea had the legs, but that was about it. Yet he felt a stirring, a tug of attraction that wasn't customary for him. It wasn't entirely because of how she looked. It was the courage she'd shown. She was feisty, and that appealed to him. So did how gentle and caring she was with the old man.

He caught himself smiling. How many people would barge into a crime scene out of concern for the well-being of an acquaintance? And, no small feat, get by a couple of burly cops to do it? He knew that the psychology of some criminals was to come back to the scene of the crime while it was under investigation. That was the reason he'd asked Miller to run her, although he hadn't truly believed Chelsea Owens had anything to do with the break-in. As he'd expected, Miller reported that other than a speeding ticket, she was clean. There was nothing on her record that suggested criminal activity.

Sam turned his attention to Rochester again. If he hadn't come in early—deviating from his normal routine because he hadn't been able to sleep and thought he'd get the month-end inventory done before the store opened—the place would've been unoccupied. Rochester hadn't seen his assailant, nor did he have any recollection of what had happened. Short-term memory loss wasn't uncommon with the type of head injury he'd sustained.

Did the perpetrator or perpetrators go ballistic because they'd expected to find the store empty, and Rochester had spoiled whatever they'd had in mind? Then again, the intruder should've known someone was inside since the alarm system hadn't been armed. If not, that pointed to an amateur again.

At Rochester's age, the blow could've been fatal. Sam's anger, immediate and intense, was unproductive, but he couldn't help it. Despite having been in law enforcement for over a decade, he hadn't become so calloused that he wasn't affected by the plight of a victim. He hated to see anyone hurt, but children, the elderly and—label him what you will, he was old-school in some ways—women getting injured bothered him the most.

On the topic of women... After his initial irritation at Chelsea, he was grateful she'd appeared. When he'd asked Rochester whom they could call, he'd been vehement that they *not* contact his wife. He'd explained she had a weak heart and he didn't want to worry her. Sam had to respect the man for caring about his wife and wanting to protect her. Instead, Rochester had given them contact information for his nephew, Adam. Adam worked at the store, too, he'd said. But both numbers he'd provided had gone straight to voice mail. Rochester had cautioned that Adam wasn't an early riser.

So, Sam was glad Chelsea had come along to soothe Rochester and keep him company until either the nephew arrived or the paramedics transported him to the hospital. Sam had been worried about the man's pallor and how fragile he'd seemed. She'd obviously eased some of his tension, and his color was much better.

Watching her smile at one of the paramedics, he felt a strange churning in his stomach. Her big green eyes were filled with warmth, and the smile accentuated her well-defined cheekbones and delicate nose and chin.

As the paramedics were helping Rochester

onto a stretcher for transport to the hospital, a slim, agitated man rushed into the store.

"What the heck is going on here?" Sam asked Miller, not hiding his frustration. "Do we have a c'mon-in sign hanging out there?"

Miller's cheeks colored again. "He's the nephew, Adam Rochester. You said to let him in when he got here."

It wasn't Sam's nature to lose his temper and take it out on members of his team. "Sorry, Joe," he said with a pat on the young officer's back. "Coffee's on me when we drive back to the station." And he hoped they could wrap up here and be on their way soon.

There was something that didn't sit right with him about the break-in, and it wasn't just that occurrences like this were rare in the small town of Camden Falls.

CHAPTER TWO

IT WAS NEARING six thirty that evening when Chelsea, balancing her dry cleaning, a large pizza box and a bag of groceries, let herself into her second-floor apartment. As she nudged the door closed with her foot, Mindy, her oversize gray-and-white cat, emerged from the bedroom. Mindy made her annoyance at Chelsea's late arrival abundantly clear with a haughty lift of her head and a testy meow.

"I'm sorry I'm late. How about salmon for dinner to make up for it?" Chelsea asked to appease the cat.

Mindy responded with a mournful grumble as she sauntered toward the kitchen.

Chelsea tossed her keys on the hall table, hung her dry cleaning in the coat closet and slipped off her shoes. Following the sound of Mindy's meowing, Chelsea headed for the kitchen. She put the pizza box on the counter, opened a can of Mindy's favorite food and scooped the contents into the cat's dish. Then she hurriedly put away the groceries she'd picked up.

With the late start to her workday because of the time she'd spent at All That Glitters and Shines, and subsequently everyone wanting to talk about the robbery, she'd left the gallery quite late. Luckily, considering all the excitement, she'd remembered Paige was coming over for dinner.

Paige and her adorable son, Jason, had been her downstairs neighbors from the time Chelsea moved in until Paige had married Daniel Kinsley. Paige was also Chelsea's closest friend. The house Paige and Daniel had bought wasn't far, but Chelsea still missed seeing Paige nearly every day, as she had for almost three years. And it wasn't just Paige. She missed Jason, too. He was ten and a half now, and how wonderful that he'd been free of cancer for almost three years.

This was one of the rare nights that Paige wasn't with her family, since Daniel and Jason had a father-and-son event at Jason's school, and Daniel's parents had insisted on watching baby Emily for the evening. Chelsea had planned to cook dinner, but she'd run out of time. Thankfully, Paige was undemanding and understanding…and it was probably for the best. Cooking wasn't one of Chelsea's strengths, which was why she liked to practice on Paige when she had the opportunity.

She selected a bottle of Cabernet Sauvignon from her little wine rack and uncorked it to let it breathe.

Checking her watch, Chelsea realized she had exactly seventeen minutes to get changed before Paige was due to arrive.

She was in and out of the shower in less than five minutes, and quickly dressed in her usual leisure wear of black leggings and a chunky sweater. She rubbed her wet hair with a towel before working a small blob of mousse into it to get her preferred style.

Chelsea heard the knock on the door just as she was rinsing her hands. She took a quick look in the mirror before rushing out of her bedroom.

"Paige, it's so good to see you," Chelsea said as she gave her friend a warm hug. Taking a step back she ran an approving eye over Paige, her tall slender frame, the long glossy blond hair and clear blue eyes. "How is it possible that every time I see you, you look better than before? Isn't a baby supposed to wear you out?"

Paige waved the compliment away. "Emily's been a dream."

"No, I'm serious," Chelsea said. "Marriage and motherhood agree with you."

"I'm very fortunate to have found Daniel," Paige admitted. "And Jason and Emily are my world."

"You're lucky to have found each other," Chelsea corrected Paige, and accepted the bottle of wine she held out. "Thanks for this. Very nice," she added, reading the label. "I already have a Cab Sauv breathing in the kitchen. Would you prefer I opened this?"

"Oh, the Cab's fine." Paige hung up her coat and bent down to stroke Mindy. She sniffed the air as she rose again. "Smells good. What are we having?"

Chelsea laughed. "Well, about that… I was planning on veal parmigiana, but you know what they say about best-laid plans." She led Paige into the kitchen and filled two glasses with wine.

"Any excuse to get out of cooking, huh?" Paige teased, then took a closer look at her friend. "Hard day?" she asked with concern.

Chelsea handed one of the glasses to Paige and took a sip from her own as they sat down at the kitchen table. "Oh, *hard* isn't the right word. More…*unexpected*. You know the nice older couple who own All That Glitters and Shines, the jewelry store next to the gallery?"

Paige tasted her wine and nodded.

"Their store was robbed early this morning. Mr. Rochester, the owner, was there at the time and he was attacked."

"Oh, no! Is he okay?"

"The paramedics said he should be. He got a deep gash in his head, and they took him to the hospital to check for concussion. He looked so pale and weak." She closed her eyes for a moment, her worry resurfacing. "I'm glad Adam, his nephew, showed up in time to go to the hospital with him. Otherwise, I would've gone."

"You were there when it happened?" Paige asked with alarm.

"No. It happened very early in the morning. The police and paramedics were already there when I...barged in."

"*Barged* in?" Paige probed.

"Yeah." Chelsea grinned. "That's exactly what I did. The detective in charge wasn't very happy about it, especially when I first got there."

At the ding of the oven timer, Chelsea hopped up. "I'll tell you more—especially about the good-looking detective—but our dinner should be warm by now. And I didn't answer your question about what we're having. Since I was running behind all day, pizza was the quickest option for me. I hope you don't mind."

"Not at all. I'm just happy we have a chance to spend time together."

Chelsea slid a couple of slices on each of the plates and took them to the table.

"I have to say, it's worrying to have something like this happen in Camden Falls," Paige said. She took a bite of pizza before continuing. "One of the reasons I originally moved here with Jason was because it was such a safe, friendly place. That was also why Daniel and I decided to stay here after we got married."

Chelsea and some of her colleagues had expressed similar sentiments during the day. "The police seem to be taking it seriously, if the number of cops at the store was any indication. I'm sure it's an isolated incident and nothing to worry about," she said, trying to mollify Paige. "I got the sense that the detective leading the investigation knew what he was doing and will get to the bottom of it soon." She thought back to all the damage in the store. "I wouldn't discount the possibility that it was kids causing trouble."

"I'm not sure that makes me feel any better," Paige responded. "Is that what the police believe?"

Chelsea shook her head. "I have no idea what they're thinking. The detective in charge—Eldridge, Sam Eldridge—was tight-lipped about it." Remembering how frustrated he'd been with her when she'd first shown up, but how he was more...tolerant, maybe even amused, by the time she'd left, Chelsea grinned.

"What's so funny?" Paige asked, wiping her mouth with a napkin.

"Not funny, really. The detective in charge has got to be one of the most intense, serious people I've ever met."

"Sounds like a recipe for a personality clash with you," Paige said, returning Chelsea's smile.

"You'd think so..."

Paige studied Chelsea with interest. "You like him?"

Chelsea swirled the wine in her glass as she considered Paige's question. When Mindy strolled over, she reached down to stroke her. "I suppose I do. I can't put my finger on why, though. He's not the sort of guy I'd usually be attracted to. He seemed so somber and...brooding." She glanced at Paige, with unconcealed amusement. "It would be an interesting challenge to see if I could get him to lighten up! As for his looks…" Her smile spread. "He's the best-looking cop—heck, the best-looking *guy*—I've seen in a while."

"You haven't been interested in anyone since you and Joel stopped dating," Paige observed. "I was hoping the two of you might get back together, especially since you see each other at the gallery most days."

Chelsea lifted a shoulder, then let it drop as she thought about the gallery owner's grandson. "Joel's okay, but the relationship had run its course. It was a little awkward at work at first, but fortunately his job in marketing and promotions frequently takes him away from the gallery."

"No chance the two of you might get back together, then?"

Chelsea shook her head. She regretted how far they'd drifted apart, but she couldn't be in a relationship without that spark, and they'd definitely lost it. She wasn't prepared to settle for anything less.

"Aw, Chelsea, he seemed to make you happy."

"He did, for a while. It just didn't last. We're better as colleagues than partners." She took a slow sip of wine. "What you and Daniel have? It's special. That's what I hope to find one day."

Paige gave Chelsea's hand a gentle squeeze. "You've got a lot to offer. Joel didn't realize how lucky he was."

"That's not fair," she said in Joel's defense. "It wasn't his fault. It just…wasn't meant to be. I'll meet the guy who's right for me one day. I'm sure of it. Yeah, Joel understands the world of art. We have that in common, even though he's not as passionate about it as I am, but he isn't particularly…sensitive. Nor did he want kids, which, as you know, is high on my priority list when I get married."

"You've always said that as an only child, you're keen on having a large, boisterous family. That shouldn't have come as a shock to him."

"He knew about that from the start. It only became an issue when the relationship began to get serious." She stared into her glass for a moment. "I don't know if that was the final straw," she said pensively and gave her head another little shake. "Something changed. He… he wasn't as attentive as he'd been at first. He seemed to become preoccupied."

"With what?"

"I don't know. He started canceling dates.

Lost track of conversations." Chelsea frowned. "He forgot the second anniversary of our first date. On the positive side, I'm glad it hasn't affected my relationship with his grandmother. Being in the gallery owner's bad books would *not* have been a good outcome, especially with my career aspirations." Chelsea clinked her glass against Paige's. "So it's all good, and I wholeheartedly believe that I'll meet the person I'm meant to be with. We'll find each other when we're intended to. In the meantime, I love my job at the gallery but I don't want to be a sales associate forever. I want to get the curator position when Charles Hadley retires in a couple of years. He's been the perfect mentor, and he's been super sweet about helping me. I'll focus on my career for now, but that doesn't mean I can't appreciate a great-looking guy like Detective Eldridge!"

"WHAT HAVE YOU got on the jewelry store robbery?"

Sam glanced up at Colin Mitchell, surprised his captain would be inquiring about the occurrence the day after it happened. "Why do you ask?"

Colin pulled back a chair facing Sam's desk

and folded himself into it. "I heard a couple of the techs talking about it in the lunchroom."

Sam raised his brow. "That's not unusual."

"No. That isn't. But what *is* unusual is that you wouldn't predict whether they'd find any evidence."

Sam nudged his laptop away and leaned back. "Yeah. That's correct."

"You want to tell me why?"

"Sure. I'd be interested in your take on this whole thing, anyway. And I'll ask you to keep an open mind," Sam added with a smile. "I believe whoever did it expected the place to be unoccupied. The fact that the owner was there at that time of day is outside the norm. Unexpected. Also, there was a lot of damage done. Too much. The time spent causing it could've been better used grabbing some pricey bits of bling. The most obvious items— engagement rings, high-end watches—were left untouched. What was taken, in comparison, is nickel-and-dime stuff. The extent of damage and low return for the effort says amateur to me, but it still doesn't make sense. The time wasted on destruction, when it could've been put to smarter use, leads me to conclude that the person either panicked or flew into a rage. Carelessness and intentional vandalism doesn't feel right. I'm leaning toward rage rather than panic."

"I agree," Colin said after a moment. "Panic due to finding the owner there could explain the attack, but would likely have caused the perp to flee. He risked getting caught by spending all that time destroying the place. We didn't find any prints, nothing we could use, am I correct?"

Sam nodded. "Yes. Most of the prints we found were those of the owners and their nephew, who also works at the store."

"But you had enough doubt not to bet on it."

"Yeah. I can't ignore the conflicting signals. My theory's a stretch, so this is where I need you to keep an open mind. I know we haven't seen this in Camden Falls—not to the best of my knowledge, anyway—but Willowbrook Avenue is where we have our concentration of high-end retailers. When I worked the beat in Boston, it wasn't unusual for pros to prepare for a major heist by creating a disturbance nearby to test police-response times. I've been wondering if that might be the case in this situation."

"As you said, it's a stretch. I haven't heard of that happening here, either. Besides, Camden Falls is a small town. No retail or commercial business is that far from us, and our department isn't large. There'd be significant variability in response times, based on what else we might have on the go at any moment and how many of us would be otherwise occupied."

"That occurred to me, too."

"Have you considered an addict, looking for some quick drug money?"

"Yeah. The cash drawer wasn't tampered with. If that *was* the case and even if the perp was flying high, he'd have gone for cash or the flashier items, in my opinion. What got me thinking about the response-time angle is the fact that it wasn't the security company that alerted us. As we both know, when an intrusion alarm goes off, more often than not, it's a failure in the system or a false alarm. It also means that the overall response time is longer, since it goes through the monitoring company, and they'll attempt to contact the premises first. If they can't reach anyone and if their standing orders specify it, they call us. That could take anywhere from five to ten extra minutes. In this case, the intrusion alarm had already been deactivated by the owner when the perp entered. The panic button, linked directly to us, was triggered."

"That makes sense, since the owner was on the premises."

"But Arnold Rochester doesn't recall activating the panic button." Sam gestured to keep Colin from interrupting. "Yeah, we could speculate that although he doesn't have a concussion, the trauma might've caused short-term memory loss. But we found him some distance from the location of the panic button, and that idea just doesn't ring true to me."

"So, how do you plan to proceed?"

Sam shrugged. "I'll have a closer look at some of the stores along that stretch of Willowbrook. And it wouldn't hurt to route some extra patrols through that area for the time being."

Colin stood up. "I can do that in the short-term, but if you're right and we're dealing with pros, who knows how long they might wait before acting. You're aware of our resource constraints. We won't be able to keep it up for more than a couple of weeks."

"Understood."

Sam was satisfied with how their discussion had gone. It probably worked in his favor that Colin had started his policing career in a big city, too. Without that, he might have dismissed Sam's theory outright. But it was the only plausible one Sam could come up with, short of a random act perpetrated by a very stupid person.

He brought up a mental image of the street

and the dozen or so stores. The Sinclair Gallery came to mind, along with a spirited woman with short dark hair. Chelsea Owens. He remembered her name without having to check his notes. She'd said she worked as a sales associate. He'd never set foot inside the gallery. His taste in art wasn't eclectic. He liked his art plain and simple, and as realistic as possible. Photographs were even better. He wasn't big on abstracts or old paintings, with their gloomy colors and depictions. He frankly found them depressing. But Sam knew some of that stuff was valued ridiculously high. He had no idea what the pieces at the Sinclair Gallery cost.

Maybe it was time to have a look and find out.

He'd read in the morning paper that there was going to be an exhibit and auction at the gallery Saturday evening. Ever since Katherine had left him and moved back to Boston, his social calendar had been meager, and he had no plans for the weekend.

The exhibit presented an ideal opportunity to check out the gallery.

CHAPTER THREE

THE GALLERY'S SHOWROOM looked perfect. Chelsea had worked darn hard to make sure it did. The annual exhibit and auction tended to draw a big crowd and was an important event for them. The gallery itself was a dominant presence on Willowbrook Avenue and in the community. It had been ever since Mrs. Sinclair established it when she'd moved to Camden Falls from Cambridge. She was already widowed at the time. Her son and daughter-in-law had died in the same tragic accident as her husband, so she was also Joel's guardian. Mrs. Sinclair was a bit of a celebrity in Camden Falls, and the gallery's annual gala was on many townspeople's social calendars, but it also attracted patrons from Boston, Cambridge and well beyond.

The event was a big deal, and Chelsea had nagged Mr. Hadley until he'd agreed to let her handle it mostly on her own. Joel had coordinated the media, public relations and advertising, but the showroom was all hers!

It was another test she'd set for herself. Despite being her own worst critic, she was pleased with how everything looked.

The hors d'oeuvre stations had been set up and the members of the waitstaff were finishing final preparations in the kitchen. The area where the auction would be held was ready and cordoned off. Nothing seemed out of place.

Chelsea relished these quiet moments before the guests started to arrive and she could be alone to take pleasure in her work.

Mr. Hadley was in his office, changing into his tuxedo, and Joel had gone to his apartment to get ready. He'd pick up his grandmother on his way back. Tina, the gallery's administrative assistant, and Deborah, the gallery's other full-time sales associate, had already changed into their dresses. The event was advertised as black-tie optional, but Mrs. Sinclair expected the gallery team to dress up, as did most of their regular patrons. Mrs. Sinclair might be a sweet old lady, but she had exacting standards for herself and the people who worked for her. And her resolve, once she'd set her sights on something, was unwavering.

No, there was no room for Chelsea to make a mistake.

She moved to where she'd positioned a wing-back chair for Mrs. Sinclair. Vital and youthful though she looked, she was nearing eighty and—as much as Chelsea knew she hated her own weakness—she could no longer be on her feet all evening. She needed short rests whenever time allowed.

After taking one last look around the room, it was time for Chelsea to get ready, too. In the women's washroom, she changed into the black cocktail dress she'd bought for the occasion. It was plain other than a sheer-lace panel across the shoulders, and some lace at the hemline just below her knees. Chelsea removed the two jewelry boxes from the case she'd brought with her. She opened the long slender one and carefully pulled out the beautiful single-strand pearl necklace. Admiring it first, she secured it around her neck. Next, she took the matching earrings out of their box and fastened them to her earlobes. The set had been her beloved grandmother's, who'd passed it on to her mother. Chelsea's mother had given it to her on her twenty-first birthday. Chelsea treasured it, because it reminded her of her grandmother, who'd died a few years back and whom she missed dearly.

Chelsea missed her mom and dad, too, but at least they were only a phone call or an hour-and-a-half's drive away in Fitchburg.

To complete her attire for the evening, she'd decided on black stockings and—although she knew she'd regret it by the end of the evening—stiletto-heeled black pumps. Rather than using mousse to get her favored spiky look, she'd styled her hair straight and sleek that morning, parted on the side and tucked behind her ears. Because she opted for a lighter shade than she usually wore, her lips were a more natural-looking shimmery rose.

She studied herself in the washroom mirror with a critical eye, much as she'd assessed the showroom earlier.

Elegant wasn't a word she usually associated with herself nor, frankly, was it something she normally strove for. But tonight? She thought she'd hit the mark.

It was important to her to set the right tone. Not just because she'd put so much personal effort into the event, but because of her goal to be the next curator. She wanted to ensure that Mrs. Sinclair found absolutely no fault with the evening…or her.

Soon after she reentered the showroom, the guests started to trickle in. By seven thirty, the gallery was packed. There were so many people, Chelsea worried that they'd run out of hors d'oeuvres. Or even more concerning, champagne.

Finding a moment to herself, she hurried to the kitchen to see how the supplies were holding up and passed several reporters along the way. She'd hoped there'd be a strong media presence, even though that fell in Joel's area of responsibility. Getting excellent earned-media coverage was an important side benefit of the event. In her wildest dreams, she wouldn't have imagined that arts reporters for two Boston media outlets and one from Cambridge would be there, along with all the locals.

Assuring herself that everything was fine in the food and beverages area, she circulated through the room, much like a conscientious hostess. She engaged guests while leaving the media to Mr. Hadley until Mrs. Sinclair and Joel arrived. When she noticed Mr. and Mrs. Rochester, from All That Glitters and Shines, she excused herself from the couple she'd been speaking with and went to greet them. Placing kisses on their cheeks, she stepped back to scrutinize Mr. Rochester. Although they'd spoken on the phone, she hadn't seen him since the robbery, because the store was closed while repairs were being made under Adam's supervision.

Chelsea was relieved that the only indication of the trauma Mr. Rochester had suffered was the small bandage he sported on his temple. "How are you feeling?" she asked him with genuine concern.

"I'm fine. As well as can be expected, at my age." He looked at his wife lovingly. "Between Carla's fussing and Adam's, I can hardly wait for the store to open so I can feel useful again."

"Now, Arnold, don't start complaining. We have every right to worry about you. It's part of our job descriptions," his wife said with a smile, slipping her arm through his.

He patted her hand. "I know, dear, but I really *am* okay. And speaking of Adam…" He turned back to Chelsea. "He's here somewhere if you'd like to say hello. I'm afraid Carla and I won't be staying long. I need my rest."

"I understand perfectly, and I'm grateful all three of you could make it, especially under the circumstances." She glanced around the room and saw Adam in conversation with someone in front of a Jose Royo painting. "Can I get you anything before I go see Adam? A glass of champagne?"

"Oh, we're fine, thank you," Mrs. Rochester replied.

"Well, then, I hope you'll enjoy yourselves," Chelsea added, before wishing them a good night.

She kept working the room and waited until Adam was alone before going to him. She'd known him for as long as she'd been at the Sinclair Gallery. They got on well enough, but with him she'd never felt the mutual affection she did with his aunt and uncle. She'd gotten to know him a little better while she and Joel had dated. Joel and Adam had been friends since they'd gone to school together. Although not as close as they used to be, they were still on good terms. Considering the hardships Adam had endured as a child, she understood why he was reserved. She told herself she should be more accepting, but their personalities were so different—Adam, being more of a loner and introspective—they'd never gotten close. Maybe part of it was that Adam didn't seem to show an appreciation for art, one of her great loves.

No matter. He was a guest, and she'd make sure he was having a nice time.

"Are you enjoying yourself?" she asked, walking up to him.

"Yeah." Adam motioned to the crowd behind them. "Impressive turnout. With deep pockets, I'll bet," he added.

"We have a good mix of people who appreciate art," was Chelsea's diplomatic response.

"As an example, how much is this piece?" he asked, turning back to the painting.

For the higher-valued works, they didn't display the asking prices. They wanted to have the opportunity to discuss the paintings with anyone who might be interested, rather than immediately scaring them off with the price. Chelsea studied the Royo, too. "It's a classic example of a contemporary artist whose work is favorably compared to old masters. The best we've had in some time. It's valued at a hundred and thirty thousand dollars."

"That's a substantial amount of money, even for the wealthy. We don't have anything in that price range at All That Glitters and Shines."

"Trust me. We don't sell many pieces in this price range, either," she said and left as soon as she felt she could do so politely.

A quick perusal of the room indicated there were even more people present now. For her own peace of mind, she decided to pop into the kitchen to satisfy herself that they still weren't running low on anything.

As she exited the kitchen, relieved that they had plenty of everything, she saw Joel with his grandmother. He was guiding her protectively into the room. One thing she'd always liked about Joel was how considerate and loving he was to his grandmother. Family was important to Chelsea, and the way Joel treated his grandmother had endeared him to her when they'd first met.

As usual, Mrs. Sinclair was elegantly dressed. Unless Chelsea was mistaken, today she was wearing a Chanel evening suit in rose, a perfect color to complement her pale and remarkably unlined skin and silver-white hair. Chelsea signaled one of the waitstaff to prepare a cup of the herbal tea Mrs. Sinclair preferred, before heading over to the entrance to greet the owner.

Chelsea was pleased by the smile that appeared on Mrs. Sinclair's face when she reached her. "Mrs. Sinclair, it's wonderful to see you. I hope you find everything at tonight's event to your liking."

Mrs. Sinclair took Chelsea's hands in her own. Her grasp was cool and unexpectedly firm. "It's all lovely, my dear. I'm certain our gala will be a success."

"I hope so," Chelsea murmured. "I've positioned your chair next to the Angelo bronze," she said, gesturing. "Oh, and here comes Sandra with your tea."

"Thank you," Mrs. Sinclair said, as she accepted the cup from the waitress. "That's very sweet of you, but enough worrying about me."

"I'll keep Grandmother company," Joel assured Chelsea. "Why don't you go mingle and sell some art," he said, not unkindly.

"I'll do that," Chelsea responded with a grateful smile for Joel. "If you need anything, Mrs. Sinclair, please let me know."

Chelsea did as Joel suggested, and she began to relax. Every indication was that the evening would be a triumph. They'd received a few advance bids above the reserve for the works that would be auctioned at the end of the evening, and she personally made a couple of minor sales. Then she saw Mr. Anderson, one of their faithful patrons, standing in front of a Babineux, obviously admiring it. If she could make *that* sale, it would be a bonus to an already fantastic event.

"Hello, Mr. Anderson," she said as she

stopped beside him to look at the painting of a woman and her child.

"Good evening, Chelsea." He smiled at her briefly before turning his attention back to the painting.

"Henri Babineux, as I'm sure you know, is one of the most renowned artists of his day. This piece was painted circa 1862. Today is the first day we're showing it. I don't think we'll have it long. Wouldn't it look fabulous in *your* collection?"

"You might be right," he replied. "Excellent turnout, by the way. I don't usually go for these types of events, but I couldn't resist coming this evening to see what new treasures you might have available."

"I trust you're not disappointed."

"As a matter of fact, I'm not."

She stepped a little closer and lowered her voice. "Should I get a sold sign for it?"

"Now, now! I might be known for impulse buying, but even I'm not quite that spontaneous." He turned shrewd eyes on her. "However, you could tell me how much it would set me back if I did decide to acquire this painting."

Chelsea named the number in the mid six figures and knew that as pricey as it was, it wasn't out of Mr. Anderson's range.

His expression turned contemplative. "Let me think about it while I help myself to a glass of champagne and see what else might capture my interest."

"Please do," she said, not in the least disappointed. If she was a betting person, she would've laid money on Mr. Anderson's buying the Babineux sooner or later. She was familiar with that look in his eyes. Once he'd moved on, she turned back to the painting. It wasn't her preferred style, but she recognized the artistic talent. More important, she knew that the Babineux was to Mr. Anderson's taste. She then studied the abstract next to it.

"Help me understand what, exactly, this painting is supposed to represent." The deep voice, with a touch of humor, had Chelsea glancing over her shoulder.

Her courteous reply caught in her throat as she found herself staring into familiar bold blue eyes. "Detective Eldridge, I didn't know you had an interest in art."

His laugh was warm and masculine at the same time. "I don't normally, no. And when I do, I tend to like…ah, the more mundane."

He was standing so close, she could see the faint stubble of a day's growth of beard, and the fine lines at the outer corners of his eyes and mouth when he smiled. There were a few strands of gray in his black hair. His scent, clean and woodsy, teased her nostrils. She let her gaze slide over him. She was sure there was a fit and impressive body under his conservative suit.

"I hope I'm not underdressed," he said.

Chelsea felt the heat rise to her cheeks. She obviously hadn't been as subtle in her perusal of him as she'd hoped. "Oh, no, you look perfectly fine." Now she could feel her cheeks burn even more. "What I meant is your attire is fine. Black tie is optional. Are you here for professional or personal reasons?" she rushed on, wanting to change the subject.

"A bit of both."

His answer perplexed her, but she remained quiet.

"I'd appreciate it if you'd enlighten me about this particular painting," he said after a moment.

"Of course, Detective. This painting is by Jackson Pollock, who's among the leaders of abstract expressionism." Noting his blank look, she went on to explain. "In abstract expressionism, the artist is mostly interested in color, movement and rhythm, rather than trying to depict specific objects. The artists also worked with new ways of applying paint. Pollock, for example, used sticks to fling and drip paint on his canvases. This piece was painted in 1934 and was in a private collection until the gallery acquired it recently through auction."

"That gives me its history, but tell me about the painting itself. And Sam is fine."

His blue eyes and the sparkle of humor in them captivated her, and she missed his concluding comment. "I'm sorry? What did you say?"

The smile became a wide grin. "I'd prefer it if you called me Sam instead of Detective."

"Oh, okay…Sam."

"Now, tell me about the painting. What is it supposed to be? Aside from blobs of color, I mean."

Chelsea should've been offended by his barely restrained mirth but was instead tempted to laugh along with him. Instead, she ran through the sales pitch she'd developed for the painting. "Well, as you can see, this is a painting of an enchanted forest shrouded in mist," she concluded and glanced up at Sam.

He was staring at the canvas intently, his brows drawn together, his eyes narrowed. She tried not to feel disconcerted by his proximity.

Finally, he shook his head. "I'm sorry, but

I can't see it at all. This," he said, pointing, "looks like a sand crab to me, but mostly all I see is spattered paint."

She was about to point out the key elements of the painting to him, but the absurdity of even trying struck her. "It's a *stylized* depiction of the forest," she conceded.

"Can we at least agree that it's *highly* stylized?" he asked.

Now Chelsea did laugh, but quickly clamped one hand over her mouth, her eyes darting around. Satisfied that no one had noticed her outburst, she looked back at Sam.

"Well, am I right? Can you see the crab?" he asked. "I should help you sell paintings here."

"Don't quit your day job," she countered under her breath when two patrons strolled over to admire the Pollock.

"I wasn't planning on it," Sam said, as they moved away to give the couple space. "We each have our strengths. Do you have the time—and the *patience*—to show me around?"

Chelsea heard the humor in his voice again and found herself drawn to him. All their guests seemed to be engaged and enjoying themselves. Mrs. Sinclair and Mr. Hadley were making the rounds, champagne glasses in their hands. Joel, Deborah and Tina were available to address any questions, and it was less than an hour before the auction started.

Happily, she noted that sold signs had been placed under a few more of the pieces. "Sure. I have some time. What interests you the most?"

"I haven't the slightest idea!" he said with a chuckle. "Surprise me."

CHAPTER FOUR

CHELSEA'S MISCHIEVOUS STREAK kicked in. Sam was someone who, by his own admission, knew little about art, and it stood to reason that he had equally limited interest. She'd see what she could do about turning him into an art aficionado.

"Why don't we start with some baroques," she suggested. "Are you on duty?" she asked, when she saw a waitress approach with a tray of champagne.

"Not at the moment. Why?"

Chelsea signaled discreetly to the waitress and she veered toward them. "Thank you, Marsha," she said, taking two flutes from the tray and offering one to Sam. "If you're not inclined to appreciate art, I thought this might help."

He accepted the glass and took a sip. "Nice. Hmm...Krug Grande Cuvée, 2013." When Chelsea raised her brows, he said, "I may not be an expert at art, but..."

"But you're an expert in fine wines and champagnes?" she guessed.

"No, but I'm a detective and I have well-honed investigative and observation skills," he said with a smug smile.

She stared at him blankly, not sure what he meant.

"There was an empty carton in the corner of the hall closet when I hung up my coat," he explained. "It was clearly labeled."

Chelsea wouldn't have thought the intense cop had a sense of humor, but it appeared that he did. And when he smiled? He went from seriously good-looking to dangerously handsome.

"Why don't we start here?" she suggested, hoping he wouldn't notice that she was blushing again, and led him to a watercolor of a Venetian canal by American artist John Singer Sargent.

"I personally like this painting," she began. "Sargent was said to be fascinated with Venice, and I think it shows in his work. He's captured the different shades of the water and the brightness of the light beautifully. It's interesting that although he turns a commonplace neighborhood into something so romantic, he didn't use much detail depicting the people on the bridge." She smiled up at Sam. "Sargent's passion for the city didn't seem to extend to its inhabitants."

Next, she showed Sam a Ralph Curtis painting, also of Venice. "Curtis was the son of Bostonians, who moved to Venice in the late 1870s. He was educated at Harvard, but then studied in Paris. We purposely juxtaposed these two paintings to allow our patrons to compare and contrast the style and emotion of the two. Sargent and Curtis were, in fact, distant cousins. It's quite remarkable, isn't it, how Sargent's work evokes romance and joy while this one… well, is quite bleak."

"Uh-huh" was Sam's noncommittal response.

Chelsea guided him to a Childe Hassam winter scene in New York next and continued talking until she could all but see his head spin. Since he'd said he was there for business *and* pleasure, she assumed the business had to do with the robbery next door, so she made a point of taking him to speak with the Rochesters. She almost laughed at the relief she saw on his face as they approached the elderly couple.

Chelsea introduced Sam to Mrs. Rochester, and he politely asked Mr. Rochester how he was feeling and just as politely answered that they still didn't have any leads on the robbery. Adam joined them and also expressed an interest in the investigation. Chelsea was aware of how concerned he was about his aunt and uncle. He wanted the matter over with as much as anyone; she presumed that was so he wouldn't have to worry about their safety, in case the perpetrator decided to return.

Adam questioned Sam until, eventually, Chelsea adeptly steered the detective away.

"The nephew, Adam, seems close to the Rochesters. What's his story?" Sam asked when they were separated by some distance.

"Oh, yes, they're close. Adam's story is a sad one, though. Adam's father—that's Mr. Rochester's considerably younger brother—was in the military and frequently deployed overseas. What I've heard is that Mr. Rochester was the principal father figure in Adam's life as he was growing up. Adam's mother was already struggling with alcohol and drug abuse by the time her husband was killed in the line of duty. His death pushed her over the edge. The Rochesters tried to get help for her, but it was futile. Although they didn't have legal custody of Adam, they tried to be positive influences in his life."

"Where's the mother now?"

"Excuse me," Joel interrupted, as he joined them. He glanced at Sam—seemed to size him up, Chelsea thought—before he turned his attention to her. "Mr. Anderson was looking for you. When we saw you were…occupied, he asked my opinion of the Babineux. I didn't know enough about it, so I steered him to Mr. Hadley."

Pushing aside her immediate concern that she'd dropped the ball, Chelsea asked, "Did Mr. Anderson buy the Babineux?"

Joel frowned. "No, he didn't. He left."

"Without buying anything? Is Mr. Hadley upset with me?"

"I smoothed it over for you. But the auction's about to start, so I thought you might want to get ready for it."

Chelsea had been enjoying herself with Sam so much, she'd lost track of time. "Thank you for reminding me," she said gratefully. "I'll get to it right away," she added, but she couldn't help noticing that Joel kept looking over her shoulder. "Oh, Joel, let me introduce you to Detective Sam Eldridge. Detective Eldridge… uh, Sam is leading the investigation into the robbery next door. Sam, this is Joel Sinclair, grandson of Nadine Sinclair, the owner of the gallery."

"The last part of the introduction is superfluous, I hope, as I like to think my role at the Sinclair Gallery is earned rather than nepotism,"

Joel said stiffly as he shook hands with Sam. "Are you working tonight?" he asked, with a meaningful glance at the flute Sam held.

"No, I'm not," Sam replied and took an un-hurried sip from his glass.

"What brought you to our gallery this evening? I don't recall seeing your name on our invitation list."

Sam glanced at Chelsea. "Curiosity." There was something in his eyes she couldn't decipher.

Joel took a sideways step toward her and ran a hand casually up and down her arm. "You enjoy art, Detective?" He continued probing, obviously not in any hurry to leave them alone, and she sensed friction between the two men.

"Not particularly."

"The filmmaker Jean-Luc Godard said, 'Art attracts us only by what it reveals of our most secret self.'"

"Very profound, but I like to keep my most secret self to myself," Sam retorted.

Chelsea felt as if she was watching a chess game, and it had started with Joel's inappropriate display of possessiveness. Two could play that game, she thought, and she moved away from Joel in a way that put her equidistant between the men. She intended to stay neutral.

"Well, Detective Eldridge," Joel said after a moment. "I hope you got some pleasure from your tour. Even if you're not a huge fan, the right work of art always adds richness and interest to a room. You should consider acquiring one of our…more traditional pieces."

Sam stuck his hands in his pants pockets. "You're correct that I *am* more of a traditionalist."

They didn't seem to want to let up, and Chelsea didn't need to stick around while they jockeyed for alpha position. She cleared her throat. "I see Mrs. Fontaine admiring the Oldenburg. Joel, if you'd attend to the detective, I'll see if she's interested in making a purchase. Good evening, Detective," she added, deliberately using his title rather than his name, before she walked away.

SAM WATCHED CHELSEA march off. March seemed to be the most accurate way to describe it. He had to give her credit for determination. There was no question she'd had enough of the verbal sparring he and Sinclair had been engaged in. His gaze still on her, he noted that she moved with poise, too.

She might not have been particularly tall, but she had long legs. Elongated by the sexy heels. How did a woman manage to stay on her feet all evening in a pair of those? And then there was her trim, shapely figure. Maybe not his type, but a man had to appreciate a form like that.

He kept his gaze on Chelsea longer than he might have, because he knew he was being watched by Sinclair. Sam could tell that it irritated him, and for some reason that gave him satisfaction. When he finally looked back at Sinclair, he wasn't surprised by the scowl on the other man's face. He hadn't missed his possessive stroking of Chelsea's arm, either. Boyfriend? They did appear to be suited, but the thought of the two of them together annoyed him for some reason.

Sam decided to test his hypothesis. "How long have you been seeing each other?" He noticed the immediate tensing, the breaking of eye contact. Both possible tells that Sinclair wasn't comfortable with the question.

"Oh, we started dating about two and a half years ago."

"Uh-huh." Well, she was off-limits to him. *Where did that come from?* He hadn't realized he'd been thinking about Chelsea in that context.

Forcing his thoughts onto a different subject, he looked at the statue on a pedestal not far from where they stood. From his discussion with Chelsea he'd gathered that statue would be priced in the six figures. With the value of the artwork displayed, if his theory about the robbery at All That Glitters and Shines was correct, the gallery could be the real target. Since Sinclair was still standing next to him, he'd take the opportunity to learn more about the gallery...and Sinclair himself. He pointed to the statue. "What can you tell me about that piece?"

Sinclair gave him the rundown. It was evident that he knew his facts, but he didn't show any of the warmth or passion that Chelsea had. Sam deduced that for him it was a job. For Chelsea? More of a calling.

Sam decided to try another angle. "Chelsea mentioned your grandmother owns the gallery."

"Yes. She does."

Sam saw Joel glance around the room, his eyes resting briefly on the gray-haired woman dressed in a muted pink—he supposed it would be called rose—suit in the far corner of the room.

"Is that your grandmother?"

"What? Yes."

"I'd like to meet her."

"I don't see why—"

"You never know when connections to the

Camden Falls Police Department might come in handy," Sam interrupted in a tone that deterred argument.

"Yes, of course," Sinclair said curtly.

Sam followed him to the corner where his grandmother was. They waited until she'd finished her conversation with a distinguished-looking gentleman.

"Grandmother, I'd like to introduce you to Detective Sam Eldridge," Joel said when she turned to them. "Detective, this is my grandmother Nadine Sinclair."

Sam noticed the slight narrowing of her eyes before she offered him a bright smile and held out her hand. Her charisma was powerful. Joel Sinclair didn't inherit his lack of charm from his grandmother.

"It's always nice to have a Camden Falls police officer visit our establishment." Her expression sobered. "Do you have news about the robbery next door? What happened to Arnold Rochester is simply horrible."

"No, I'm sorry, I don't, but we're doing our best."

"I'm the one who needs to apologize. How rude of me to ask about such a terrible incident when you're a guest at our little gallery. I imagine your line of work is often thankless, but I'm grateful for what you and your colleagues do to keep our community safe and free from crime. I trust the investigation is in good hands." The glint in her eye made Sam think she would've been a force to reckon with in her younger days, and probably still was. Age hadn't dulled her intelligence or her perception. Although she made him feel as if he was her focus, she kept a vigilant eye on the room behind him.

"No apology necessary. I'm never entirely off the clock."

She angled her head. "As I said, we're grateful for your service and dedication. I noticed Chelsea showing you around. You haven't been in here before, have you?"

"No, ma'am."

"I hope you like our gallery and will visit us again."

"Thank you. You have an impressive place. I expect you have a sophisticated security system, too."

"We do, supplemented by security guards and patrols," Joel responded, drawing his attention. "But it's also something we avoid discussing in public. Part of the system's effectiveness has to do with the fact that it's unobtrusive. If would-be thieves were to know the details of the system, it would be that much easier for them to disable or circumvent it."

Mrs. Sinclair patted her grandson's arm. A subtle sign of admonition perhaps?

"Joel can get very protective of the gallery... and me. So, Detective Eldridge, can I interest you in any of our works of art?"

"You'd be the third one to try," Sam said with a smile. "And the one most likely to succeed, but no. I came more out of general interest today."

Activity in another part of the room had all three of them turning in that direction, and Sam guessed the auction was about to begin. It was time for him to go—before an innocent scratch of his head ended up costing him a year's salary for something he didn't need or want. He thanked both Sinclairs and started to navigate through the crowd toward the door.

He'd ascertained that the gallery would be a viable target, if his theory held. Whether related or not, his gut told him not to trust Joel Sinclair. The grandmother seemed nice enough, but there was something about Joel that rubbed him the wrong way.

Chelsea came to mind, and he nearly laughed at himself.

No, it wasn't because Sinclair had a relationship with Chelsea.

Sam admitted to a certain fascination with her, but she wasn't available and Sam never poached.

Still, he couldn't resist pausing before he left the room to search her out. She was near the podium he assumed the auctioneer would use, in animated discussion with another young woman. When she glanced in his direction and smiled, he returned her smile and waved goodbye.

Wondering if he'd see her again, he astonished himself for the second time that evening with how much he wanted to.

Business. He had to focus on business, he reminded himself. And he had the answer to his question, he thought, as he pulled away from the curb a short while later. The gallery housed valuable art. The most expensive pieces on display far exceeded the highest-priced items in the jewelry store. But while jewelry and watches could be easily fenced, priceless and readily identifiable works of art could not. Private collectors with immense wealth, a disregard for the law and secret collections would be the only potential purchasers of stolen art, in Sam's opinion. He presumed that was a very limited group.

Since he was here, he'd take a drive down Willowbrook Avenue to see if there were any other probable targets for a major heist.

As soon as the thought occurred to him, he chuckled.

Major heist and the quaint, peaceful little town of Camden Falls was a contradiction in terms. He wondered if he was looking for something big he could sink his teeth into, because—admittedly—the job here didn't present the challenges that being a cop in one of the seedier areas of Boston had. And without a personal life to speak of, the job was all he had, he mused as he drove slowly by a gift shop and a pet food store, neither of which he considered a viable target.

But then *peaceful* and *crime free* were two of the reasons he and Katherine had decided to relocate to Camden Falls when they'd learned Katherine was pregnant. They'd also wanted a strong sense of community, and Camden Falls offered that, too. They'd been ecstatic at the prospect of raising a family here.

Well, that didn't turn out as planned, Sam thought ruefully as he passed a ladies' clothing boutique and a shoe store. And the big city had lured Katherine back to reestablish her career as a financial planner, while he'd stayed right here in Camden Falls, consumed with grief. They hadn't spoken since the divorce.

With their son, Nicolas, gone, there hadn't been any reason.

By the time Sam reached the end of the retail section of Willowbrook Avenue, he'd narrowed potential targets down to the Sinclair Gallery and an electronics store—*if* his theory was correct. He would've put the gallery at the top of the list, except for the challenge of fencing stolen works of art. So, the jewelry store struck him as the best of the possibilities, after all. And that negated his response-time-testing theory.

Maybe he was grasping at straws.

This wasn't Boston.

He thought about the people he'd met that evening and wondered if any of them could have been responsible for the jewelry store robbery.

Sam considered Joel Sinclair and his lack of passion for the business. He wondered how much Joel made from the gallery in comparison with his grandmother. Sam's thoughts returned to Chelsea Owens as he took a right onto Cedar Lane to head home. There was an irresistible quality to the quirky, upbeat, high-spirited young woman. But was his interest professional? Was he drawn to her because his instincts told him she might have a connection to the robbery next door? Or was the attraction personal?

He had to be overtired if he was thinking along either of those lines.

She wasn't his type. He wasn't interested in a relationship, even if she was. And she wasn't available, anyway.

He'd get a good night's sleep and talk his theory through with Colin on Monday.

But try as he might, he couldn't get Chelsea out of his thoughts.

CHAPTER FIVE

CHELSEA SAID GOODBYE to Sharon Robinson, the third-grade teacher at Camden Falls Public School, and the kids in her class for whom she'd conducted a tour of the gallery that morning. Chelsea loved kids and loved teaching them about art. Their insatiable curiosity and the way they saw everything so differently from adults never ceased to amaze and inspire her. She was always more than willing to organize and run the tours, but that didn't mean the kids' limitless energy didn't take a lot out of her.

Still, when the time was right, she wanted to have kids. A number of them.

She'd have to work on her stamina, though, she decided.

Chelsea was glad the showroom was empty so she could have a well-earned lunch break. Deborah was off today, but Tina could keep an eye on things and Joel was due back from the Nightingale estate auction anytime now. Then he could attend to any walk-ins, although that wasn't his favorite task.

Grabbing her sandwich, a bottle of water from the fridge in the lunchroom and one of the fashion magazines Tina habitually left on the counter, she sank down in a chair. She flipped the magazine open to a random page and had barely unwrapped her sandwich when she heard footsteps in the corridor. She glanced up to see Joel lean against the doorjamb. He'd crossed his legs at the ankles and tucked his left hand in his pants pocket.

It was his *GQ* look, as Chelsea used to think of it. She knew it to be contrived.

"How was the tour?" he asked.

Chelsea smiled. "Great kids. As entertaining as always."

"Any damage?"

"Oh, Joel! Can't you forget about that one isolated incident?" She didn't bother to hide her irritation. "That incident was more than a year ago, and you make it sound as if it was malicious. The poor kid tripped on his shoelace and, thankfully, fell against a promotional banner rather than a display case or stand. There was no harm done. And to answer your question, *no*, there was no damage today."

His glower persisted and caused her to look away.

"I'm sorry. That was unwarranted," he finally conceded, drawing her gaze back to his. "The children's program is important to my grandmother and therefore the gallery. You've always been terrific with the kids. And since you handle it, I don't have to be involved. So, I'll apologize again."

"Apology accepted." As far as Chelsea was concerned, the discussion was over. She finished unwrapping her sandwich, but she could feel Joel's eyes on her and looked up again. The expression on his face was inscrutable and made her uncomfortable. Looking down, she took a bite of her sandwich.

"Chels, have dinner with me tonight."

The invitation, unexpected and spoken so softly, had her glancing at him with astonishment. It reminded her of his odd behavior the evening of the exhibit and auction, and made her wonder what was going through his mind.

Joel was still leaning casually against the doorjamb, his blond hair tousled, a playful smile spread across his face. The dimple she'd once found so sexy flickered on his right cheek.

"C'mon, Chels," he said when she hesitated. "For old times' sake. What do you say?"

For a moment—just one moment—she was tempted to say yes. The boyish grin had always drawn her in and she hadn't been on a date since…well, since she and Joel had stopped seeing each other. But then she thought about some of the reasons she'd broken it off with him.

At first, he'd made her feel special. But by the end of their relationship, she felt he'd lost interest in her. There always seemed to be other priorities, and she'd begun to feel like an obligation.

Chelsea considered herself relatively easygoing and flexible, but she couldn't be in a relationship in which she wasn't valued.

Remembering how it had been between them when they'd first started dating, she felt a twinge of sadness over what they'd lost, but was careful not to let it show. She didn't want to inadvertently encourage him. "Sorry, Joel. I don't think it's a good idea."

He straightened. "Have it your way."

She wasn't sure if it was disappointment or anger that sparked in his eyes before he turned and stalked away.

Well, that was fun. She sighed. This was justification for why she tried to avoid workplace romances. If they didn't work out—which in her experience was usually the case—it could be awkward. She thought back to the easy friendship she and Joel had shared before they began dating. She wished they could recapture it but suspected that was unlikely, at least in the short-term.

As much as she regretted how everything had turned out between them, she hoped again that her relationship with his grandmother would remain unaffected. Not only did she *like* Mrs. Sinclair, but ultimately it would be Mrs. Sinclair's decision whether to give her the curator position once Mr. Hadley retired. Joel had made it clear that he wasn't interested in running the gallery, so it was either promote her or Mrs. Sinclair would have to go outside the organization to hire someone.

Chelsea didn't want to lose Mrs. Sinclair's friendship—or the opportunity to be the next curator.

No dating people in the workplace ever again! she resolved as she took another large bite of her sandwich.

When Tina called her from the lunchroom doorway, she wondered if she'd ever get a chance to finish her lunch.

"Sorry to interrupt, but Mr. Anderson is here and would like to talk to you about the Babineux."

Chelsea put her sandwich down and dabbed at her mouth with her napkin, careful not to smear her lipstick. "He didn't have an appointment, did he?"

"No," Tina assured her. "But as you know, he does most of his buying on the spur of the moment."

"Yes, that's true. Please tell him I'll be out in a second." Chelsea rewrapped the rest of her sandwich and stuck it back in the fridge. Looking in the mirror behind the door, she rubbed off a smudge of lipstick with her index finger.

Mr. Anderson was standing in front of the Babineux when she walked into the showroom. His back was to her, his head slightly tilted. He had a sparse frame, was shorter than average, and was impeccably dressed and groomed, as always. Chelsea had often thought that for the price of one of his elegant suits, she could've paid the rent on her apartment for at least a month.

"Mr. Anderson," she said as she approached. "It's nice to see you so soon."

He spun around and smiled. "Chelsea, my dear, how are you?"

"I'm fine, thank you." She glanced at the painting. "I thought it would be only a matter of time before the Babineux graced your walls. Is this the day you make it yours?" she asked.

"Yes, I think it might be. I hadn't planned

to stop in today, but I was in the area with a few minutes to spare." He grinned and spread out his hands. "I couldn't resist. I suppose it's meant to be."

"That's what I thought, too! Shall I get the paperwork?"

He stroked his chin as he considered the painting. "Why not? Let's do it!"

Chelsea felt like doing a fist pump, but knew it would be unseemly. The commission on the sale would cover a brake job and new tires for her car. Both were very close to becoming a necessity. "Please have a seat in the sales office. Would you like a cup of coffee? A glass of champagne, perhaps?"

"As delightful as champagne sounds, it's too early in the day for me. Let's make it a coffee, and we'll both have a glass of champagne when I come to pick up the painting."

"Sounds perfect. I'll be right back."

With the folder in one hand and a cup in the other, Chelsea rejoined Mr. Anderson a few minutes later. "Here you go," she said, placing the cup and a napkin in front of him before sitting down in the opposite chair. She reviewed the documentation with him. Once he was satisfied that all seemed to be in order, he handed her his credit card for the deposit. While Tina ran the card, she made copies of the appraisal and authentication documents for Mr. Anderson's insurance company.

"I'll call you if my schedule changes," he said. "Otherwise, I'll see you on Friday to pick up the painting."

"We'll have it packed and ready for you, Mr. Anderson." She held out her hand. "Congratulations on adding another magnificent piece to your collection."

He took her hand in his. "Always a pleasure doing business with you, Chelsea."

As soon as he was out the door, not only did Chelsea do that fist pump, she did a little dance. Embarrassment warmed her cheeks when she turned around and noticed Joel watching her. "I sold the Babineux," she said, to explain her behavior.

"Good for you," he responded, but his tone was incongruous with the congratulatory words.

"Do you have a minute?" Sam asked Colin from the doorway to his captain's office.

Colin dropped the report he'd been reading on his desk. "Sure. What's up?"

Sam took a seat on the other side of Colin's

desk. "We still don't have anything on the jewelry store robbery."

"You're not bringing me a problem without a solution, are you?"

Sam knew his boss was half joking. He was always on them not to just come forward with a problem but to bring the options to solve it. "I'm working out the alternatives. First of all, if we go with the theory that the break-in was to test our response time because there's another target in the area, my bet would be the Sinclair Gallery."

"Why?

"The value of some of the pieces in there could pay for a small house."

Colin leaned back and crossed his arms. "No kidding?"

"Nope."

"I can't see how there'd be a market for that kind of art in Camden Falls."

"Good point. What I learned is that the gallery's clientele is from a much larger catchment area. It's international, in fact. When you're dealing with rare works and there's only a limited number of people with deep enough pockets and a desire to spend that much money on art, it doesn't matter where the gallery is situated. There isn't a critical mass of potential clients in any one location. They go where the art is."

Colin nodded thoughtfully. "Regardless of what we find on the jewelry store break-in, I'll have to think about increasing patrols in the area on a permanent basis."

"Not a bad idea. Now here's another long shot. I discovered that the jewelry store owners' sister-in-law is estranged from her kid, who's been raised mostly by them, his aunt and uncle. She has addiction issues, and was recently released from a mental health institution. You'd mentioned the possibility of an addict looking for easy money. Her last known address was Springfield, but she hasn't been there for a while. There's no record of employment. What if she resents the Rochesters for what might, in her eyes, amount to taking her only child away from her? And what if she's desperate for a quick fix? Would she consider the jewelry store as a means to an end?"

Colin was silent for a moment. "I agree it's a long shot, but I have to say that between the two alternatives, I'd consider the sister-in-law breaking in more probable. Where do you go from here?"

Sam shrugged. "I'll try to determine the sister-in-law's whereabouts. Continue to pursue the other avenues of investigation and so on."

"What about the young woman who showed up at the store? We know the stats on how often perps return to the scene of the crime."

"Not possible." Sam was startled by the vehemence of his response. Colin was, too, if the look on his face was any indication. "What I mean is that she was too caring about Rochester. I don't believe she'd hurt him." Or anyone.

"Okay. Keep me informed."

"Will do," Sam said and rose to go.

CHAPTER SIX

THURSDAY THE FOLLOWING WEEK, Chelsea was discussing the merits of a Keith Hamilton sculpture with a couple when she heard the gallery's front door chime. Turning, she saw Mr. Anderson hurrying through the front foyer.

"Chelsea! This is outrageous!" he called to her the minute he stepped into the showroom.

Excusing herself, she left the couple she'd been with and hurried to Mr. Anderson. He hastened toward her, too, waving a document.

"This has never happened to me in all the years I've been collecting!" His face was flushed, and his nostrils flared with each rapid breath he took. "As soon as I got this, I drove straight here from Boston."

Worried more about the fact that he seemed to be hyperventilating than what her potential new clients might think, Chelsea touched his arm placatingly. "Please calm down, Mr. Anderson. Why don't we go into the office? You can explain to me what happened. Whatever it is, I'll do my best to fix it."

He let out a loud harrumphing sound.

Chelsea apologized to the couple she'd been with as she led Mr. Anderson past them, and signaled to Deborah to take over.

She got him seated in the sales office, but he declined refreshments.

"Please tell me what's wrong," Chelsea said.

"What's wrong? What's *wrong*?" He flapped the papers at her. "You sold me a forgery!"

Chelsea was sure she hadn't heard him correctly. "I'm sorry. Could you repeat that?"

"Here," he said and thrust the papers at her. "Have a look at that. I had the Babineux authenticated myself, as I always do, and as my insurance company requires. And that!" he said, motioning at the document. "*That's* what I got back. You tell me how this could've happened!"

Chelsea quickly scanned the document and felt the blood drain from her face. "This…this can't be right. There has to be a mistake."

Mr. Anderson's jaw jutted out. "Murphy & McGuire is one of the most reputable art authentication and valuation companies in the nation. Their people have never been wrong for me before. If there's a mistake, it's on your end."

"Would you excuse me for a moment?" she asked. "I'd like to get Mr. Hadley."

"Go on. Go get him."

She left the document on the table and rushed out. As she reached Mr. Hadley's office, Joel grabbed her arm. "Are you okay?"

"Yes. No. I have to get Mr. Hadley."

Joel's eyes narrowed. "What's wrong?"

"I'm not sure." She shrugged out of his grasp. "I'll tell you later."

Fortunately, Mr. Hadley was in his office. She explained what had happened and remembered to pull the file with their copies of the authentication and appraisal reports. When they entered the sales office, Chelsea let Mr. Hadley take the lead.

"I'm terribly sorry about this," he said, his British accent more distinct than usual. "I can't imagine how it might have happened, but I'll get to the bottom of it. In the meantime, please bring the painting back. We'll have it reauthenticated and I will in good faith refund the full purchase price until we sort everything out."

Mr. Anderson's color was returning to normal and his voice didn't sound quite as shrill. "That'll be fine. I'll have the painting brought in tomorrow. I've spent enough of my time traveling back and forth from Boston."

"I understand. Why don't I make it easier for you and arrange to have it picked up?"

"That would be appreciated."

Mr. Hadley's solicitousness and offer of transport seemed to appease Mr. Anderson, at least temporarily. The two men shook hands, neither paying much attention to Chelsea. She felt it was deliberate and wondered why this had become *her* fault, when she didn't have any responsibility for acquisition, valuation or authentication.

She stayed back and waited until Mr. Hadley had seen Mr. Anderson out. When he came back, Joel and Tina were both with him. Mr. Hadley's brow was furrowed, his mouth a thin, straight line.

"Can anyone venture a guess as to how this could've happened?" he demanded.

Joel seemed to know what he was talking about, but Tina looked perplexed. Chelsea gave a brief overview of the situation. Tina grabbed the file folder from the table and leafed through it. "Ridley's did the authentication. They're one of the most respected houses in the state. They wouldn't make a mistake like that."

"Well, *someone* did. Anderson used Murphy & McGuire. It's equally unlikely that they'd make such an enormous error. If this leaks out, especially before we get to the bottom of it, our reputation will take a huge hit." Mr. Hadley turned to Joel. "I'll need you to prepare for a media onslaught." At Joel's nod, he continued. "I'm going to have to tell your grandmother about this. I'd much rather she hears it from me than other sources—like the press."

Joel raised his hands. "I have to agree. She won't be pleased, I can tell you that. You know as well as I do that the gallery is her passion, and she cares deeply about it. This gallery is everything to her."

"Other than you," Chelsea added softly.

Joel shifted his gaze to her. "Yes. Thank you."

MR. HADLEY DECIDED it would be best to deliver news of this import to Mrs. Sinclair in person. Joel went off somewhere shortly after their meeting, and Tina was arranging for the top authentication expert in New York State to have a look at the Babineux.

Chelsea and Deborah were covering the showroom. Not that there was a lot of walk-in traffic. Frankly, Chelsea wanted to go home. A headache was beginning to pound behind her temples and she was facing the possibility of losing a substantial commission. A commission she'd already spent on her car for the much-needed maintenance work.

As the front-door chime sounded, she sincerely hoped Deborah would take the customer. With the mood she was in, it was highly unlikely she'd be able to make a sale, anyway. When she saw Detective Sam Eldridge, her heart did a little skip. She glanced at Deborah, who was already sashaying over to greet Sam.

Chelsea felt an unexpected and unreasonable pang of jealousy as she watched Deborah turn on the charm for Sam. She really couldn't blame Deborah, since a man's looks were a priority for her, and Sam had them in spades. But she didn't have to hang around and watch this, she thought, and turned to go.

"Chelsea!" She heard Sam call her name. "Do you have a minute?"

She swung around and saw the mildly annoyed expression Deborah gave her. "Yes. Certainly." She walked back toward Sam.

"Is there somewhere private we could talk?"

"Sure. The sales office."

Sam glanced over at it. "Somewhere without glass walls?" he asked.

It had been a long day, and the throbbing behind her temples was intensifying. "Can we—"

"Let me buy you a coffee," he interrupted.

She was about to refuse, but before she had a chance, he added, "official police business."

It must've been loud enough for Deborah to hear. With a satisfied smirk, she tossed her long blond hair over one shoulder and walked back to the office area.

"All right. Give me a minute to get my things." And take an aspirin.

Chelsea went to her desk and pulled her handbag from the bottom drawer. She took the painkiller first. With the drawer still open, she noticed the high-heeled pumps she'd worn to the gallery's gala. Headache be damned, she took off her more practical shoes and slipped on the pumps. Using the small mirror she kept in her desk, she touched up her lipstick. Sam might want to talk police business, but that didn't mean she couldn't look her best.

By the time she spritzed on some perfume, her headache was fading.

THE FIRST THING Sam noticed when Chelsea walked out of the back was that she looked… taller. He slid his gaze down and saw the shoes. Unless he was mistaken, they were the same shoes she'd worn the night of the exhibit, but they worked even better with the skirt she wore today.

Caught in the act, he realized when he looked up and saw Chelsea's amused smile. "Ready to go?" he asked, proud of how smoothly he managed to recover from his lapse of professionalism. He helped her with her coat and walked her to his vehicle, having agreed that he'd drive her back to the gallery to get her car when they were done. "How was your day?" he asked as he pulled away from the curb.

She leaned back against the headrest. "Don't ask. One of the worst."

He thought of Joel Sinclair and how unpleasant he'd seemed and glanced at her. "Boyfriend trouble?"

"What?"

"Sorry. Too personal." And where the heck did *that* come from?

"Oh, no. It's not that at all. Just something... unusual happened at work today."

He glanced at her again. She had her eyes closed and seemed unwilling to elaborate.

He drove into The Coffee Shoppe's parking lot and took a spot close to the entrance, and let her precede him into the café

They both had coffee and Chelsea ordered an enormous cinnamon bun.

"What's wrong?" she asked him after swallowing a generous bite.

He watched her tear off another sizable portion. "Where do you put all that food?" he asked.

"I get plenty of exercise walking around at work, and I try to do yoga a couple of times a week," she explained. "Fortunately, I'm also blessed with a high metabolism," she added with a flash of even white teeth. "But you said this was official police business. Do you know who's responsible for the robbery at All That Glitters and Shines?"

"I did say it's police business," he replied, although he'd nearly forgotten, enjoying her company as much as he was. "It's about the robbery, although regrettably we haven't caught the responsible person yet."

Chelsea had been about to put another bite of the pastry in her mouth but paused. "Does it usually take this long with a robbery of this sort?"

"Generally not. The longer it takes, the lower the odds that we'll be able to catch the perpetrator. This case is somewhat out of the norm. And that's part of the problem." He preferred not to tell her outright what he was considering, for two reasons. He didn't want to worry her unnecessarily; she looked troubled enough as it was. Also, if he was going to share his theory with anyone, it should be the curator or owner of the gallery. His purpose in meeting with Chelsea was to get her take on whether there'd been anything out of the ordinary that could indicate the gallery might be a target.

Or so he told himself.

"What's unusual about it?" Chelsea probed. "Is it that Mr. Rochester was hurt? There aren't many incidents like that in Camden Falls. Not that I've heard of, anyway."

"You're correct. We don't see a lot of crime like the jewelry store break-in. Generally, that makes my job a lot easier," he said with a smile. "But since it did happen, we don't want to see a recurrence. Catching the perpetrator will not only keep him or her from a repeat performance, but it'll also act as a deterrent to other potential thieves."

"Sounds like a plan. How can I help?"

Her hands were wrapped around her mug, and her smile was warm and inquisitive. She looked so appealing, he had to force himself to remember what he'd been about to say. "Uh, Willowbrook Avenue is home to most of Camden Falls's retail stores, the most likely targets for a thief. I couldn't help noticing," he said, smiling again, "that you seem to be aware of what goes on in the neighborhood and don't mind getting involved, if the need arises. I don't mean that as a criticism," he added quickly, when he saw her eyes narrow. "I was wondering if you'd seen anything suspicious in the area, either before or after the robbery."

Her brow furrowed. "Not that I recall. The store owners and employees along that stretch of Willowbrook all know each other and we're a close-knit group. We tend to look out for each other. If anyone had seen anything, I would've found out."

"Have you seen or heard of anyone unfamiliar or someone who seemed out of place visiting the gallery or any of the other stores?"

She took a sip of her coffee but kept her eyes steady on his. Finally, she shook her head. "You're asking me because you don't think the robbery at All That Glitters and Shines was an isolated incident. You think the gallery or one of the other businesses on Willowbrook might be targeted."

It wasn't posed as a question. Her agile mind impressed him. "We haven't discounted the possibility. We've arranged for extra patrols along Willowbrook for the time being. Just in case."

Chelsea nodded. "Thank you. There wasn't

much of value stolen from All That Glitters and Shines, was there?"

"No."

"But there *was* a great deal of damage. I can't imagine Mr. and Mrs. Rochester having enemies. So, I don't think it was targeting them." Sam assumed she was looking for confirmation or denial. Careful to give her neither, he was again struck by how bright she was. He was starting to respect her intelligence as much as her courage, kindness and humor.

"It wasn't strictly vandalism, though," she continued. "There are easier, less risky ways to accomplish that than breaking *into* the store. What was the motivation, then?"

"Interesting line of reasoning," he said. "You've taken courses in criminology?" he teased.

Her delighted smile caused a twinge—like extreme hunger—in his gut.

"No, but I love reading crime novels." Her expression turned serious. "I can put two plus two together well enough to know that if you considered it a routine robbery, we wouldn't be here having coffee."

The thought of them doing just that, but for personal reasons, ran through his mind. "Maybe I used it as an excuse to get you here."

She rolled her eyes, but not before she smiled at him again—flirtatiously this time. "I understand you can't tell me more," she said, "but I honestly don't know what I can say that would help. Believe me, I want the person who hurt Mr. Rochester caught." The intensity in her voice underscored her words.

"You care about him," he said, stating the obvious.

She raised her hands. "*Of course* I care about Mr. Rochester. And Mrs. Rochester, who's been worried sick about her husband. They're a sweet couple. The way they are with each other, you'd think they were in the honeymoon phase of their relationship. They've been married more than forty-five years."

He mentally added *romantic* to the list of her attributes. And the list was getting long. She had intelligence, warmth and compassion. She had a spirit of fun that he readily admitted he was lacking but admired. And, needless to say, he loved the way she looked.

But she had a boyfriend and he had to stay focused on the case. "Another question, if you don't mind. Is there anything more you can tell me about Adam Rochester or his mother?"

"Not really." She stared down at the table. "I told you everything I know the other night."

He'd been watching her intently—couldn't take his eyes off her. So he'd noticed that the warmth fizzled out as she talked about the nephew. "You don't like him."

She raised startled eyes to meet his. "What makes you say that?"

"I'm a detective, remember. Well-honed observation skills," he responded, trying to put her at ease again and lighten the mood. It had the desired effect, making her smile again. "So, why is that?" he asked.

She seemed to consider his question for a moment. "I don't *dislike* Adam. We've just never…connected."

"How long have you known him?"

"Since I started working at the gallery. Nearly five years ago now."

"That's a long time not to connect with someone."

"Perhaps," she acknowledged. "But I don't think connecting is a function of time. We're too different."

Soon after, Sam ran out of questions, and he needed to take Chelsea back to the gallery. He dropped her off there and said good-night.

But he found himself thinking about her as he drove home.

He was drawn to her in a way he couldn't

remember being drawn to anyone else...other than Katherine. He'd been tempted to ask Chelsea about her relationship with Joel again, but he didn't want to cross the line from business to personal. Her reaction to his impromptu question in the car had told him she was sensitive about it.

Didn't it just figure that when he finally met a woman he could be interested in, it was during an investigation *and* she was in a relationship. Even if those obstacles didn't exist, he recalled her comment about not connecting with Adam Sinclair because they were too different.

Weren't *they* too different? Sam wondered grudgingly as he let himself into his apartment. Not from his perspective. And her comment about connecting not being a function of time? His own reaction to her had been almost immediate, so he had to agree.

It was only when he closed the door behind him that he realized he'd neglected to ask her what she'd meant about this being one of her worst days.

CHAPTER SEVEN

VERY GENTLEMANLY, CHELSEA mused, how Sam had walked her to her car at the gallery and waited until she'd pulled out of the parking lot. It was a thoughtful gesture.

Although Detective Sam Eldridge was about as far from what she considered her "type" as she could imagine, he intrigued her. He was undeniably attractive, but it was more than that. She found his personality appealing, so steady and solid—and her complete opposite.

Wouldn't it be fun to throw him off his game? Get him to be a little more spontaneous?

And she was known for her spontaneity!

There was no ring on his finger—she'd checked—and she was sure he'd be the kind of man to wear one if he *was* married. She went into her apartment, hung up her coat and scooped Mindy into her arms as she headed to the kitchen. She placed the purring cat on a kitchen chair and searched through her handbag for the business card Sam had given her.

Samuel D. Eldridge.

The name suited him. She wondered what the *D* stood for but wasn't surprised to see the use of his middle initial. He just seemed to be the type. *Stuffy* was the wrong word. *Proper* was more like it.

Mindy meowed and Chelsea scratched her behind the ears.

Sam looked like someone who could use some fun in his life, she decided.

It was less than a half an hour since he'd dropped her off. Chances were that he'd be home or wherever he'd been going.

She tapped the card against her fingers and grinned.

Grabbing the phone, she dialed his cell number.

"Eldridge here," was the brusque response.

"Owens here," she said, mimicking him.

"Is everything okay? Did I forget something?" He sounded confused. Point for her!

"Yes and no."

"Did you think of anything else that might help the case?"

She was tempted to laugh, his reaction seemed so in character, but she didn't think he'd appreciate it. "No, and before we play twenty questions, here's one for you. Are you busy after work tomorrow?"

His pause told her she'd surprised him. She could all but *hear* him ask "why?" "I don't have any plans."

This was it. She'd either get what she wanted...or embarrass herself. But, hey, what was life without risk? "I thought we could have a drink together."

"A drink?" No question she'd surprised him.

"Yes. You know. Share conversation over an adult beverage."

"But don't you..."

"Don't I what?"

"What about you and Sinclair?"

"What does Mrs. Sinclair have to do with this?"

"Not *Nadine* Sinclair. I meant *Joel* Sinclair."

"I'm sorry, I'm not following you."

"Aren't you seeing Joel?"

Now he'd surprised her. "No. What made you think..." Before she'd finished the question, she recalled Joel's strange behavior the night of the gala. "Oh, no! You misread things. Joel and I dated for a while, but that ended almost four months ago."

"I'm sorry. I didn't mean to pry. It's just—"

"That I was asking you out, and you didn't

want to tread on anyone's toes." That was something else she could admire about him. A core of decency she'd sensed even when she'd first met him. The way he'd obviously cared about Mr. Rochester. Letting her comfort him, although it had been clear to her that it was contrary to police procedure.

"That sums it up."

"Can I assume you aren't seeing anyone, either?" She was being direct, even for her, but she might as well get it out there while they were on the subject.

She heard a choked laugh. "It's safe to say I'm not."

"Well, then?"

"Well, then what? Oh… Sorry, I'm not used to being asked out by beautiful women. Yes, I'd like to have a drink with you."

She smiled.

"But there's a condition."

Her smile wavered. "A condition?"

"That I buy."

A lot of guys—in her experience, anyway—expected the woman to pay her own way. Joel had been one of them. While she liked to think of herself as being on equal terms with any man she dated, she didn't have an issue if that man wanted to hold a door open for her or, as in this case, treat her. "I can accept that condition."

"Glad to hear it. Do you have a place in mind?"

"How about Sorley's on Eden Avenue?"

"Sounds good. What time?"

THEY'D AGREED TO meet at five thirty, allowing each of them to finish work and drive the short distance to Sorley's. After the initial shock had worn off, Sam had to admit he'd liked the fact that Chelsea had taken the initiative to ask him out. It had also cleared up his misconception about her and Joel Sinclair.

Sinclair had intentionally misled him. Yeah, Sinclair and Chelsea might've *started* dating two and a half years ago, but he'd neglected to mention that they hadn't been involved for nearly four months.

Sam had been pleased to discover from Chelsea that there was no longer a personal relationship between her and Sinclair, although he wasn't entirely sure that Sinclair would dismiss it as readily as Chelsea had.

He'd have to exercise some caution there.

At work, Sam made a point of wrapping things up on time for a change. In the station's locker room, he took off his tie and stuck it in his pocket. He washed his face, cleaned his teeth and ran a brush through his hair.

As he pulled up in front of Sorley's fifteen minutes later, he saw Chelsea's car. One more thing to like about her. She was punctual. If things went well, maybe he'd be able to talk her into having dinner with him.

One step at a time, he cautioned himself, as he walked into Sorley's.

She was sitting in a booth, facing the door, and noticed him right away. Smiling, she waved to him, and he felt that strange sensation in his gut again.

Shortly after he sat down, a waitress came to take their order.

"Thanks again for getting together with me," she said after they had their drinks.

"Thanks for inviting me. But I have to ask—why did you?"

She shrugged. "I'd like to get to know you."

He was about to ask why again but held back. "Okay. What would you like to know?"

She laughed. "Just like that?"

"Yeah. Just like that."

She pursed her lips, appearing thoughtful,

and he couldn't stop staring at her, she looked so darn pretty.

"Oh, I know! What does your middle initial, *D*, stand for?"

Now *he* laughed. "That's it? That's what you want to know about me?"

Her grin was big and bright. "It's a start. I wondered when I saw it on your business card."

"It's Dorian."

He hadn't thought her smile could've been any sunnier, but he'd been wrong.

"Dorian? As in *The Picture of Dorian Gray*?"

"The movie, right?"

She nodded. "And the book. By Oscar Wilde."

"Well, yes, I suppose so."

She touched the top of his hand with hers. "See, you *do* have a connection—tenuous as it might be—to the art world!"

"I don't have a picture of myself at home that ages instead of me, if that's what you mean. Speaking of art, how did you first get interested in it?" he asked, wanting to get off the topic of his unusual middle name.

She took a sip of her wine. "Oh, I loved to paint from the time I was old enough to hold a brush."

He smiled, picturing her as a child with a brush in her hand and paint smeared on her face.

"Before you get too caught up in that fantasy, I have to say I had no talent."

"I find that hard to believe." His opinion of her was that she could probably do anything she set her mind to.

She laughed, and the joyous, carefree sound touched something deep inside him that had been dormant too long.

"Okay, maybe *no* talent is a bit harsh. But little talent is as generous as it can get."

"Then why did you choose to work in the field?"

"Ah, well. I may not have the talent to execute, but I developed a strong love of art. My parents supported and encouraged me, so I took art history and other related courses in college. Just about anything to do with art, without actually having to *do* art."

There was that determination he respected about her. "You discovered something you loved and you found a way to make it work for you." Her eyes widened and her mouth softened. "I admire that sort of resolve and perseverance."

"Thank you," she said. "My turn to ask you

a question. Are you originally from Camden Falls?"

"No."

"How long have you lived here?"

He didn't have to think about it. He could give her the answer, almost to the day. "Just over six years."

"Where did you live before?"

"Boston."

"What made you decide to move here?"

"That's more than one question," Sam said, wanting to buy time. He drank some of his beer, and thought about Katherine and Nicolas and tried not to show the grief, which still had the power to debilitate him. He could see she was waiting for an answer, so he gave her part of the truth. "The small-town aspect of Camden Falls appealed to me, and there was a job opening with the police department at the time." He could tell that she was puzzled by his curt response to what was essentially a simple question, but she had no idea what lay beneath it.

He realized she was just trying to get to know him, but the answer—what had precipitated the move, and Katherine and Nicolas—was too painful for him. It was a part of his history he wasn't prepared to discuss with her. At least not yet.

And if he decided against pursuing a relationship with her, maybe never.

CHAPTER EIGHT

WINTER MIGHT HAVE been just around the corner, but the early-morning sunshine slanting through the blinds and spilling across Chelsea's bed felt warm and comforting.

She stretched before snuggling back under the blanket in a happy and contented state, thinking of her evening with Sam.

That thought had her bolting up. It was a workday!

She wasn't sure if it was the sun or Mindy's plaintive meows that had awakened her, but both were indications that she'd overslept.

And that meant she was late for work.

She pushed off the covers, got out of bed and picked up Mindy as she headed out of her bedroom. She fed the cat and made a toasted bagel and coffee for herself, while she left a voice mail for Tina, explaining she'd be a little late…due to unforeseen circumstances.

Ten minutes later, she was on her way to work. Despite her shorter-than-normal sleep, the hurried start to her morning and the regrettable fact that she'd be late for work, Chelsea had to acknowledge that she felt refreshed, relaxed and happy.

And her date with Sam was the reason for it.

After they'd finished their drinks, Sam had suggested they have dinner together. Not the most romantic of invitations, but it worked for her.

They had a leisurely meal, and despite the lateness of the hour when Chelsea got home, she'd called her mother to let her know she'd met someone she was interested in.

Yes, it was early stages yet, but her mother was always encouraging her to get out more. Chelsea knew she longed for her only child to get married and have children. She'd been happy and excited, and had wanted to share it with her mother.

Chelsea almost danced into the showroom.

"Chelsea," Tina called from the back office.

Immediately feeling guilty again about being late, Chelsea hurried over to Tina. "I'm so sorry. Thanks for covering for me. I'll make it up to you. I promise. If Mr. Hadley's okay with it, I'll stay late today so you can leave early."

Tina waved that away. "Don't worry about it. Mr. Hadley is out. So is Joel. No one knows you got here late except us. It's not a big deal. But I do need to speak with you. Do you have a minute?"

"Sure. Let me hang my coat up first."

The look on Tina's face suggested that whatever she wanted to talk about wasn't good news. When Chelsea returned, Tina was sitting at the meeting table in the open area of their office, a white envelope in front of her.

"We got the authentication report back from Hartfield's for the Babineux painting," she said as soon as Chelsea slid into the seat across from her.

She'd believed that Mr. Anderson's consultant had made a mistake. But looking at Tina… she wasn't so sure anymore. Chelsea's heart thumped heavily against her ribs. "And?"

"You better read it yourself," Tina said, pulling the document out of the envelope and handing it to Chelsea.

After a rapid perusal, Chelsea lowered the papers. "This can't be right."

"Oh, it is. I called Harry Stein," she said, referring to one of Hartfield's most respected and senior experts. "There's no mistake. The Babineux we sold Mr. Anderson is *not* the original."

"It's a forgery?"

"That's the upshot."

"How is that possible? We have strict procedures in place to authenticate every piece we acquire to avoid a situation like this. We weren't careless with the Babineux. How could this happen?" she repeated.

"Your guess is as good as mine," Tina replied.

Several thoughts ran through Chelsea's mind, from how she was going to make up the lost commission she'd already spent, to—more important—the impact this could have on the Sinclair Gallery. "Does Mr. Anderson know?"

"No. I wanted to tell you first. Mr. Hadley doesn't know, either. He's got meetings this morning, then he's having lunch with Mrs. Sinclair." Tina winced. "I can only imagine how *they'll* take the news."

Yes, Chelsea could picture that conversation, too. "Okay. Thanks," she said to Tina and rose to go back to her own office.

They now had independent verification that Mr. Anderson's authenticator was correct. They'd have to get back to Ridley's, the company that had done the original authentication. How was it possible that they'd made such a major error?

Technology had advanced to the point that it was virtually impossible to conceive of an error like that by even the most inexperienced person.

And if it wasn't an error, then what?

Chelsea sat down at her desk and stared out the window.

Was it possible that the painting had been stolen and replaced with a forgery? Could Mr. Anderson have had it replicated and exchanged the forgery for the original? No, that was impossible. He wouldn't have had enough time.

"Stop letting your imagination run away with you," she hissed to herself. But if not Mr. Anderson, who could have switched it? When and how?

She was jumping to silly conclusions.

First, she had to break the news to Mr. Hadley, then call Mr. Anderson. She didn't relish the thought of either conversation.

Minutes later, Chelsea reached Mr. Hadley on his cell phone. He was outraged by the news and said he'd cancel the rest of his meetings, go see Mrs. Sinclair right away and be back at the gallery as soon as possible to help with damage control.

How she handled the discussion with Mr. Anderson could have a serious impact. She worried that the gallery would lose one of its best clients; however, the call with him wasn't as challenging as she'd expected. He took the news reasonably well. Better than Mr. Hadley.

Chelsea supposed it had to do with the fact that he'd had time to become accustomed to the idea. Since he trusted the company he used for authentication, he'd already accepted that the painting he'd purchased wasn't the original. He declined the offer of a private showing to choose another piece to replace the Babineux. Chelsea hoped that, eventually, he'd come around.

Her duty done, she turned her mind to what could have happened to the painting. Regardless of how she tried to rationalize it, she kept coming back to the idea that someone had intentionally switched the paintings.

If that was the case, that meant the original had been *stolen*.

And that brought Sam to mind. He'd be able to help her sort through it.

Or did they need to formally report a theft?

Chelsea thought that would probably be the next step, but it would be Mr. Hadley and Mrs. Sinclair's decision, not hers.

Right now, she wanted to talk to Sam and get his take on it, informally if possible. As she was about to call his cell, Tina stuck her head in the door.

"Chels, I thought you might want to know that Mr. Hadley called. He and Mrs. Sinclair have talked and they're on their way to meet with the insurance adjustor. They wanted to discuss the situation with him, to see if they're covered for the loss."

"Thanks for telling me." Chelsea assumed that taking that step meant they'd be reporting the situation to the police, too, probably after their meeting. It made her even more anxious to talk to Sam.

His cell phone went to voice mail. She called his number at the police station next. When it went to voice mail, too, she pressed zero to reach an admin person, and was told he was at the station but in a meeting.

Chelsea had no idea where Joel was, but Deborah had arrived for her shift, and she and Tina could handle any walk-ins. She grabbed her handbag from her bottom drawer, then pulled the file containing the various authentication reports and appraisals for the Babineux. She made copies, put on her coat and rushed out.

The police station was only a fifteen-minute drive from the gallery. Chelsea parked in a visitor's spot and entered through the front door. She'd never been in a police station before. Having always respected and appreciated the dedication and sacrifices of law enforcement personnel, she was a little awed to be there.

"May I help you?" a young woman with long auburn hair asked from behind a reception counter. There was a glass partition separating her from the entrance vestibule.

Chelsea stepped up to the opening and returned her smile. "Yes, please. I'd like to see Detective Eldridge, if he's available."

Her smile brightened. "You're the person who called a short while ago. Chelsea Owens, correct?"

"Yes."

"I told Sam to expect you." She glanced surreptitiously behind her. "I shouldn't be sharing this with you, but when I told him you'd called and would be stopping by to see him, he got a bit frazzled." She leaned closer to the opening. "I haven't seen that before with steady-as-he-goes Sam!"

"Um…okay." Chelsea might say that kind of thing to a total stranger, but she didn't encounter too many other people who were quite that open. Marla, as the receptionist's name plate identified her, was someone she could get to like.

"I'll let him know you're here," Marla said.

"Great. Thanks."

While she waited, Chelsea looked around. There were photographs of honored officers on the walls and even some of police service dogs. Her smile faded and she felt a tightness in her chest when she noticed that a couple of the photographs were in memoriam. Camden Falls might be a small town but, sadly, bad things happened everywhere. She said silent thanks to the men and women who dedicated their lives to law enforcement as she read the plaques under a few more pictures on the walls.

"Chelsea. Hi. What brought you here?"

She could see amusement—and was it pleasure?—on Sam's face. She could also see over his shoulder that Marla was watching them intently. "There's something I'd appreciate your opinion on," she said in a subdued voice.

"Okay," he said with a quizzical look, and led her through the door to the back and into his office.

"Do you remember me showing you the Babineux painting the evening you were at the gallery?" she asked once they were seated.

"I remember you showing me a *lot* of paintings," he said with a laugh. "I couldn't tell you which one was the Babineux."

"It was one of the first ones I showed you. Anyway, one of our best patrons bought it." She frowned. "Or it might be more accurate to say he *used* to be one of our best patrons. Well, he admired the painting at the gala—"

"Now I remember the painting," Sam interrupted. "And the guy who bought it is the one Joel Sinclair made such a big deal out of leaving without seeing you?"

"Yes." Chelsea nodded rapidly. "Anyway, he came back and bought the painting. Because of the value, his insurance company wanted an independent appraisal done. As part of the appraisal process, they authenticate the work to ensure it's the original." She went on to give Sam the details, then pulled the photocopies from her handbag. She placed everything in front of him and watched as he flipped through the pages.

He had strong, capable hands. Long fingers. She wondered what it would be like to link her fingers with his.

She shifted in her chair.

He glanced up, and when his eyes met hers, there was a warmth in them that caused a pleasant tingling along her spine. When he focused on the papers again, she took the opportunity to study him further, the chiseled jaw, dark brows and firm mouth that had just drawn into a frown.

When he looked up again, the warmth was gone from his eyes.

"Is it possible that Ridley's was mistaken in their authentication?" he asked.

She shrugged. "Anything's possible, but it's highly unlikely. Authentication of paintings has come a long way in recent years. It used to be an art, but with current-day technology it's more of a science. Authentication may be a year or two off, if we're talking about old masters, but not centuries. The composition of paints is so dramatically different, I can't see how an error like that could be made. It would be beyond incompetence. Regardless, we'll have Ridley's reauthenticate the painting."

Sam nodded thoughtfully while he stacked up the papers and handed them back to her. "When do you expect the results?"

"They'll be concerned. Understandably. It's their reputation as much as ours. I expect they'll make it a top priority. We should have the results in a day or two."

Sam nodded again. "What do you think happened?"

Chelsea tried to ignore the fact that Sam was all business now. She laughed to calm her nerves. "You're asking me?" She pointed to herself. "That's why I came to see *you*!"

He settled back in his chair. "I don't have sufficient information to come up with a hypothesis. How easy is it to replicate a painting like that and make it convincing enough to fool industry experts?"

"It would take considerable skill and time, but there are plenty of talented artists out there who aren't making money from their painting. There's a lot of money at stake. It's doable."

"And timewise?"

Chelsea thought back to how long they'd had the painting. "That would be more challenging. We only had the painting for a couple of weeks before we sold it. Its first showing was at the exhibit you attended. I suppose it could be done, but it would take a lot of focus."

"Could Anderson have switched it? Taken the original home, brought the forged one back?"

"It's plausible from the perspective that it was under his control, but I don't see how he could've done it in the available time. He would've had to know that we had the painting and somehow managed to get a replica produced in advance. And we didn't publicize that we'd acquired it. I'm quite certain that seeing it the night of the gala wasn't something he expected."

"Okay. How did the gallery acquire the painting and is there any chance it could've been duplicated *before* you had it?"

"We acquired it through auction. Prior to that, it was in the private collection of a Russian billionaire. But that's a valid question. Although working from the original would be preferable, a good forger wouldn't necessarily require it. A high-resolution photograph, zoomed in, would show the brushstrokes, for example."

"Can I assume that even with the gallery's security system and guards, it would be easier for someone to break into the gallery than a Russian billionaire's home...or palace, whatever his accommodation would be called?"

"Yes, this particular billionaire lives in a palace and, yes, I suppose you're correct. There's another possibility, though. The gallery owns a warehouse space. It's seldom used, but I believe the Babineux might have been part of a shipment that was stored there before we put it on display."

"How secure is the warehouse?"

"I've never been there." She thought back to the time she'd heard Joel talk about it. "It has a security system with motion sensors throughout. I imagine the security system would have to be a good one, if Mrs. Sinclair and Mr. Hadley felt comfortable leaving expensive pieces there. It would have to be at least as secure as the gallery. The advantage, if someone wanted to get in, is that it's not in a high-traffic area, especially after normal business hours."

"That's a good thought. Do you want me to open a case file?"

"Mr. Hadley or Mrs. Sinclair should make that decision. They'll probably want to wait until we get the results from Ridley's to make sure it wasn't a mistake." Thinking it through, she realized that she might have been premature in bringing it to Sam's attention. "I'm sorry to have bothered you with this."

He smiled, and she was glad to see the man rather than the detective. "It's no bother. It gave me a chance to see you." He brushed a hand across hers, and that made her think again about holding his.

Shortly after, he walked her to her car. Before she could get in, he touched her shoulder, causing an odd little flutter in her chest.

"I'd like to see you again…on a personal basis."

The sensation intensified. "I'd like that, too," she said, which was a significant understatement. She enjoyed being with him.

"How about Saturday night?"

"Great—" Her smile faded. She'd been so excited by the prospect, she forgot that it was the night of Mrs. Sinclair's annual charitable event at her home, and she'd already confirmed her attendance. The annual event at the gallery and the one at Mrs. Sinclair's home tended to happen in quick succession, as part of the buildup to the holiday season. "I'm sorry. I just remembered a prior commitment."

"No problem. We can make it some other time."

"Or...would you like to join me at Mrs. Sinclair's place for a charity function?"

"Not more art!" he exclaimed, but she could see he was joking.

"Given half a chance, I'll turn you into an art lover!"

"Will it hurt?"

"Only if you don't develop an appreciation for art," she responded with a grin as she climbed into her car and closed the door.

CHAPTER NINE

"WITH ALL THE excitement because of the forged Babineux, the week flew by," Chelsea explained to Sam as they drove to Mrs. Sinclair's home Saturday evening. "That's the house. On the right," she said, pointing to the stately Victorian.

The long driveway was already full of cars so Sam took the first available spot at the curb. He helped Chelsea out of the passenger side and, with a hand on the small of her back, guided her toward and up the front steps.

Joel opened the door for them. "We're glad you could make it," he said, quite obviously to Chelsea, and placed a kiss on her cheek. "Detective," Joel added, but with considerably more reserve.

"Quite the place," Sam commented as they followed Joel into a spacious black-and-white marble-floored vestibule.

"It's seen better days."

Sam shot a look at Chelsea behind Joel's back. She simply rolled her eyes.

Joel took their coats and led them into a large living room, with high coffered ceilings and tall windows. "Let me get you something to drink. What would you like?" he asked Chelsea first.

Chelsea glanced at the other guests to see what they were drinking. "I'll have a glass of champagne, please."

Joel turned to Sam. "And you?"

"A Coke with ice would be great."

After Joel walked away, Sam checked out the room—the old, expensive-looking carpets, the elegant if somewhat threadbare furniture and, most striking, the plethora of art throughout. Judging by what Chelsea had shown him at the gallery, he surmised that the art in this room had to be worth a small fortune. It didn't surprise him to see the motion sensors at the corners of the ceiling. It was prudent of Mrs. Sinclair to have a solid security system. "What would all this be worth?" he asked Chelsea, gesturing to the works of art.

"Oh, not as much as you'd think. Some are originals, but she also has several replicas. For example, that one over there? The man in the top hat, writing…" She took his hand—he felt a jolt at the touch—and led him over to a small oil painting. "This is by Manet, painted circa 1880. The original is worth millions, but this is a flawless replica."

Sam stepped up to the painting, examining it more closely. "Looks like a real painting to me. How do you know it's a replica?"

"Oh, it's a real painting, all right, meaning someone painted it. It just isn't the original." She smiled. "The reason I know is that the original disappeared during the Thompson Museum art heist. It was one of a group of works of art stolen from the museum, and none of them have been recovered, despite everyone's best efforts." She looked up at him. "You've heard of the Thompson heist?"

It'd happened well before Sam's time as a police officer, but you couldn't work in law enforcement and not know about the theft. "Yes." He tried to recall the details. Sam turned back to the painting. "And this is a replica of one of the stolen paintings?"

"Yes. In total, those thirteen works of art are valued at over five hundred and eighty million dollars. I'm not sure of the exact breakdown, but I did the simple math once and came up with roughly forty million apiece."

He took a last look at the painting and shook his head. "I do know that the Thompson art heist is the biggest art theft—in fact, the biggest property crime—in the United States to date. Not only has the art never been recovered, the identities of the thieves are still unknown."

"Here you go," Joel interrupted, and handed them their glasses. "Admiring the painting, Detective?"

"Call me Sam, please, and yes. Chelsea was just explaining its history to me."

"Being an art lover, my grandmother has an avid interest in—even a fascination with—the Thompson heist. She was living in Cambridge at the time. She's often talked about the shock waves that went through the art community when it happened. And again, when it became clear that the thieves wouldn't be apprehended."

Joel paused. Sam suspected he was waiting for a rejoinder, but Sam was reluctant to engage in more verbal fencing. Joel seemed marginally less antagonistic toward him, and more accepting of his being with Chelsea. Sam wasn't interested in provoking him and didn't take the bait.

"Anyway," Joel finally continued, "make yourselves at home and talk to some of our other guests. If there's anything I can do so that your evening is more enjoyable, let me know. Please consider donating, Sam. Any amount is appreciated. The proceeds will be split between the Cambridge Children's Hospital and Camden Falls General. There's a collection box in the library around the corner there." Joel gestured toward an archway at the far end of the room and, with a nod of his head, left them.

As Sam watched Joel work the room, he recalled a comment he'd made when they first arrived. "What did Joel mean by this place having seen better days? It looks like there's a lot of money here."

"I've heard him allude to that before. When we were seeing each other, he told me about his concern that his grandmother had invested a great deal in art, but wasn't investing in the upkeep of her home."

Now that Chelsea mentioned it, Sam could see the faded water stain on a portion of the ceiling and adjoining wall, and some peeling paint on the window frame closest to them. "I can understand why he'd be concerned about his grandmother. Does he live here with her?"

Chelsea sighed. "No, he has his own apartment, and I'm sorry to say this, but I honestly don't know if he's more worried about her or his inheritance." She shrugged. "Don't get me wrong. He cares deeply about his grandmother. It's one of the traits I like and respect about him. But there's a mercenary aspect to his nature, too. He's his grandmother's only living relative and therefore her sole beneficiary. I feel he resents it when she donates large amounts to charities, as she will after tonight." Her eyes rested on Joel, and Sam saw a sadness in them. "He's basically a good person," she concluded. "Let me show you around and introduce you to people who might be of interest to you. I see that some of the other Willowbrook business owners are here. We should start with our hostess, though."

"Mrs. Sinclair," Chelsea called to her just as she was disengaging from a small cluster of people."

"Chelsea, my dear. I'm glad you could make it."

"I wouldn't miss one of your charity events," she said with sincere affection in her voice. "Mrs. Sinclair, do you remember meeting Detective Sam Eldridge at the gallery exhibit and auction?"

Nadine Sinclair gave Sam an enchanting smile, and once again he noticed her beauty, despite the lines of age. "I hope it's not business that brought you here this evening."

"Not at all. It was Chelsea. A pleasure seeing you again, Mrs. Sinclair. You have a beautiful home and an impressive art collection."

"Chelsea's gotten you to appreciate art, Detective?"

He glanced at Chelsea and saw the smile she was trying to hide. "Call me Sam, please, and let's say that my appreciation is…developing."

"I'm glad to hear it. I saw you were admiring my Manet earlier. It's a beautiful piece, isn't it? I can imagine that young man sitting on that patio, admiring all the lovely young women passing by. The original painting was stolen." She moved to the painting. "Quite romantic, I think."

"The painting or the theft?"

Mrs. Sinclair turned faded but undeniably astute blue eyes back to Sam and chuckled. "Oh, the painting, of course." She squeezed Chelsea's hand. "Make sure Sam develops an appreciation for my pieces, Chelsea, and I hope you both enjoy yourselves. I should pay attention to my other guests now. Thank you again, Sam, for coming."

"She's very charming," Sam observed, once Mrs. Sinclair was out of earshot.

"Yes, she is, but underneath the charm, there's a backbone of steel and a well-honed business mind." Chelsea smiled up at him. "I like working for her…and for Mr. Hadley. I hope she'll give me the chance to be curator when Mr. Hadley retires."

"I hope so, too, but wouldn't it make sense for Joel to do it, since he's family?"

The shake of her head had her silver earrings dancing with a muted tinkling sound. "Joel's not interested. He likes marketing and promotion, but not the actual dealing with patrons. He doesn't like handling the financial end of things, either." Her eyes clouded. "He used to say he supported me completely, but that was before we ended our relationship. I hope he'll still want me as curator. Mrs. Sinclair might have a mind of her own, but the one blind spot she has… No, that's wrong. She's smart enough to see Joel's strengths and weaknesses. So, it's not a blind spot as much as a *soft* spot for Joel."

"That's understandable, isn't it? Since he's her only relative. Her only grandchild." And sole heir, he reminded himself.

"Yes, I suppose."

"Well, why don't you continue my cultural education?" he asked with a smile.

"As long as you don't end up laughing at any of Mrs. Sinclair's prized pieces!"

He sent a pained look at an abstract across the room. "I'll try, but I can't make any promises."

Chelsea grinned at him as they moved to the next painting. He felt her stiffen slightly when a man he recognized from the night of the exhibit at the gallery approached them.

Chelsea made the introductions. "Mr. Anderson, this is Sam Eldridge."

"Pleasure to meet you. This is a lovely piece, isn't it?" he said to neither of them specifically.

"It is," Sam responded, sensing Chelsea's discomfort. "Mrs. Sinclair has many...lovely pieces." Not a word he'd generally use, but it seemed appropriate under the circumstances.

"Yes, she does, indeed." Anderson looked down at Chelsea. "I wonder if she'd be willing to do transactions with me through her private collection, now that my confidence in the gallery's been shaken. A pleasure," he repeated to Sam and walked off before Chelsea could answer.

Chelsea had paled noticeably. Not wanting to add to her discomfort, Sam decided against asking if Anderson was the man who'd bought the Babineux. His recollection was that it was the name Joel had mentioned when he'd told Chelsea at the gallery event that the potential purchaser had left. He made a mental note to ask her about it, and the odd exchange, later.

"I see Arnold Rochester, the owner of All That Glitters and Shines, is here," Sam remarked.

Chelsea turned in the direction he'd indicated. "Oh, yes. He's here with his wife and..." She glanced around the room. "I imagine Adam's here, too, somewhere. Over the years, the Rochesters and Mrs. Sinclair have developed more than a business relationship. Joel and Adam used to be close friends, as I told you. The two families socialize together and support each other in their business endeavors when they can."

Knowing what Adam looked like, Sam glanced around the room to see if he could locate him. He found him on a settee next to Mrs. Sinclair, a glass of wine in his hand. Chelsea introduced Sam to several other people and tried her patient best to educate him about the works of art.

By the time the evening was winding down, he'd had enough art and was more than ready to leave. He'd realized earlier that Chelsea was much more of a people person than he was, but spending the evening with her had impressed him. He admired how charismatic and vivacious she was with everyone present. Just watching her wore him out. And on the topic of *watching*... He'd caught Joel doing that on more than a few occasions. The looks he gave Sam when they made eye contact were far from friendly. It reinforced in Sam's mind that Joel was obviously not over Chelsea.

"Feel like a coffee?" he asked as they walked back to his car.

He was pleased when she agreed, as he wanted to spend some time alone with her.

They were sharing a booth at The Coffee Shoppe when Sam remembered to ask Chelsea about Anderson and their brief exchange. "Is Mr. Anderson the person who bought the painting with the authentication problem?"

"Why do you ask that?"

"Remember? Well-honed detective skills," he said jokingly before turning serious again. "I assumed as much when he said his confidence in the gallery was shaken."

"Oh, that's right. He did say that." She stared down at her coffee mug. "It's the first time we've ever had anything like this occur at the gallery, at least that I'm aware of. It's crazy! We still don't know what actually happened or how. We've made it right with Mr. Anderson, but we're trying to keep this quiet, since it could hurt our reputation."

"Has it been reported formally to the police?" He recalled that she hadn't wanted him to open a case file when she'd come to see him at the station.

"I don't believe so. Mr. Hadley is dealing with the insurance company and he's asked, through the gallery's lawyers, to have Ridley's take another look at the painting. I think he and Mrs. Sinclair want to have the result first, to make sure it wasn't simply a mistake. *Should* we have reported it to the police already?"

"Not necessarily, but I expect the insurance company will be doing their own investigation. There's a substantial amount of money at stake, correct?"

Chelsea nodded.

"Based on what you've told me about the authentication process, isn't it most likely that the company doing the authentication in the first instance wasn't wrong? That someone switched the paintings?"

"I know we discussed that, but…I don't know how it could be possible. I was probably overreacting." She smiled weakly. "I can't imagine that happening in our gallery. Someone defrauding us. That would be a criminal act."

"Yes, it would. As for whether it's possible, unfortunately that's what keeps people in my line of work employed, small town or not. You showed me a painting tonight that you described as a flawless replica of a Manet, the original of which you estimated to be worth millions of dollars." He shook his head at that.

"I know. Hard to believe, but true."

"With a lot of money on the line, I know we discussed this but why wouldn't it be possible for someone to have a replica created of the Babineux quickly?"

"It would be possible. Naturally. But it would take a great deal of talent…and it couldn't be done too fast."

"Hmm. Okay." Sam could tell she was getting agitated. He decided to change the subject. "You mentioned the other night that you organize tours for schoolkids at the gallery."

"Yes, I do. They love it!"

"Huh. Really?"

"Why does that surprise you?"

"I didn't think kids that age would like… *that* kind of art." He was backing himself into a corner.

"Kids have such wonderful, open minds. Why wouldn't they?"

"I just thought the art at the gallery would be more appealing to adults." That sounded credible, he congratulated himself silently.

"The kids are generally quite taken with most of our pieces. My guess is they focus on the colors and the movement, not so much on the execution or realism that most adults might."

He was skeptical.

Chelsea's smile widened. "You haven't spent much time around kids, have you?"

He understood she meant it in a teasing way and couldn't possibly know about Nicolas, but the pain of loss ripped through him. He doubted he'd ever get over the death of his son. But it didn't mean he didn't like kids. "I'm a wish granter for the Wish I May Foundation, and I try to interact with the kids whenever I have the chance. For example, if an ill child wants to go to a New England Patriots game, or go up in a police helicopter, I try to arrange it."

"You do? That's wonderful!"

"Now it's my turn to ask why that should surprise *you*."

She shrugged. "I guess I wouldn't have thought of you as being big on kids."

"I like helping these kids and their families. The kids often have only a few months to live. If I can put a smile on their faces or get them to forget their pain for a short while, it's worth it. Have you heard of the organization?"

"Oh, yes!" Chelsea replied. "My best friend, Paige, met her husband through the Wish I May Foundation, when he became a wish granter for her son, Jason, who'd been diagnosed with brain tumor."

A child's illness—any child's—affected Sam deeply. He'd thought this would have been a safer topic, but apparently not. "I'm very sorry…" he murmured.

"No, no. It's a happy story!" Chelsea assured him. "Paige and Daniel are married, and it'll be the third Christmas this year that Jason will be cancer-free."

There were examples of critically ill children whose stories did have happy endings, Sam reminded himself. It hadn't worked out that way for Nicolas, but wanting to make a difference for kids trying to beat the odds was one of the reasons he volunteered with the Wish I May Foundation. "That's good. I'm glad," he said, but he was struggling to shake off the depression that engulfed him whenever he thought of Nicolas.

"Anyway, that's not all," Chelsea continued, oblivious to his mood. "One of my former neighbors married the organization's executive director, Laura Armstrong. Well, she's Laura Weatherly now. She's an angel, and boy, did she ever bring Mr. Weatherly out of his shell! You must know Laura if you work with the foundation."

"I do know Laura, and I like and respect her. She has a way of getting people to commit to things before they realize they're doing it."

Chelsea laughed. "Yes, she does. You should ask Paige's husband, Daniel, about that!"

Sam's good mood was being restored by Chelsea's enthusiasm and beguiling chatter.

"Paige and Daniel are having a dinner next weekend. Why don't you come?"

"Because I don't know them and I haven't been invited," he said with a quick grin.

Chelsea gave him a playful swat on the hand. "Very funny. They…ah, they'll have a bunch of people there, I think. Probably Laura and her husband, too. I'm allowed—in fact, *encouraged*—to bring a date. Consider yourself invited!"

He pulled out his cell phone and checked his calendar. He wasn't working that evening. "Then I'll accept the invitation. Now, back to these schoolkids enjoying the art at the gallery—do you think I should take some of the kids I sponsor through the Wish I May Foundation to the gallery?"

She smiled. "You're more than welcome to. I'm not sure, though, if it's because of the art rather than getting a day off school that these kids are so enthusiastic, but I've yet to meet a kid who didn't have a great time."

When Chelsea yawned, he suggested they call it a night.

"I'm sorry. It's not the company. I promise," she said, quick to apologize. "Thanks to the issue with the Babineux and the additional duties I've taken on to learn about the operation of the gallery, I suppose I've been burning the candle at both ends."

"No offense taken. I'm glad I drove so I can get you home safe and sound and not have to worry about you falling asleep behind the wheel."

Twenty minutes later, he pulled up in front of her apartment building.

He walked her to her door. When she looked up at him, her smile was sleepy. "Thank you for joining me this evening. I hope you didn't find it too boring."

"Not at all." He didn't think he could ever be bored by being with her.

"Well, good night." She placed her palm on his chest, rose up and kissed him lightly. "Thank you for a nice night, and for driving me home."

The feel of her lips on his—as brief as it

might have been—stayed with him as he watched her let herself into her apartment.

Maybe he hadn't completely closed himself off to the prospect of a relationship.

Maybe there was still hope for him…with Chelsea.

CHAPTER TEN

CHELSEA VISITED PAIGE after work the following Monday.

"I'm always happy to see you, but to what do I owe this unannounced visit?" Paige asked.

"Does there have to be a reason?" Chelsea responded as she crouched down to greet the family's black Lab mix. "Hey, Scout. How're you doing?" She scratched the dog behind his ears and along his back, prompting him to lean into her and whimper with pleasure.

As Chelsea straightened, Paige watched her closely. "What's that saying? You look like the cat that got the cream? Or is it the canary?"

"Do I?" Chelsea's grin broadened, and she followed Paige into the kitchen.

"Uh-huh. Want to tell me why?"

Chelsea did a little pirouette. "You remember I told you about the detective I met?"

"Yes."

"We've gone out a couple of times." She

plopped down on a stool by the center island. "I really like him."

Paige scrutinized her friend even more closely. "This *is* serious, isn't it?"

Chelsea pressed a hand over her heart. "It's early days, but I think it could be. He's the opposite of the kind of guy I thought I'd fall for. He's reserved and serious." She snickered. "He wouldn't know a Picasso from a kid's finger painting. It's my heart and not my head that's telling me he *might* be the right one."

Paige rubbed Chelsea's arm. "Trust your heart, Chels. You remember how hard I tried to fight falling in love with Daniel?" Paige had the dreamy expression on her face that she always did when she spoke about her husband. "Where would I be...and how much would I have missed out on if I hadn't given in to my heart?"

"You two are perfect for each other. And Daniel is so wonderful with Jason and Emily, too."

Paige nodded.

"I'd like you to meet Sam," Chelsea said.

"I'd love to meet him."

She gave her friend a sheepish grin. "I told him you were having a dinner this weekend. With the whole gang. The Bennetts, Laura and

Harrison Weatherly. I know you only invited me, but I got carried away. I wanted Sam to be comfortable. He already knows Laura, and I thought it would be fun if he could meet everyone. Not that I've invited any of them, of course. If it's too much trouble, I'll tell him…something."

"Don't worry about it. I'll call everyone. It'll be nice to see them. Let's just hope they can make it on short notice."

"You're the best friend anyone could wish for!" Chelsea jumped up and hugged Paige. "I'll help in any way I can. Cooking. Whatever."

Paige laughed. "It must be important if you're offering to help with the cooking. Why don't we agree that you'll leave that to me, okay?"

"Happily. But I do want to contribute—and I want to know what you think of him."

"Would how I felt about him make a difference?" Paige asked softly.

Chelsea took a moment to think about it. "Please don't take this the wrong way. Your opinion matters a lot, but considering how *I* feel about Sam, probably not. Having said that, I do hope you'll like him, because you and Daniel are very important to me."

"LOOK AT THAT, the house has an actual white picket fence!" Sam exclaimed as he pulled his car up to the curb in front of Daniel and Paige's home on Saturday evening.

"Great, isn't it? When they were dating, Paige told Daniel she'd always dreamed of a house with a white picket fence. After they got engaged, Daniel found one for her. Wait until you see the rest of the place," Chelsea said as she climbed out of Sam's car.

Paige must've been watching for them, because she opened the door as they stepped onto the front porch. Before Chelsea had a chance to make introductions, Jason ran up to her, Scout at his heels.

"Hey, Aunt Chelsea!"

She bent down to hug Jason, then ruffled Scout's fur. "Hey, squirt. It's good to see you."

"You, too, Aunt Chels."

The honorary title always made her feel warm because without siblings, she'd never have a niece or nephew except possibly through marriage.

She placed her palm on Jason's head. "Have you grown again, squirt?"

"Uh-uh. I don't think so."

"No. I'm sure you have." She lowered her hand by about five inches. "I believe you were this tall last time I saw you."

Jason laughed. "You're wrong! Tell her she's

wrong, Mom. I was that tall a couple of years ago."

Paige brushed Jason's hair back from his forehead. "Not a couple of years, but not last month, either, so you're both wrong." She held her hand out to Sam. "I'm Paige. It's a pleasure to meet you. And this is our son, Jason. Jason, this is Mr. Eldridge."

"Sam is fine with me, if it's okay with you," he said.

"Sure," Paige agreed. "Say hi to Sam, Jason."

Jason held out his hand as his mother had.

Sam shook it and bent down to pet Scout. "And who's this?"

"That's Scout. He's my dog."

"Great dog," Sam observed.

"Paige, would you mind showing Sam your house?" Chelsea asked. "I told him how wonderful it is."

"Of course."

It was evident how much Paige loved the house, and not just because it had the white picket fence she'd dreamed of.

"The three-car garage is perfect for Daniel, since he has a small workshop in there. And here," she said as she led them into an office area, "is my office. Daniel had it initially when he started his company, Heartfelt Legal Services, shortly before we got married."

"Heartfelt Legal Services? I haven't heard of it."

"Daniel will tell you all about it, Sam, if you give him half a chance. It's a legal aid business. He started small, but it took off, and the home office was no longer sufficient for him. Convenient for me, since I set up a business, too, and I needed a place to work."

"What do you do?" Sam asked with interest.

"She's *amazing*!" Jason, who'd tagged along with them, enthused before Paige could answer. "She makes websites for companies. Really cool ones. I designed the logo for Dad's business."

"That's impressive," Sam told him.

Paige touched Jason's shoulder with affection. "He's my best salesperson and all-around cheerleader. I have a web design and maintenance business."

"Her company has done very well and Paige could get a lot more work if she hired staff and found office space somewhere else, but she prefers to operate from home," Chelsea explained.

"The latter part is definitely true. I like keeping the business small and home-based so I can spend as much time with Jason and Emily as possible. Emily's our baby. She's in the family room with the others."

Paige led them through the bright, spacious kitchen.

"Isn't this a fantastic room?" Chelsea asked. "Better yet, Paige knows how to cook really well, unlike someone else standing in this room right now."

"Daniel, come and meet Sam," Paige called to her husband as he entered the kitchen with a couple of empty glasses in his hand.

They soon joined the others in the family room, and Chelsea took baby Emily from Laura and held her lovingly. Paige introduced Sam to her friends and former neighbors, the Bennetts. The elderly couple who lived in Chelsea's building a floor below her greeted Sam warmly.

"Chelsea is a wonderful, kind young woman, and a dear friend. She'll make a great wife and mother someday," Mrs. Bennett said to Sam, which made Chelsea's face flush.

Paige took Sam over to where Harrison Weatherly and his wife, Laura, were seated.

"Sam, I'm so happy to see you," Laura said as she rose to hug him. "This is my husband, Harrison," she said.

"Chelsea did mention that you know Laura," Paige commented. "You're probably aware that

Laura's the executive director for the Wish I May Foundation. It was through the foundation, and Laura's miraculous work, that Daniel and I met. Actually, everyone here today was partially responsible for us getting together."

"How so?" Sam asked.

"Oh, that's a long story," Paige said, taking Emily from Chelsea. "It's best saved for another day."

"What do you do, Sam?" Mrs. Bennett asked him.

"I work for the Camden Falls Police Department."

Jason looked up at Sam with wide eyes. "You're a police officer?"

"Yup."

"That means you do real dangerous stuff to keep people safe, right?"

"Sometimes it can be dangerous."

"Will you tell me about some of the stuff you've done?"

SAM NOTICED THAT all conversation had stopped and everyone present was now focused on him. The center of attention was *not* his favorite place to be. "How about we save that for some other time, too, and you tell me what you want to do when *you* grow up."

Jason grinned. "I want to be an architect."

"Wow! That takes a lot of talent, I'll bet."

"Jason," Chelsea interjected. "Why don't you show some of your drawings to Sam?"

"Okay!" he said and ran off to his room, Scout scampering after him.

"One day that kid'll be exhibiting at the Sinclair Gallery," Chelsea added.

When a timer went off in the kitchen, Chelsea glanced at Paige. "Do you want me to take care of…whatever needs taking care of? Or, my preference, I'll hold Emily for you and you can go do whatever needs to be done."

"I think we'll both be happier if you hold Emily and I go to the kitchen," Paige said with a grin.

"Works for me." Chelsea took Emily and rubbed her back gently until she stopped fretting. "Let's have a look," she said to Jason when he returned. She got the boy settled between her and Sam, and Jason showed them his sketches.

Sam was impressed by his talent. Although he tried to focus on what Jason was showing him, he couldn't help watching Chelsea from the corner of his eye. She was such a natural with both kids. Somehow, at that moment she was the most beautiful he'd seen her. She seemed radiant. She looked up and offered him a warm smile.

Sam forced his attention back to Jason and his drawings. "Those are terrific," he said after Jason had reached the last page in his pad.

"Thanks!" Jason's face shone with pleasure.

"Why don't you go put your pad away so your drawings don't get damaged?" Chelsea suggested.

"'Kay. I'll be right back."

Sam turned his attention fully to Chelsea. She was swaying back and forth, cooing to the baby whenever she made fussy noises. Somehow, the rest of the people present had drifted away, leaving the three of them—him, Chelsea and the baby.

His mind transported him back in time. To a day when the sun was beaming down from a cloudless sky, a gentle breeze ruffling the leaves of the trees. And Katherine was holding baby Nicolas, just like Chelsea was holding Emily right now. Sam remembered vividly the expression on Katherine's face. Her eyes were closed, her smile so achingly sweet it tore at his heart, and she'd swayed and clucked and hummed to their son.

That day they'd both been so incredibly

happy. Elated with life. Desperately in love with each other and their son.

And only days later, their world had come crashing down...

Sam felt a nudge on his shoulder. He looked up at Chelsea.

"Where did you go?"

"What?"

"I was talking to you, but you seemed to have gone somewhere else."

He thought back to the vision of Katherine and Nicolas. "I'm sorry. My thoughts must have wandered."

"It's okay. Paige said dinner's almost ready. Would you like to hold Emily while I help her with the final preparations?"

Sam glanced at the beautiful baby, and the image of Nicolas superimposed itself on her. "How about if you keep holding her? She seems to be comfortable. There's no reason to upset her. I'll go help Paige."

Chelsea's smile dimmed.

"Well played, Eldridge," he mumbled under his breath as he headed into the kitchen. She'd looked at him as if he'd lost his mind. Maybe he had.

The rest of the evening passed uneventfully. Sam had to admit that he liked Chelsea's friends and neighbors. He and Daniel established an immediate rapport. Paige was extremely pleasant and intelligent. He did his best to avoid the kids and by the time they were preparing to leave, he felt guilty about it.

"Don't forget you said you'd come back and tell me stories about being a police officer!" Jason reminded Sam when they were saying their goodbyes.

Yeah, he'd said that earlier. Before the memories of Katherine and Nicolas had barraged him. "What if I do one better?" he asked as an idea occurred to him. A way to ease his feeling of guilt.

"How?"

"Wait here for a minute." Sam went outside and jogged over to his car, unlocked the trunk and pulled out something that he kept behind his back as he returned to the others.

"What did you get?" Jason asked.

Sam held out a black ball cap with the Camden Falls Police Department logo on the front.

"That's a cool cap!" Jason exclaimed. "Can I see it, please?"

"Sure. You can have it."

The kid's face lit up. "Really?"

"Yes, really." Sam adjusted the strap at the back and put it on Jason's head.

Jason placed his hands on top of it, grinning. "Thank you very much!"

A simple gift seemed to have made the kid's day, Sam mused as he drove Chelsea to her apartment.

And what great kids both Jason and Emily were. He tried to pay attention to Chelsea's conversation, but an incredible sadness descended on him as he thought that he'd never again know the joy of having a child.

He walked Chelsea to her apartment but avoided kissing her good-night, regardless of how much he'd wanted to.

At home, Sam went straight to bed, however sleep eluded him. He stared up at the ceiling with unseeing eyes.

He couldn't get the images of Chelsea with Jason and Emily out of his mind. The kids seemed to sense that she loved them, because they kept gravitating to her the entire evening.

Katherine had been like that, too. If things had turned out differently, Nicolas would've been just a few years younger than Jason.

Sam squeezed his eyes shut. It didn't matter how much time passed. The pain of loss might have become almost bearable, but it hadn't gone away.

Seeing Chelsea this evening had made him think. More than that, it had made him yearn for something he hadn't yearned for in a long time. Something he couldn't have.

Family.

There was no question he was falling for Chelsea. He'd liked her from the first time he'd met her, but wasn't it ironic that seeing her with her friends' kids—the very thing he couldn't give a woman—had made him realize that he could lose his heart to her. He owed it to her to let her know about himself...and his background.

No point procrastinating. He'd tell her the next chance he got.

Despite recognizing how he felt about Chelsea, it was Katherine and Nicolas on his mind as he finally drifted into a restless sleep.

CHAPTER ELEVEN

SAM CALLED CHELSEA at work on Monday and made a date to take her to lunch.

"I'm so glad you could meet Paige, Daniel, Jason, Emily and all the rest of my friends," Chelsea said as they sat in a booth at a nearby diner.

"I enjoyed meeting them."

"Aren't they terrific? And you wouldn't believe the change in Mr. Weatherly since he married Laura. He's proof that people should never say never. He was a confirmed bachelor before he met her." Her eyes were steady on his and shone with sincerity. "I'm confident there's that one special person out there for everyone. For Mr. Weatherly, it's Laura. You just never know when you're going to meet that person."

If that wasn't the opening Sam was searching for, he didn't know what was. "Chelsea, you're a very special person. You have so much to offer. I should have told you this sooner, but the timing wasn't right."

Chelsea's eyes turned misty, and her smile was soft and sweet as she reached for Sam's hand. "When it *feels* right is the right time."

Belatedly, Sam realized he'd gone about it all wrong. His preamble had misled her, perhaps understandably. "What I meant to say…"

The anticipation in her eyes made him want to groan. He'd better get it all out before he inadvertently set her up for a bigger fall. "Chelsea, I was married."

Her smile faded and her hands tensed but she didn't pull them away. "You were married?" she echoed. "For how long?"

"Nearly six years."

"Oh…"

"We got divorced years ago, but we had a son."

Now she did pull her hands back. "How… how old is he?"

Her voice sounded hollow. He could tell she was trying to process what he'd said, since it wasn't what she'd expected. "We lost Nicolas when he was one."

Conflicting emotions played across her face, until compassion won out over shock. She reached for his hands again. "I'm so very sorry, Sam. I don't know what to say. I'm not sure there *are* words for something like this.

I know it's ineffectual, but I'm sorry," she repeated.

"Thank you." He had no idea what else to say, either. Never had.

"Why didn't you tell me sooner?" Her voice was gentle. Caring. Not accusatory.

He shrugged. "It's a painful part of my past and I don't talk about it much."

"Do you mind if I ask what happened? Unless you don't want to talk about it," she added hurriedly.

"That's okay. It happened years ago." Not that it made any difference to him. "Katherine, my ex-wife, and I…" he began. "We started dating in high school and eventually got married." He knew that some of what he was going to say would hurt Chelsea, but he had to get it out. It was only fair. "We were deeply in love and were thrilled when Katherine became pregnant two years into our marriage. We agreed that we wanted a family, and we were glad to be starting early. When Nicolas was born…" He paused to take a drink of water. "When he was born, he was happy, beautiful, exuberant." Sam rubbed a hand over his mouth. "Katherine and I were over-the-moon happy. Our world couldn't have been brighter.

"But in just a few months, Nicolas began to

show some concerning symptoms. We got him the best medical care possible, but Nicolas...he never celebrated his second birthday. He passed away of spinal muscular atrophy."

Chelsea had tears coursing down her face. "I'm so very sorry..." she whispered. "How horrible for you. For both of you."

He nodded and tried to swallow the constriction clogging his throat. "With Nicolas's passing, our relationship changed. Subtly at first and then more dramatically. Instead of turning to me in her grief, Katherine became progressively more withdrawn, until she announced one day that she was leaving me. She claimed she still loved me, but said I was a constant reminder of little Nicolas, our loss, and she couldn't endure it anymore."

"I don't know what to say. Did you consider having another child?"

Sam shook his head sadly. "Katherine and I were both diagnosed as carriers of the recessive gene that resulted in Nicolas's illness." What he didn't say was that even if he married a woman who tested negative for the condition, *he* could still pass on the defective gene to their child. After what he and Katherine had gone through with poor little Nicolas, he wasn't prepared to risk that, and had resolved a long time ago that he would never have children of his own again.

Neither one of them said much for a while, and they both had to get back to their jobs. He paid the bill for their lunch and walked her to her car.

Chelsea's eyes were still shining when she rested her palms on his forearms. "I'm so sorry for what you had to go through. I'm really sorry." Rising on her toes, she placed her lips briefly on his. When he didn't pull away, she kissed him again, lingering over it this time.

She said goodbye, got into her Honda and was gone before he'd even taken a step.

Climbing into his own car, he started the engine to get the heater going but didn't put the transmission in gear.

Telling her about Kathryn, Nicolas and his own condition had been the right thing to do.

But now that he had, where did it leave them?

He could see how much Chelsea loved kids and what a terrific mother she'd make. She'd been open about wanting her own children.

Seeing her with Jason and Emily, he couldn't blame her one bit.

Sam was afraid that if his feelings for Chelsea continued to grow, somewhere along the way, he'd face a decision that he knew would leave him brokenhearted. He was anguished by the hurt he'd inflict on Chelsea as well, regardless of the fact that it was in her best interests.

He rested his head against the back of the seat and closed his eyes.

Should he continue seeing Chelsea but keep the relationship casual to ensure that neither of them would plan on a long-term commitment? A commitment which, to his way of thinking, would naturally lead to marriage and, in her mind, children.

Or should he end the relationship, despite his growing feelings for her, freeing her to find a man who *could* give her the children she longed for?

Either choice was a no-win, and he wasn't ready to contemplate that decision yet.

The churning her kiss had caused in his stomach told him he was already in deep.

CHELSEA SENSED A change in Sam.

She attributed it to the mounting pressures of his job. There was no progress on the investigation of the robbery at All That Glitters and Shines, and she knew that frustrated Sam and added to his heavy workload.

He'd called her the day after they'd had lunch to apologize for dumping his history on her and to let her know how much he appreciated her listening to him.

Thankfully, her own job kept her so busy she didn't have much time to dwell on the fact that she hadn't heard from him since and wondered why. Ridley's had taken another careful look at the Babineux and submitted a letter, through their lawyer, categorically denying that the painting they'd just seen was the same one they'd originally authenticated. They provided copies of all their work product and maintained adamantly that it was a replica. The allegation, though not explicitly stated, was that someone had switched the paintings.

Joel had his hands full managing the industry and media fallout. He was doing the best he could, but the news was spreading and having an impact on the volume of sales. Oddly, they had more walk-ins. As sales volume declined, Chelsea concluded that they were mostly gawkers, wanting the thrill of seeing the "scene of the crime."

Mrs. Sinclair was spending more hours at the gallery than Chelsea could remember her doing in the past. Understandable, in her opinion, since it was Mrs. Sinclair's and her gallery's reputation at stake. For the first time since she'd known Mrs. Sinclair, Chelsea thought that she looked her age. She was also seeing a different aspect of her personality. Previously comfortable delegating responsibly to Mr. Hadley, she was now taking charge with a tenacity Chelsea wouldn't have expected her capable of. She might have *looked* her age, but her energy seemed to have increased.

When Mrs. Sinclair wasn't occupied at the gallery, she would disappear for long stretches of time. Tina mentioned to Chelsea that she'd seen her going into All That Glitters and Shines on more than one occasion. Chelsea rationalized that Mrs. Sinclair's dear friends, the Rochesters, brought her comfort, since she came back after her absences reinvigorated and with a sense of purpose.

Under the circumstances, the theft of the Babineux had to be reported to the police. It didn't surprise Chelsea to learn that Sam was chosen to lead the investigation.

He called her to explain that since he'd been assigned the Babineux case, it might be a while before he could see her again.

Her disappointment had been acute, but there wasn't much she could do about it.

After the initial flurry of activity, with the decline in sales, and without a personal life to speak of, Chelsea had additional time to educate herself about the gallery's operations. The situation with the Babineux added to her resolve to learn about authentication and valuation, and not just because of her hope of becoming curator one day. She appreciated more than ever the importance of these aspects of the business.

In the days that passed, she hadn't seen Mr. Anderson at the gallery. Fortunately, Mr. Hadley hadn't asked her to repay the commission on the Babineux. They'd agreed that her future commissions would be used to offset the amount until they were even.

Although Chelsea, Deborah and Tina weren't nearly as occupied because of the decrease in business, Mr. Hadley seemed busier than ever, working to reestablish credibility and industry confidence in the Sinclair Gallery, along with Joel and Mrs. Sinclair. He was out at meetings more than he was at the gallery.

On a particularly slow day, Chelsea sat in her office reviewing the financial statements. She was self-aware enough to admit that numbers weren't her strength. Still, she was interested in learning about every facet of the gallery's operations. That included bookkeeping. As curator, she'd have to understand the financial aspects of the business, and be accountable to

Mrs. Sinclair for profit and loss. Of all the areas she'd been learning about—from media and public relations to valuation and acquisition—the number crunching was the most challenging for her.

She was struggling to understand the balance sheet when she'd much rather have been out front selling art to affect the bottom line. Well, at least she was getting the hang of the terminology.

She was so absorbed in studying the columns of numbers, she jolted when Mr. Hadley called her from the doorway.

She glanced up, but it wasn't Mr. Hadley who drew her attention. Sam was standing beside the curator.

She hadn't seen him since they'd had lunch together, and she felt a flutter in her belly at the sight of him now.

"Chelsea, I'm sorry to interrupt, but Detective Eldridge stopped by to see us about the Babineux. He wants to speak to each of us individually."

"Oh, sure." She put her laptop in sleep mode, rose and tugged her short leather skirt downward in what she hoped was an inconspicuous manner. She gestured to a chair at the small round meeting table in the corner. It was less formal than having her behind the desk and Sam in front of it. It was disconcerting enough seeing him again—and in an official capacity—after the kiss she'd given him the last time she'd said goodbye.

"Have a seat, please," Chelsea offered. *Wow, was this ever uncomfortable!*

As she walked over to join him, she realized her palms were damp. Nervous was not the impression she wanted to make, since he was here to see her because of an active police investigation.

Thankfully, he lowered his tall, muscular frame into the chair she'd indicated, taking the decision of whether she should shake hands with him away from her. "Can I get you a coffee? Some water?"

"I'm fine, thanks." His eyes were kind, and she felt he was trying to put her at ease. But being interviewed by the police, regardless of how she felt about the detective doing it, was not something she could take lightly or be relaxed about.

She pulled out the chair opposite Sam and sat, too. Linking her fingers to keep from fidgeting, she placed her hands on her lap.

Sam glanced over his shoulder, presumably to satisfy himself that Mr. Hadley had closed the door behind him. "Chelsea, I'm sorry about this. I know it must feel awkward for you. Heck, it's awkward for me, but we have a serious matter to deal with. I have to interview you, the same as I do everyone else who works here."

She nodded. "I understand." But did she? Was she being considered a possible suspect or did he just need to gather background information? As much as she longed to, she couldn't ask him. She didn't want to put him on the spot, or unnerve herself even more, if his answer didn't alleviate her concerns.

Sam ran her through a series of questions. Some of them they'd already talked about, but now it was on the record. He asked her about gallery procedures, security and so forth. Chelsea tried desperately to remember what she'd told him before to make sure she didn't inadvertently contradict herself. She wouldn't lie intentionally, but what if she said something different because she was uncertain? Or nervous?

"Chelsea?"

"Sorry. What?" She'd been so preoccupied with her own thoughts that she'd stopped paying attention to Sam.

"I asked if you could tell me about your colleagues, and if any of them might have contact with a person capable of forging the painting."

The idea that one of them might have stolen the original Babineux was appalling. She knew and liked them all. "I don't think any of them could have done this."

His bold blue eyes searched her face. "That wasn't my question, but let's leave it for now. What about Mrs. Sinclair, then?"

"Oh, gosh, no! She's a sweet lady and loves the gallery. No, *lives* for it is more accurate."

He leaned forward. "Chelsea, there was no break-in. No alarms tripped. No video footage of anyone switching the painting. That might mean it was an inside job and the person responsible knew what he or she was doing to circumvent the security system and get away with it undetected."

Chelsea sucked in a breath and raised her hands. "Sam, I'm sorry, but I really can't see anyone here doing that. If I knew anything that I thought would be helpful, I'd tell you."

"Okay. Let's try this. Do you know if anyone who works here has recently run into family or financial issues? A significantly ill relative? A debt they incurred that they don't have the means to repay?"

Chelsea thought about the commission she

couldn't refund but understood that wasn't what Sam was concerned with. Besides, it was a paltry sum compared with what they were talking about. As for the others? Mr. Hadley's sister had a health issue, but she lived in London and Chelsea hadn't heard anything to imply it was that serious. "No. I really don't know of anything like that."

Sam sighed. "All right, Chelsea." He rose and she did the same. "I'm sorry to put you through this. We're dealing with a felony. The value of the painting makes it grand theft." He briefly touched her upper arm. "Please contact me if you remember anything that might be relevant. Never mind how insignificant you might think it is. Okay?"

Not trusting her voice, she nodded.

He stood watching her for a long moment. "Chelsea, I want you to know how much I enjoyed being with you…but it's not a good idea for us to see each other personally until I have this case wrapped up." He walked to the door. When he turned back to her, his eyes looked sad.

Chelsea took an uncertain step forward. She tried not to think of how much she'd started to like him, and the question she hadn't wanted to ask earlier tumbled out. "You believe *I* might have done this? Am I a suspect?" The chill she felt had her wrapping her arms around herself.

She could see he was having a silent debate with himself. "No, I don't. But this is a significant occurrence in our town. Perceptions can be harmful. I need to be unbiased and *seen* to be unbiased."

Eyes wide, she nodded, but couldn't find any words as she watched Sam walk out her office door.

CHAPTER TWELVE

CHELSEA SAT DOWN heavily on a stool in Paige's kitchen after work that day. "Why can't I have a normal relationship with a nice man?" She dropped her hand on Scout's head when he trotted over and leaned against her leg.

Paige turned away from the coffee machine and gave her friend a startled look. "I thought things were going well with you and Sam. What happened?"

"Well, you know about the problem with the painting and that the police are now treating it as theft?"

Paige nodded as she carried two mugs of coffee to the island and handed one to Chelsea.

"The police figure it was an inside job. There're only six of us who work at the gallery, and that's including Mrs. Sinclair, the owner. With such a small number, the police are looking at each of us."

"Oh, no…" Paige was immediately sympathetic.

"Yeah, that's bad, especially when I can't imagine any of them getting involved in something like this, much less doing it themselves. It's a process. I understand we have to go through it. But here's the kicker. Sam is the lead investigator."

"Seeing him under the circumstances must be difficult."

"Yes and no. I mean, yes, it's difficult, but no, I'm not seeing him. At least not now and not until the investigation is over."

Paige reached for Chelsea's hand. "I'm so sorry. You two seemed so good together, and I sensed you were really getting to like him."

Chelsea made a tsking noise. "Yeah, I really was." She forced a smile. "I thought he was getting to like me, too. Maybe we can pick up where we left off—which is really just the beginning—when the investigation's done."

"I don't want to add to your problem, but what if they don't solve the theft? From what you've told me, there's no evidence, and not all crimes get solved, do they? I'm thinking of the Thompson Museum heist, for example, which was years ago. Or closer to home, the All That Glitters and Shines robbery. That's still unsolved as well, am I right?"

"Yes, you are." Chelsea slumped forward and

folded her hands around her mug. "I'm not sure what would happen if it remained unsolved and if Sam stayed on the case. But that would be so far into the future that whatever's been developing between Sam and me would've puffed into thin air, just like that." She emphasized her words with a snap of her fingers.

"Let's stay positive and assume it'll wrap up soon."

"Yeah," Chelsea said with cheer she didn't feel.

They heard a commotion in the front hall, and Scout abandoned Chelsea to investigate. A minute later Jason, with Scout at his heels, came skidding into the kitchen. Just seeing her honorary nephew lifted Chelsea's spirits.

She slid off the stool. "How's my favorite squirt doing today?" she asked as she hugged him.

Daniel arrived home shortly after Jason, and baby Emily woke from her nap a little while later. Paige and Daniel tried to convince Chelsea to stay for dinner, but she knew how precious family time was for her friends. She didn't want to intrude and excused herself.

At home, she fed Mindy, made a salad for herself and, with the cat snuggled up against her on the sofa, called her mother.

"I'm glad to hear from you," Margaret said. "I was planning to call you, since we hadn't heard from you for a couple of days. Is everything okay?"

"Mostly, yes."

"Chelsea…?"

She should've known better than to try to avoid leveling with her mother. Subconscious, perhaps, but that had been the reason she'd put off calling. Even though she knew she'd only hurt herself. No matter what, her parents were always there for her. Solid and dependable.

She let it all spill out. Her father got on the phone for a while, too.

"I love you, Mom," Chelsea said at the conclusion of the call.

"We love you, too, honey," Margaret told her. "It'll all work out the way it's meant to," she added reassuringly.

Those words echoed Chelsea's own thought.

If it was meant to be, she'd have a relationship with Sam. And if it wasn't, she was blessed to have fantastic parents, great friends and a job she loved.

It wouldn't be a hardship for her to make do with everything she was fortunate to have.

She rubbed a hand over the ache in her chest and wondered how long it would take to subside.

WITH CHELSEA'S NEW outlook of taking pleasure in what she had rather than bemoaning what—or more aptly *whom*—she didn't have, she focused on her job.

Mr. Hadley had been perfectly willing to teach her everything he knew. She respected his vast knowledge, which he'd gained working in the industry for over forty years, but the recent events had put her lessons with him on the back burner. His priorities had changed since the Babineux affair. Mrs. Sinclair's presence at the gallery had gradually dwindled and its running fell mostly on Mr. Hadley's shoulders again.

Although Chelsea had to accept that her budding relationship with Sam had fizzled out, she didn't give up on learning. She wouldn't let Mr. Hadley's reduced availability deter her. She was skilled with computers, so while Mr. Hadley didn't have time, she'd teach herself through online research.

With her personal life in a shamble, she was even more determined to pursue her career aspiration. Recognizing the pressures on Mr. Hadley and Mrs. Sinclair, Chelsea hoped there'd be an opportunity for her to accomplish her own goal and at the same time lessen their burden. She wanted to let Mr. Hadley know that she was prepared to help in any way she could.

"Where's Mr. Hadley?" Chelsea asked Joel as she entered the back-office area.

He shrugged his shoulder toward the curator's office but didn't say a word.

His moodiness since they'd split up had been getting worse and was beginning to annoy her. "You know, if you talk to me your tongue won't shrivel up and fall out," she said testily. "For someone who works in marketing and promotion, you'd think he'd have better interpersonal skills," she mumbled under her breath as she headed to Mr. Hadley's office.

His office door was open and Tina must have been on lunch, since she wasn't at her desk. Chelsea was about to knock on the door frame, when she heard Mr. Hadley exclaim in an uncharacteristically aggravated tone, "I said no! It's not possible for me to do it."

Chelsea lowered her hand and peered around the corner. She could see Mr. Hadley pacing back and forth in front of his window. With his free hand, he scratched the top of his head, mussing his thick salt-and-pepper hair. She could only assume that he was talking to Mrs. Sinclair, and the discussion was *not* going to his liking. Still, raising his voice at her was out of character for him.

"It's not my fault the shipment is arriving early…Uh-huh. I understand, but it can't be helped. This is a large shipment and I don't have time to do the inventory." He paused to listen again. "Look, if it was anything other than my sister…" His voice dropped and she could hear the emotion break through. "I don't know how much time she has. I must catch that flight to Heathrow today. As it is, I'm hoping I'm not too late…"

Chelsea was aware that Mr. Hadley's sister, who lived in London, was ailing and he planned to go see her, but she hadn't known how ill she was. If that was Mrs. Sinclair on the phone— and who else would he be discussing a shipment with—Chelsea was shocked by her lack of sympathy to Mr. Hadley's sister's plight. That was also out of character.

Admittedly, all of them were on edge.

Sam's question about family illness came to mind, but she was certain there was no money issue, and Mr. Hadley would never do anything illegal or damaging to the reputation of the gallery. And what a terrible time for him to have to worry about his sister! Not that there ever was a good time, of course.

The conversation had upset him, by the sound of it. This might be the perfect opportunity for her to demonstrate what she was capable of, by inventorying the shipment and completing all the paperwork for Mr. Hadley to review on his return.

"No. You don't have to worry about that. When is the shipment due to arrive?" she heard him ask, then there was a pause. "The Mackenzie warehouse? Why there?" Another pause followed. "Uh-huh. Yes, I suppose that makes sense. I'll take care of it as soon as I get back."

Chelsea realized that the conversation was coming to an end. Yes, she wanted to talk to Mr. Hadley about her idea, but she was reluctant to have him discover that she'd been eavesdropping on his conversation. Odd that they'd ship to the Mackenzie warehouse, though. That was Joel's domain; he used it to store marketing materials, displays and packing goods. To the best of her knowledge, it wasn't climate-controlled to the exacting standard they required for fine art, so they only used it for that when it was unavoidable. All the more reason she should take the initiative to deal with the shipment, she thought, as she hurried toward the showroom.

"Hey, Chels," Joel called to her as she passed

his office. Sure, *now* Joel was talking to her. She noted he was with Adam Rochester.

"That woman who looks like a crow? One of your top customers?" Joel said.

She frowned at him. That was one of the things she'd come to *not* like about him. How he could be critical and mean. "Mrs. Duffy?"

"Yeah. Her. She's here and asking for you. Deborah offered to help, but she wants you. Something about an important purchase."

Mrs. Duffy had been eyeing the Angelo bronze for some time. Could she be here to purchase it? If so, thank goodness she hadn't let Deborah help her. The commission on the bronze would go a long way to make up what she'd lost on the Babineux. "Thanks," she said to Joel as she rushed out of the office area.

As it turned out, it *was* the bronze that Mrs. Duffy was interested in and she bought it! It took well over an hour to get her to commit, but Chelsea finally had the deposit, and the paperwork was signed. This was their first major sale since the whole Babineux fiasco.

It would be icing on the cake if Mr. Hadley let her do the inventory of the new shipment. Telling him she'd sold the prized bronze sure wouldn't hurt the likelihood that he'd agree to it!

Entering the back-office area again, she noticed that Mr. Hadley's door was closed. "Is he with someone?" Chelsea asked Tina, who was now at her desk.

Tina glanced up. "Oh, no. He's gone."

"Gone?"

"Yeah. You knew he was leaving to visit his sister. There was a report of a major accident on Interstate 93. To make sure he didn't miss his flight, he headed for Logan Airport earlier than he'd planned." Her face brightened with a smile. "Congratulations on being acting curator while he's gone." The smile spread into a grin. "Can I have tomorrow off?"

Chelsea returned the grin. "Not on your life! I need you here."

"It was worth a shot. When he saw you were with Mrs. Duffy, he didn't want to disturb you." Tina reached into the top drawer of her desk, pulled out a set of keys and card keys and passed them to Chelsea. "He left these for you, in case you need them while he's gone. Oh, and this, too." Tina handed her an envelope with her name on it.

"Thanks." Chelsea turned to go but paused. "Do you know if we've done some upgrades to the warehouse on Mackenzie Avenue? Enough to store paintings there?"

"No, I don't. I haven't heard Mr. Hadley mention it."

"Do you know the street number?"

"No. I haven't seen it on any statements. I don't think I've heard Mr. Hadley mention that, either, but I do recall him complaining that he had to park his car on Addison when he went there. So I assume it's near the intersection of Addison and Mackenzie. Joel could tell you."

"Yeah. Thanks," Chelsea repeated as she walked out of the office area.

Given how strained her relationship with Joel had been lately, she didn't feel comfortable asking him about it.

She'd just have to find it on her own.

CHAPTER THIRTEEN

CHELSEA BELIEVED IN FATE. She was convinced that she was *meant* to overhear the call Mr. Hadley had presumably with Mrs. Sinclair.

With Mr. Hadley gone, she saw it as an even greater opportunity than she'd originally thought to demonstrate how much she'd learned about the overall operations of the gallery.

Not knowing the exact location of the warehouse didn't deter her and, no, she didn't want Joel to find out what she was planning. With the information Tina had given her about the intersection, she'd surely figure it out.

The note Tina had passed her contained clear instructions regarding her priorities while Mr. Hadley was away. There was no mention of the new shipment. Obviously, it had been news to Mr. Hadley, and she'd heard him state clearly that he'd take care of it on his return.

Yes, this could work out very well for everyone. It was also an opportunity for her to show initiative, she rationalized, a true sign of a good leader. Since she was acting curator and they were down a person, she couldn't leave the gallery during normal work hours, but her evening was free, once she'd stopped by her apartment to feed Mindy. She worked impatiently through the remainder of the workday.

Eager to get started, Chelsea left the office right at five. She drove home in the first snowfall of the season, fed Mindy and—to appease the cat for hurrying back out again—gave her a catnip mouse she kept hidden for just such occasions.

By the time Chelsea left her apartment, there was a light blanket of snow on the ground.

It was nearing seven in the evening when she arrived at the intersection of Addison and Mackenzie. There was no sign identifying the warehouse as one used by the Sinclair Gallery, which made sense since it wasn't a public venue. Being discreet was a prudent security precaution, because they didn't want possible thieves to think there might be something of value inside the nondescript building.

The other doors near the intersection did have signs, so through the process of elimination, she decided that the door she was looking for was the second one from the corner.

A nearby streetlamp flickered as she parked

adjacent to the curb. Glancing down the dark, deserted street sent a prickle of apprehension coursing up her spine. Her imagination playing tricks on her, she imagined that the elongated shadows cast across the pristine blanket of snow by security bollards were menacing loiterers. Grabbing her handbag from the passenger seat, she locked her car and, suppressing the urge to run, strode purposefully to the door.

She tried her master key in the lock, jiggled it around, but without success. Futile, maybe, but she pushed at the door, then gave it a bad-tempered kick. She felt a moment of unease and checked for security cameras. Relieved that none were discernible, she berated herself for not having thought things through—something she was admittedly guilty of at times because of her impulsive nature. Maybe she had the wrong building or the wrong door. She seriously considered getting back in her car, driving home to curl up with Mindy, a cup of chamomile tea and a good book, and forgetting the whole idea.

Then she remembered Mr. Hadley's keys, which Tina had given her. He must've been in a big hurry, because he'd left his entire key chain, instead of just the keys he thought she might need. Rummaging through her handbag, she found them. Trying the keys at random, she got to a shiny, relatively new one. Not having high hopes since the lock on the door looked anything but new, she was surprised when it slid in smoothly and turned without a hitch.

"Well, what do you know?" she murmured to herself. The lock must have been rekeyed recently and this most definitely *was* the right unit.

She pushed the heavy metal door open.

The screech it made as it swung on its hinges was worthy of a horror movie and had her glancing down the empty street again.

Intrusion system! she thought suddenly and held her breath until she was satisfied that at least there was no audible alarm. If she'd triggered a silent alarm, she couldn't do anything about it now. She searched in her bag for her iPhone and switched on its flashlight. Locating the alarm system panel on the wall beside the door, she saw that it had no lights flashing and appeared to be unarmed. If that was the case, it was careless of whoever had been here last. If not, and the security company personnel or the police were dispatched, she'd just have to explain who she was and her motives when they showed up. She had the letter from Mr. Hadley in her handbag, to attest to the fact that she was the gallery's acting curator, which should help.

Oh, she hoped whatever happened, it wouldn't be Sam she'd have to explain herself to.

She walked farther inside, the clicking of her heels on the concrete floor echoing around her. Using the flashlight on her phone again, she found the switches for the lights. Flipping them on, she immediately felt self-conscious in the bright glare of the overhead fluorescents. Still feeling some misgivings about being in the space without explicit permission, regardless of how noble her cause, she quickly tested the various switches and decided to leave on only a set of low-wattage incandescent lights. For her own comfort, she nudged the door shut behind her and locked it. She didn't want someone wandering in off the street while she was working.

She glanced around the room. What she saw wasn't what she'd expected.

Yes, there were several packing crates lined up along one wall—probably the shipment Mr. Hadley had talked about—but the center of the space resembled an artist's studio more than a storage area. She took a few more steps into the room. Annoyed by the harsh sound of her heels, she yanked off her boots and walked around on stocking feet.

She trailed a finger along a work surface littered with tubes of paints, brushes, palettes, palette knives, and all manner of rags and solvents. There were high-quality canvases stacked against a wall, and a couple of professional-grade easels.

Sniffing the air, the faint but distinct smell of oil paints and turpentine filled her nostrils. Odd, since oil paints were rarely used these days. Checking the tubes, she found that most did contain oils. Her mind was spinning with possibilities, not the least of which was whether this could be the place where the Babineux had been duplicated. That would mean it *had* to be an inside job, as Sam had speculated.

Not possible, she told herself. Joel was loyal to his grandmother and he, personally, had no artistic skills to speak of.

Classes, maybe? Mr. Hadley had mentioned doing that as a possible extension of their school program, but why here instead of on school premises? And why wouldn't she have been informed, since she ran the children's programs? Everyone at the gallery knew she loved working with kids, and would've wanted to be part of it.

She had no appreciable talent, she reminded herself with chagrin.

Noticing another door at the back of the

warehouse, leading to a protruding, fully enclosed area, she walked over to it. After pushing the door open, she fumbled around on the wall until she found the light switch. She wasn't worried about the brightness of the lights attracting attention this time because the room had no windows.

It was a relatively small but elegantly decorated exhibit space. The lighting—warm and moderately bright like that at the gallery—was ideal for showing works to maximum effect. There were display stands and easels with velvet draping and a couple of comfortable upholstered chairs. The walls were covered in a rich brocade. The room, however, didn't contain any art.

She ran her hand along a velvet settee.

Why would there be an exhibit space inside a warehouse? The Sinclair Gallery was known for pampering its patrons, especially those who were regular clients and tended to buy the most expensive pieces. Nice as this small room was, she couldn't imagine bringing any of their discriminating patrons here.

No rational explanation for what she was seeing came to mind…unless it was connected to what had happened with the Babineux. She didn't know how that could be or who was responsible, but she didn't like what she was seeing.

She looked behind the wall drapings, to be sure she wasn't missing anything. She found only unpainted drywall. Turning off the lights, she left the room.

It occurred to her to call Sam—but what did she really have to go on? The artist's area could just as easily have been for touching up works of art when necessary, which would also explain the oils. Still, she was feeling more exposed, and thought about the footprints she'd left in the snow outside. Glancing out one of the high windows, she saw that the snow had intensified, and her footprints had probably been obscured. But her car was parked in front of the warehouse, and she had lights on inside the building. Dim as they were, they'd be noticeable from outside in the still, dark night.

She returned to the private exhibit space at the back of the room, and her eyes narrowed. Maybe the space *wasn't* intended for their regular customers.

Was it possible that it was used to display original paintings to potential black-market buyers, and the Babineux wasn't the only forgery shown at the gallery? If someone had gone to the trouble of setting all of this up, Chelsea suspected the Babineux wouldn't have been an isolated incident!

No, there had to be a logical explanation. She couldn't let her overactive imagination run amok and have her jumping to conclusions.

But if there *was* something illegal going on…

She looked furtively around. She did *not* want to get caught in here on her own. Mr. Hadley might be out of the country, but as urgent as it had sounded to her during his telephone conversation that the paintings be inventoried, it could be possible that Mrs. Sinclair would send someone else.

With potentially hundreds of thousands— if not *millions*—of dollars at stake, unsavory people might be involved.

No, she didn't want to get caught in the warehouse.

She glanced at the crates again. Under the circumstances, her plan to do an inventory of the paintings would have to wait.

But she had to take a quick peek to see if there was anything unusual about the contents of those crates.

Having expected the customary wooden shipping crates used for transporting artwork, she'd had the foresight to bring along a screwdriver set, a small hammer and a chisel.

Excitement, anticipation and nerves coursed through her in equal measure.

She uncrated the first paintings she assumed were part of the shipment in question, then examined the contents of a couple of the other crates.

Dropping back on her heels, she released a huge breath.

Everything seemed to be in order. The contents appeared to be consistent with the bills of lading attached to the crates. There didn't seem to be anything out of the ordinary here.

Overactive imagination. Overactive imagination, she chanted to herself.

She'd tell Sam what she'd found, but the more she thought about it, the more she was convinced there was nothing untoward going on. It all related to the operations of the gallery. Granted, she didn't know all the uses for the warehouse. She'd been aware of its existence but she hadn't had any reason to go inside, since it was seldom utilized.

Putting the paintings back, she secured the crates, leaving them the way she'd found them.

She slipped on her boots and was about to leave, when a thought occurred to her. She hurriedly pulled out her phone again and snapped pictures of the workstation. She'd show the pictures to Sam and let him draw his own conclusion.

Opening the entrance door slightly to look outside, she struck by how silent everything was. Large flakes of snow drifted gently down.

But there was a set of footprints on the ground.

Not hers, which the snow *had* covered, as she'd guessed. The prints stopped some distance away from the entrance and backtracked the way they'd come, disappearing around the street corner. Had the person stopped to peer into the warehouse through the barred window?

Her first inclination was to follow the footprints to see where they led. Feeling a tingle on the back of her neck, she thought better of it. Slipping out the door, she locked it and hurried to her car.

The footprints—and the possibility of someone having seen her inside the warehouse and maybe recognizing her car—made her rethink once more what she'd found and what it might mean.

She needed to talk to Sam, she decided, with a mixture of excitement at the prospect of seeing him and hurt that he'd so effortlessly shut her out.

He'd made her promise to contact him if she

thought of anything that might pertain to the investigation. Well, she'd be following his instruction.

Chelsea took a final look at the front of the warehouse before buckling her seat belt and driving away. She'd tell Sam what she'd discovered and get his take on it. She might as well mention Mr. Hadley's sister's condition in response to his question about family illnesses. She was certain it was unrelated to the switching of the Babineux, but he *had* asked.

Regardless of what it might mean to her career aspirations at the gallery, she had to do what she considered right.

According to the clock on her dash, it was almost eight.

She had no idea if Sam was working the evening shift or not. That saddened her because it reminded her of the distance that had grown between them—and what she'd hoped they'd have together.

As to whether he was on shift, there was one way to find out and that was to call the station. She didn't feel right using his cell number in case he was off duty. Since it was after normal work hours, it wasn't Marla who answered the phone. The person who did insisted on knowing who was calling before she'd tell Chelsea if Sam was in or not. That meant Sam would know she'd called. She supposed it was better than showing up unannounced. Fortunately, he was working and at the station rather than out in the field.

Traffic flowed smoothly, although slower than normal because of the steadily falling snow. Twenty-five minutes later, she parked in a visitor spot behind the Camden Falls police station. Despite everything, she felt a sense of anticipation about seeing Sam. Flipping down the visor to access the little mirror, she fluffed her hair and ran a finger under her eyes to wipe away a bit of smeared mascara. Noticing that she'd managed to chew off most of her lipstick while she was in the warehouse, she applied a fresh coat of her trademark red.

Once inside the station, she checked in with the receptionist at the front desk. The woman looked at her assessingly, then called Sam to let him know she was there.

A few minutes later, Sam entered the vestibule where she was waiting. When she saw him, all she could think of was what it would feel like to step into his arms.

"How are you?" he asked, dragging Chelsea out of her musings. He reached out and brushed at her shoulder. Her heart did a little skip and she tried her best to ignore it. When she could only stare at him, he explained, "Snow. You had snow on your coat."

"Oh. Oh, thanks. Sam…I'm sorry to bother you, but there's something I need to discuss with you."

"No bother." His voice turned businesslike. "Is everything okay?"

"Yes. No… I don't know." She ran her hand over her hair, feeling the dampness from the melted snow. "If you're not too busy, could we talk somewhere?"

"Absolutely. Kim, the admin meeting room is available, isn't it?"

Kim tapped a few strokes on her keyboard. "Yes."

"Thanks. Let's go," he said to Chelsea.

"Okay," she replied, and followed him through the security door.

Sam led Chelsea to the administrative area of the station and into a small meeting room. He'd missed her, being with her, talking to her, *laughing* with her, but the impact of seeing her again—the feelings it evoked—astonished him. "Uh, can I get you anything?" he asked as he pulled a chair out for her.

"Water would be great. Thanks," she added

as he placed a paper cup he'd filled from a cooler in front of her.

She fidgeted with the cup instead of drinking from it, which fueled his curiosity about this impromptu visit. He wasn't going to rush her, because he was enjoying her presence far too much.

He didn't think he'd ever get tired of simply looking at her. She wasn't what he'd call conventionally beautiful. Her looks were more… exotic. Striking. Had he noticed before how clear and expressive her eyes or how soft and full her lips were? When she scraped her teeth over her lower lip, he almost groaned.

He wanted to kiss her, to touch her, but knew it would be out of line. After all, he'd been the one to put the distance between them, and he had no right to arbitrarily renege on that now.

She finally took a sip of water and turned her gaze to his. Those bright green eyes were troubled. Whatever this was about, it wasn't easy for her, either.

"Thanks for making time for me," she began.

"No problem."

She exhaled heavily. "So, today I was at work. And Mr. Hadley left for England. He's originally from London."

Sam nodded.

"Anyway, he was on the phone. I happened to listen. That doesn't sound right. It sounds as if I was eavesdropping. There was no one else there. So I stopped outside his office and...listened." She paused to take a breath. "Well, I suppose I *was* eavesdropping, but—"

Sam placed a hand on her wrist. "Chelsea, slow down. I'm having trouble keeping up."

"Yeah, okay." She slowed her pace considerably. "Like I said, Mr. Hadley left for England today to visit his sister. First off, you'd asked if I was aware whether anyone associated with the gallery has a family member who's ill. From what I understand, Mr. Hadley's sister is seriously ill. She had a stroke recently and there've been complications. Other than her son, she has no immediate family in England."

Chelsea's pace had picked up again, and he could see that she'd noticed and moderated it once more.

"I know you asked about that to see if anyone was in dire financial straits. His sister's son is a lawyer. Successful from what I understand, so I don't think it's a matter of needing money for her care."

"Okay." He sensed that wasn't all. He couldn't see her getting agitated over that bit of information, nor did he think she'd come to see him to deliver it. But, since she had, it made him realize again how much he'd missed her. "Was that it?" he prompted.

"No. As Mr. Hadley was getting ready to go, I overheard him talking on the phone, probably to Mrs. Sinclair, about an important shipment that needed to be checked, but he had no time to take care of it until he returned. I'm acting as the curator while he's away." She smiled at him hesitantly.

He couldn't help feeling proud of her, because he remembered how much she longed to be the next curator. "Congratulations."

"Thanks." She glanced down. "Anyway, I thought I'd do something extra to prove myself…" She went on to explain how she'd gone to the warehouse and what she'd discovered. "I really don't want to believe there's anything illegal going on, but when I was driving over here, I tried to come up with another explanation." She threw up her hands. "I just couldn't."

Sam considered everything Chelsea had said. She'd been excited at first and her words had tumbled over each other, but she'd calmed down as she explained her suspicions to him. He didn't know what to make of her far-fetched idea. He was aware of her excitable nature and vivid imagination. They were aspects of her character that he found fascinating and so much a part of who she was. But especially in view of those character traits, he was dubious of what she suspected. Even considering what had happened with the Babineux, what were the odds of her having unearthed a possible counterfeit art operation in premises leased by the Sinclair Gallery?

Still, implausible as her suspicions seemed, he respected her shrewd mind and quick wit. It wasn't just because he'd been falling in love with her that he couldn't categorically dismiss her claim.

Falling in love with her?

The realization stunned him but not in an unpleasant way.

He looked back at her and suddenly he was seeing her differently.

But he couldn't think of her in those terms. At least not while the investigation was ongoing. With no plausible suspects but all indications suggesting it was an inside job, he couldn't eliminate her despite what his gut told him.

He forced himself to focus on what she was doing.

She had her iPhone in her hand and was tapping and swiping the screen.

"What are you looking for?" he asked.

"I just remembered I took some pictures of the work space with the paints and other things." She looked up briefly with a self-deprecating smile. "Foolish of me not to have shown you the pictures. Okay, here's my photo gallery. Scroll through them and see what you think." She handed him her phone. *Handed* wasn't the right word, he thought; it was more like *shoving* it at him. That made him smile.

He glanced at the phone, scrolled through a couple of pictures and gave her a questioning look.

"What?" she asked.

He held the phone out to her.

She grabbed it back and studied the pictures herself. Dropping the phone in her lap, she raised her eyes to his. "The last time I'd taken some pictures, it was through a window and I'd turned off the flash to avoid getting a reflection. I must've forgotten to reset the camera to auto-flash," she mumbled, dejection evident in her tone and in her features. "That's why the pictures are all dark. The lighting in the warehouse was very low." She propped her elbows on the table and rested her head in her hands. "I'm sorry I wasted your time."

The tenderness Sam felt for her was uncharacteristic and potent. He held out his hand. "Let me have your phone for a couple of minutes. I'll download the photos and have our IT people brighten them." He saw her hesitate and wondered with amusement what other pictures she might have on her phone. "Are those the only photos you took today?"

She nodded.

"I'll just download those." He smiled reassuringly. "I promise."

Returning a few minutes later, he handed her phone back to her.

"Now what?" she asked.

"It's quite late. Why don't you go home and get some sleep? You've had an eventful day. I bet you haven't had dinner."

"No, I haven't. But…"

"Chelsea, there isn't enough evidence for a search warrant," he explained. "Even if we're able to brighten the photos, I don't think it would give us enough for a warrant. Some painting materials in space leased by the gallery wouldn't be sufficient to justify it. Right now, for me to inspect the inside of the warehouse, I'd have to have someone with authority provide access."

"I can give you access!" she insisted. "I'm acting curator this week."

"Chelsea, be careful, please. Unless you have explicit permission to enter that warehouse, not only can you *not* give me access, you shouldn't go back in."

"But—"

"You might have the key, but it's not part of your normal work space. I'd hate to have to charge you with trespassing if we receive a complaint from the owner."

"But Mrs. Sinclair wants the matter of the Babineux solved more than anyone, because it's her gallery and her reputation!"

Her expression showed her dismay, and her shoulders had drooped, too. He understood he was disappointing her by not doing anything about the warehouse and what she suspected. The urge to gather her in his arms was powerful.

"Chelsea, go home. Have something to eat and get some sleep," he repeated. "We'll have clearer images from your phone tomorrow. We can talk about it then."

He rose, and she did, too. He was sorry about his part in causing her spirits to plummet, but there was nothing he could do. And if it *was* an inside job and what Chelsea had seen in the warehouse was somehow related, the fewer people who knew she'd been there, the better.

CHAPTER FOURTEEN

WHEN CHELSEA'S ALARM SOUNDED, she hit the snooze button. She rolled over on her side, stretched much like Mindy would and curled up again, tucking an arm under her head. The cat sprang up on the bed and butted her head against Chelsea.

Chelsea wasn't a morning person. Never had been.

She wanted to stay in bed with the happy dream she'd had about dancing on a moonlit beach with Sam. It was so tempting to try to recapture the dream that she thought about drifting back to sleep for a few more minutes.

Instead, she bolted up in bed. She'd nearly forgotten that she was acting for Mr. Hadley. That meant she had to be at the gallery early. Well, if not early, at least she had to be on time. She tossed back the covers, eliciting an annoyed grumble from Mindy. She made coffee and took her first hit of caffeine, then showered, dressed and hurriedly did her hair and makeup. After opening a can of cat food for Mindy, she fixed herself a bagel with cream cheese.

Despite the few extra minutes she'd spent luxuriating in bed, Chelsea was at the gallery and preparing the first pot of coffee in the staff kitchen before eight. She had paperwork to do, so a second cup was called for.

As the coffee brewed, she leaned against the counter and let her thoughts drift back to her dream about Sam. Her recollection of the imagined brush of his lips across hers made her skin tingle. She jerked when her phone vibrated in her pocket, almost simultaneously with the machine signaling that the coffee was ready. That was a rude way to end her fantasy, she thought irritably.

Pulling her phone out of her pocket, she felt her annoyance subside at seeing Sam's name and number on the display. She held the phone to her ear as she poured her coffee.

"Hi," she said cheerfully. "Did you have a good night?"

"I didn't get much sleep," he admitted.

"Oh...?" She loved the sound of his voice, especially when it seemed a little reserved. A little uncertain, as it did just then.

"I probably shouldn't be saying this, but I couldn't stop thinking about you."

That tingle she'd felt speared straight to her stomach. "I'm trying to feel bad about that, but I can't." Then she remembered why she'd seen him the evening before. "Did your IT people have a chance to brighten the photos?"

She heard him clear his throat. Not a good sign.

"One of the guys had a look at them. When he brightened them, he lost definition. I'm sorry, Chelsea, but he couldn't bring sufficient clarity to the photos because of the muted ambient light in the warehouse. We can make out the work counter and that there are things on top of it, but no detail. We can see the easels, but they don't mean much since there are no paintings on them, and even if there were…"

"Oh…" Chelsea couldn't hide her disappointment. "I'm sorry."

She thought back to their conversation the evening before. "This means there's still nothing you can do?"

"That's right."

They chatted uneasily for a couple of minutes, then Chelsea thanked Sam and said goodbye. She was sorry that a conversation that had started on a happy, hopeful note had ended with tension between them. Taking her coffee to her office, she finished the paperwork just as the other staff began to arrive. She hated the fact that she looked at each one of them carefully, wondering if they could be involved in a forgery operation.

She took a couple of telephone calls, spent some time on the showroom floor, then retreated to her office again. "I've got to concentrate on a couple of things," she explained to Tina and closed her door.

In the privacy of her office, Chelsea got out her phone and tried to enhance the photographs herself. After twenty frustrating minutes, she tossed the phone on the table.

How ridiculous to even try. Did she really believe she'd be able to do something the IT experts working for the police department couldn't?

Why didn't she check the flash setting? Or notice that the flash hadn't gone off?

She'd been too tense. Too distracted. And not thinking logically, she berated herself.

And on the topic of thinking…how likely was it that she'd stumbled on a forgery or smuggling ring? There *had* to be a rational explanation for what she'd seen. It wasn't out of the question that her imagination had run wild. Grudgingly, she admitted that it wouldn't be the first time.

She remembered with more than a little embarrassment that shortly after Paige had started dating Daniel, she'd read a story in a Boston paper about a Mr. and Mrs. Daniel Kinsley, and she'd convinced herself that it was the same Daniel Kinsley Paige was seeing. She and their neighbor Mr. Weatherly had gone on a reconnaissance mission to determine if she was correct.

She rolled her eyes at the ceiling.

Boy, had she been wrong! It hadn't been Daniel. It had been his parents. Daniel was a sweet, honest, straightforward and considerate guy.

Thank God she hadn't ruined her friendship with Paige when she'd confessed to her what she and Mr. Weatherly had done.

Was it possible that she was wrong in this case, too?

She considered talking to Joel about it. Asking him what the setup in the warehouse was for. He'd know, if anyone did. He'd probably give her a very plausible explanation, and she'd feel foolish. The most prudent course of action was to let it go.

But she couldn't!

She'd seen what she'd seen.

She just had to figure out what it meant and what to do about it.

OVER A WEEK had passed since Sam had seen Chelsea. He'd been tempted to call her more times than he could count, but he'd resisted.

To add to his frustration, both the All That Glitters and Shines robbery and the Sinclair Gallery cases had stalled. He didn't have any leads for either. When he heard that Charles Hadley had returned from England after his sister passed away, he saw that as an opportunity to follow up on what Chelsea had told him.

He wasn't doing it simply to appease Chelsea, Sam reminded himself as he parked his vehicle in the gallery's parking lot. He'd checked with the gallery's administrative assistant, Tina, regarding work schedules. He purposely chose a day when Hadley would be at the gallery but Chelsea wouldn't to avoid running into her. Tina had told him that Hadley had given Chelsea a couple of days off in appreciation for the extra workload she'd handled while he was gone.

That worked to his advantage.

Since the showroom was empty, Sam took the time to get a better feel for the place. It was sparsely but tastefully decorated. That made sense, since they'd want everyone's focus on the art. The lighting was subdued and also drew attention to the artwork. His predominant impression was of understated elegance. He imagined the environment would appeal to people who were affluent but unlikely to flaunt it.

He glanced at the art on display. To each his own, he thought, then watched Joel Sinclair emerge from the office area. Joel must have been thirty or thereabouts. Not much younger than Sam. He had a slight build, topped out probably around five-ten, short blond hair and brown eyes. Sam sensed the same animosity from him that he had when they'd first met. It belied the casual smile he offered as he approached. "Welcome back, Detective." He held out a hand. Sam shook it and decided there was resentment as well as the animosity. "Are you interested in making a purchase today?"

"Oh, I doubt it. Most of this stuff is out of my price range."

Joel's expression remained stoic.

"How much would one of these pieces cost?" Sam asked, motioning to the paintings closest to where they were standing.

"As the saying goes, if you have to ask the price, you probably can't afford it. They're likely beyond the means of one of Camden Falls' finest," Joel added with a smirk.

Sam realized that he didn't mind getting under Joel's skin. He slid his hands in his coat pockets and smiled tightly. "Seeing I *am* one of Camden Falls's finest, humor me." He observed the irritation in Joel's eyes. "I'll ask again. How much would one of these be?"

"Each piece is assessed and appraised on its own merits," Joel responded.

"I get that. How much on average? Or if that's too difficult..." It might have been small of him, but Sam felt a brief sense of satisfaction that Joel's irritation was becoming more evident. He pointed to a particularly gloomy painting of a hunting scene. "How much is that one?"

"Oh, that's a Frederic Remington, painted circa 1902. Shortly before his death. It's appraised at four hundred and fifty thousand dollars. From the right buyer, we may get half a million. Remington's paintings and sculptures have gone up dramatically over the last decade."

Sam managed not to sputter. Just barely.

Although he'd expected it to be expensive, the fact that it was half a million dollars astounded him. He took a moment longer to study the painting. If it'd been ten dollars, he wouldn't have wanted it. He wasn't a fan of hunting, and just looking at it depressed him. "Thanks," he said, turning his attention back to Joel. "But this isn't a personal visit. As it turns out, I'm here on police business."

Joel took a step back. Sam could see his nerves build and wondered what he had to hide. "I'd like to speak to Charles Hadley, if he's in."

"Does this have to do with the Babineux?"

"I'll share what this is about with Mr. Hadley, if you don't mind getting him for me."

"Sure, Detective Eldridge. I'll see if he's available." The cockiness was gone.

Sam thought about throwing his weight around and clarifying that he hadn't asked if Hadley was available, but rather if he was *in*; however, he restrained himself. There was no point other than to mess with Joel. Sam knew Joel disliked him. He just hadn't figured out if it was all personal because of Chelsea, or because he had something to do with the theft of the Babineux. Irrespective, the dislike was mutual. Joel seemed to make a special effort to rub him the wrong way.

Alone again, Sam stopped in front of a sculpture. The creature had a man's head and torso, and the body of what appeared to be a horse. He knew such creatures existed in mythology, but he wondered how people came up with these things.

"Detective Eldridge." He heard Charles Hadley's cultured, English-accented voice from behind him. Turning, he watched the distinguished-looking man, probably in his midsixties, walk toward him.

"I'm sorry to keep you waiting," he said, extending a hand to Sam.

This time, Sam sensed curiosity, nothing more. "Thank you for seeing me."

"Naturally. How might I help?"

Sam inquired about the warehouse—how and when it had been leased by the gallery—and skated on some thin ice as he explained that there'd been "concerns" raised about it. He concluded by asking if it would be possible for him to see it.

"As you wish. Is now convenient?"

Sam didn't detect any hesitation or subterfuge, and wondered how much time he was wasting. But he was in it now and had to follow through. "Works for me."

"I'll get my coat and keys and be right back."

Sam considered whether he should've let Hadley out of his sight. He'd agreed so readily, Sam speculated what the odds were that he was on the phone, alerting someone to their visit. He counted off the seconds until Hadley returned, and decided if he had made a call, it was a very brief one.

Sam knew where the warehouse was, but he followed Hadley's late-model Audi and pulled up next to the curb behind it. Trailing Hadley into the warehouse, he immediately heard the security alarm signal, and watched as Hadley turned on the lights and, with his body blocking the panel so Sam couldn't see the code he entered, disarmed the system.

Chelsea hadn't mentioned anything about encountering an alarm system. Would she have known the code?

"Who, other than you, has the code to the security system?" he asked when Hadley had rejoined him.

"Joel Sinclair. He uses this space the most, for storage of displays and staging generally. I suppose the gallery's owner, Nadine Sinclair, would have it written down somewhere."

"What about your sales associates? Deborah or Chelsea? Or your assistant?"

Hadley shook his head. "They wouldn't have any need to come here."

"Is the code the same as for the gallery?"

Hadley smiled. "No, that would be unwise, and it would mean that anyone who had the gallery code—and the sales associates and Tina have that one—would automatically have this code, too." Sam still didn't sense any deceit or defensiveness. He nodded thoughtfully. So how would Chelsea have gotten into the building without setting off the alarm? "Is the alarm always armed, regardless of whether you have anything of value in here or not?"

"Yes, of course."

"Always?" Sam prompted.

"Yes...well, unless there's a problem with the system."

"Does that happen often?"

"No, but shortly before I left for England, there was a power failure at the warehouse. Actually, the power for the whole block went down for an extended period of time, because one of the transformers blew. The security system has a UPS—an uninterrupted power supply—backup, but the length of the failure drained the battery, so the system failed."

"Wouldn't someone have been notified by the monitoring company?"

Hadley exhaled. "Yes. They notified me, but I was focused on my sister at the time and when they sent the reminder, I was already in England. At my sister's deathbed. I wasn't checking email or voice mail. Since low battery is not deemed to be a critical response condition, the company didn't dispatch anyone. Nor were the police notified."

"I'm sorry about your sister."

Hadley nodded.

"And sorry to be asking these questions at what must be a difficult time... But shouldn't the system have reset automatically, once the power came back on?"

"I'm not sure. I would think so."

That was what Sam expected, too. "Has anyone been in here that you know of since you left?"

"Not that I'm aware. As I said, Joel uses the space the most, and we haven't had any events or other initiatives that might have required him to be here. Oh...wait. I completely forgot that Nadine Sinclair called just before I left to tell me that we had a shipment. So he would've come here to receive it, but that would've been before I went to England. No. No, I'm wrong. Joel had an appointment that day. It might have been Nadine who received it. I didn't ask, so I'm not sure." He gestured toward the side wall, where there were several wooden shipping crates. "As I forgot all about it, the shipment is still here, crated, so I don't think anyone's been here since it arrived."

The power failure might explain why Chelsea didn't trip the alarm when she entered, but only if it didn't automatically reset when the power came back on. But the system was armed when they'd arrived just now, so if it *hadn't* automatically reset, someone had been in the warehouse between the time Chelsea had been and their arrival. Someone who might or might not have noticed that the alarm wasn't set, but did set it when he—or she—left.

"Mind if I look around?" Sam asked.

"Not at all."

Sam had already assessed the overall surroundings when they'd first walked in. Now, he noted again that the workbench Chelsea had described was there, but it was clean and clutter-free. He went over to have a closer look. "May I?" he asked Hadley, indicating the under-counter drawers and cupboards.

"Go ahead."

Instead of paint or other art supplies, he found tools and packing materials. The easels were there, but empty. There were no canvases.

Next, he pointed to the shipping crates along the wall. "Okay if I have a look?"

"Be my guest."

Again, Sam sensed no reservation, no discomfort. In contrast, he thought of Joel Sinclair's demeanor and wondered whether he had something to do with whatever might be going on.

Sam knelt in front of the crates. They seemed

to be in good order, although a couple of them looked as if they had been opened and resealed. Chelsea's handiwork, no doubt.

"Would you like to see inside any of them?"

Sam glanced over his shoulder. "Thanks for the offer, but it's not necessary."

He rose, walked around the open space and entered the room that he assumed Chelsea had described as an exhibit space. It was nothing more than an empty shell of drywall. Instead of the concrete floors throughout the remainder of the building, it had hardwood, although...

He took a few steps in and crouched to look more closely at the floorboards. There were some fresh scrapes, possibly indicative of a hurried move. He looked up to where the walls met the ceiling and noticed screw holes, possibly for curtain rods or draping?

It wouldn't have been possible for anyone to clear out the room in the time it took him and Hadley to get here from the gallery. If it *had* been set up as Chelsea claimed, it'd been cleared out before he'd asked to see the place.

"Thank you for your time," Sam said as he watched Hadley reset the alarm on their way out.

"No problem. Is there anything I should be concerned about?"

"No. I don't think so. Thanks again," Sam repeated before walking to his car.

Reconnecting with Chelsea would have to wait until she was back at work.

Under the circumstances, he didn't feel comfortable contacting her at her home.

CHAPTER FIFTEEN

As Sam had anticipated, the discussion with Chelsea wasn't a pleasant one.

He went to see her at the gallery on her first day back.

She'd been so excited to learn that he'd gone to the warehouse, he regretted having to tell her that he hadn't seen any of the things she'd described.

He wasn't entirely convinced that she'd been wrong, however. He couldn't ignore the security alarm issue, nor what he'd noticed in the enclosed space.

"I wasn't imagining it. I'm certain of that," Chelsea said emphatically.

"There were no art supplies and the back room was empty. No furniture. No wall coverings." He didn't tell her about the scrapes on the floor and the screw holes high up on the walls. Although he had questions about them, he didn't want to give her false hope. If he ended up finding something, okay, but until then it would be better if Chelsea put her suspicions aside.

"But I *saw* it. How could it be completely different a little more than a week later?"

"I don't know," he responded gently. "Did you tell anyone about what you'd seen? Or having been in the warehouse?"

"No. You're the only person I said anything to. You're thinking that if I told someone—the *right* person—they would've moved everything out?"

"Correct. It's not possible that the space would've been emptied out like that in the twenty minutes from when I asked Hadley to take me to the warehouse and when we got there."

Chelsea threw her arms up. "But it *was* emptied out. Doesn't that support the supposition that something illegal or at least inappropriate was going on there? That whoever's responsible didn't want to get caught?"

"True. If someone had known that you'd been there."

"We're going in circles here," she observed with a pout.

That had occurred to him, too.

"Oh…wait! It was snowing the evening I was there. The street was deserted when I arrived, but when I came out, there were fresh foot-prints in the snow in front of the warehouse."

He looked at her sympathetically. "Chelsea, I'm sorry, but that's grasping at straws."

She hissed out a breath and stared through the window.

"I do have a question, though," he said. "Did you disarm the security system when you got there?"

She turned back, her expression thoughtful. "No. I worried about it at the time, but I forgot. I didn't hear an audible alarm. At first I was afraid someone—a security guard or a police officer—would show up." She raised her hands again. Let them fall. "Then, like I said, I forgot about it."

"And you didn't set it when you left?"

"No. I didn't think of it, but even if I had, I don't know the code."

"Okay. Thanks. That's it for now." He didn't want to leave her like this.

He didn't want to leave her at all…

Chelsea walked Sam out of the office area.

He'd noticed that Adam had been with Joel in his office when he first arrived. He was still there, which had Sam questioning how much time he spent at the gallery. Adam called out to Sam as he passed Joel's office.

"Detective Eldridge, do you have a minute?"

Sam paused and waited for Adam to reach him.

Adam shot an apologetic look at Chelsea. "I'm sorry to bother you, but my uncle and I've been wondering if you've made any progress with the break-in at our store."

Sam watched Adam transfer his weight from one foot to the other and wipe his palms down his jeans. He'd pegged Adam as the nervous sort at the best of times, and Sam acknowledged that he tended to intimidate people.

"No. I'm sorry, I don't have anything to tell you. The investigation is ongoing."

Adam shifted his gaze away. "Oh, okay. Thank you for your time." Stuffing his hands into the front pockets of his jeans, he shuffled back into Joel's office.

"Is he always that uneasy?" Sam asked Chelsea as they walked through the empty showroom.

"Pretty much," she said with a small smile.

Sam turned to her. "I'm sorry about how things are right now."

She clasped her hands together. "I understand," she assured him, but he wasn't entirely certain that she did, as he watched her walk back to her office.

"GOT A MINUTE, COLIN?" Sam asked.

Colin swiveled his chair away from his computer. "Sure. Come in."

"I'm still troubled by the jewelry store robbery and the art forgery case at the Sinclair Gallery. And I *hate* not having a viable lead on either one."

Colin took a sip of his coffee and grimaced.

The look on his face made Sam smile. Colin had obviously been absorbed with the computer longer than he'd thought, and the coffee must have gone cold.

"Are you still of the opinion that the jewelry store robbery was to test our response time?"

Sam exhaled heavily. "I don't know what to think anymore. It's been weeks, and nothing's happened. If it *was* to test us, odds are there would've been another break-in by now. In my experience, the perps wouldn't wait this long. Too much can change and invalidate whatever they learned."

"You don't think it had anything to do with the switching of the Babineux?"

"Whoever's behind that wasn't worried about police response, in my opinion."

"All right. Is it possible that the theft of that painting caused the perp to rethink his plan? You've been in and out of the gallery a few times since that happened. Could be a deterrent."

"Yeah. Can't argue with that."

"What's your theory?"

Sam dragged his fingers through his hair. "That's just it. I *don't* have a theory. It's annoying the heck out of me."

Colin raised a brow, but Sam appreciated not getting the customary speech about bringing problems to his captain without solutions.

"I can't shake the feeling that the two incidents are somehow connected."

"A break-in at a jewelry store with lots of damage and negligible loss, and the possible theft of a very expensive piece of art from a gallery—with no sign of break-in and no damage. How do you figure there's a connection?"

"It's too coincidental otherwise. We agree that there's no such thing as coincidence in our line of work?"

Colin nodded.

"Willowbrook Avenue might be the main retail street in Camden Falls, but it hasn't experienced a lot of crime. In the past five years, there's been some minor shoplifting, the theft of a tourist's wallet and an altercation between two college students. That's it. I checked. Although crime rates aren't on the rise overall, in the last couple of months we've had two major incidents on Willowbrook, and the two establishments affected happen to be next door to each other."

"I wouldn't put much weight on the proximity aspect," Colin said. "The argument could be made that any store along that stretch of Willowbrook is in close proximity to any other."

"Point taken. But my gut tells me there's a connection. I just don't know what it is yet."

Colin started to lift his coffee mug again, then thought better of it and put it back down. "Yeah, it does seem too coincidental, although I can't imagine, either, what the connection would be."

"There's something going on at that warehouse. I know it," Sam said with conviction.

"Are you sure Owens isn't yanking your chain? Or involved in the theft of the painting and trying—in a not-too-sophisticated way—to throw you off the track?"

Sam pushed out of the chair and strode to the window. "No. She's not involved. And no, she's not as flighty as you seem to think." He faced Colin. "She's passionate and excitable, but she's smart, too."

"And you've fallen for her."

"That's irrelevant!"

"Relax. Just an observation. I'm not suggesting it would compromise your professional objectivity. I know you too well. With you, it's always duty first. Maybe too much so," Colin added in a conciliatory tone. "I also know you haven't seen anyone seriously since Katherine left. I'd be the first to say good for you, if you were interested in someone."

Sam tried to gather his thoughts while processing what his boss and, yeah, friend had said. Yes, Chelsea was the first woman he'd had feelings for since Katherine. It was true.

And sad.

"Back to the point," Sam said. "I'd like to get into the warehouse again, but we won't get a warrant until we have something concrete to go on."

"Safe assumption."

"I know Chelsea didn't imagine what she saw. That means whatever had been in that warehouse was moved out and in a hurry. The intrusion alarm wasn't operational when she was there, but it *was* armed when I went in with the curator. That means between Chelsea's visit and mine, someone moved a lot of the contents out. Judging by the look of the one room, it was done in a hurry. A very limited number of people have the security system code for the warehouse. According to the curator, Chelsea isn't one of them."

"Go on," Colin encouraged when Sam paused.

"It was snowing the night Chelsea was in the warehouse. She said that when she left, there were fresh footprints on the sidewalk. They seemed to have turned around just past the door and headed back in the direction they came from. I checked the security camera the landlord has on the exterior of the building for the time frame in question, although none of them are aimed at the gallery warehouse."

Colin sat up straight. "And?"

"The street's quiet that time of night, but there was a car that drove by while she was in there."

"Were you able to ID the car? See a person?"

He groaned in frustration. "Ha! You'd think! Unfortunately, the camera's a cheap one and with the snow, the lens was obscured. All I could see was a tan-colored vehicle. Although, as I said, the camera isn't aimed at the entrance of the warehouse, someone did walk along the street soon after. Probably male."

"Can we enhance the images? Get a plate?"

"No. I've tried. I checked with the security-monitoring company. Since the system was down the day Chelsea was inside the warehouse and it didn't reset automatically, they were of no help. With nothing conclusive picked up by the camera, we don't know if anyone was in who might have been in there between the time the UPS ran out and the following Tuesday night, when the system was rearmed. But someone was in there Tuesday evening, if not before. Hadley claims not to know who."

"So what are your next steps?"

"I'd like to set up after-hours surveillance. I don't care who goes in and out during normal business hours when the area's busy. I do want to know if someone goes in at night, when that part of town is as quiet as a morgue."

"Sam, you're aware of the cost of overnight surveillance. I'd have to pay overtime out of a budget that barely accommodates our regular expenses. If it was just one night, I could swing it. If there *is* something going on there—and that's a big *if*—even you won't be lucky enough to catch whoever is responsible the first night."

"How about a better camera?"

"That would be affordable but we'd need the owner's permission. Are you okay asking for it?"

"Hmm. You make a good point. Not knowing the relationship between the landlord and the gallery's management, it might not be wise to ask. I didn't have to elaborate why I wanted to look at the video footage, but if I go back and ask for permission to install a better camera, I'd bet the landlord would want to know why."

"And I'm assuming you don't want to take the chance of the landlord talking to the gallery's management about it, since you suspect it's an inside job."

"Right. But we wouldn't need permission if it's a traffic camera. We did have that DUI farther down that street a couple of years back."

A sly smile spread across Colin's face. "Good point. It's stretching it a bit, but we might be able to swing a temporary traffic camera."

"I'd appreciate it." Sam got to his feet. "Thanks for not reminding me about bringing you a problem without a solution."

"Sam," Colin called before he walked through the door.

Still frustrated and angry at himself, Sam turned back. "Yeah?"

"Don't beat yourself up. Neither of these cases is an easy one."

SAM LIKED THE idea of a camera monitoring the comings and goings on Mackenzie Avenue, but he was impatient. He didn't want to wait until it was approved and set up.

He wanted the case over and done with.

He wanted it closed.

Not only because justice needed to be served, but he was anxious to explore what was between him and Chelsea. He thought of Nicolas and his own condition. That would be another bridge he'd have to cross with Chelsea, if things unfolded between them the way he hoped.

Damn it all, he *missed* being with her!

He also hated the thought of losing out on evidence because of a delay. He had time; he might as well put it to good use.

Unwilling to risk alerting whoever it might be by the presence of a police cruiser in front of the warehouse, even an unmarked one, he took his personal vehicle.

He thought a reasonable precaution was to park a block down from the warehouse behind several nondescript cars and on the opposite side of the road. Surveillance through his rear-view mirror might not be ideal, but it was better than being made.

As time passed, he'd responded to every email he had in his inbox, called his parents, had a good long chat with his mother and finished a novel he'd had on the go for the better part of a month. Despite his winter boots and gloves, his hands and feet were getting numb from the cold, and he was thinking of calling it a night, when he saw a beige Acura MDX turn onto Mackenzie. It approached slowly and parked a couple of car lengths down from the warehouse entrance on his side of the road.

Sam hunched down to avoid being seen and adjusted his mirror.

Whoever was in the MDX was in no hurry to get out. The engine kept running and the exhaust puffed fat plumes of smoke into the chilled air.

While Sam sat in the cold, teeth chattering. Go figure!

Then the person finally stepped out, walked up to the warehouse door, slipped a key into the lock and entered. Once he was inside, Sam got out of his car and made his way toward the building, hoping to get a glimpse at whoever it was through a window. Before he'd crossed the street, the man—yes, it was a man—exited again. As he looked both ways, Sam had no place to hide.

Damn. He'd been seen and—based on how quickly the man ran back to his SUV—he'd been made.

No question.

Sam hurried forward, wanting to get a license plate, since he'd never be able to ID the man, bundled in a heavy winter parka, a ski cap pulled low over his forehead. The engine roared to life and the vehicle's tires spun as its driver sought purchase on the ice-slicked edge of the road.

It shot away from the curb.

And barreled straight toward Sam.

CHAPTER SIXTEEN

SAM LEAPED BACK as the MDX careened toward him.

But he wasn't fast enough.

Pain exploded in his right hip as the vehicle's right front fender grazed him.

Stumbling, he landed hard on the asphalt.

Although the pain blurred his vision, he kept his wits and got a partial plate before the SUV took a sharp turn down Addison and disappeared from his sight.

"WHAT THE HELL HAPPENED?" Colin demanded as he rushed over to Sam in the emergency room. Sam was slipping his shoes back on, with a great deal of difficulty because of the stiffness in his hip.

"I got hit by a car," Sam muttered. He stood up, balancing against the gurney, and glanced down at his pants. There was a horizontal tear near the knee, where he'd hit the pavement.

"This was one of my favorite pairs," he complained.

When he tried to put weight on the leg, he nearly collapsed. Fortunately, Colin gripped his elbow and kept him upright.

"We'll talk about what you were doing there later," Colin said darkly. "At least, this should expedite the approval of the traffic camera. My immediate question, though, is should you be walking on that leg?"

"Yeah. It's okay. They x-rayed it. There's no fracture. Just soft-tissue injury. A heck of a lot of bruising. But it hurts like a—" He watched a woman walk in with her daughter. "Hurts a *lot*," he amended, out of deference to the little girl. To make matters worse, his left leg wasn't in great shape, either, because he'd landed hard on his knee.

Out of necessity, Sam let Colin help him outside. Only then did he realize that his car was back at the warehouse, since the paramedics had brought him to the hospital in an ambulance. "Would you mind dropping me off at the corner of Addison and Mackenzie?"

"Why?"

"That's where my car is."

Colin released Sam's elbow and he staggered. "You plan to drive?"

"Point made. How about driving me home, then? And if you could get someone from the department to pick up my car, I'd appreciate it." He dug in his pocket and handed his keys to Colin.

"I can do both. And on our way to your place, you can fill me in on what went down."

By the time Sam got out of Colin's vehicle in his driveway, he'd been berated for having done the stakeout without authorization or backup, and on his own time. But he'd also gotten Colin's commitment to expedite the traffic cam. He wrote down the partial plate for Colin, and the make and model of the vehicle. Colin had promised to have it run and hopefully have the owner identified by the next morning.

Sam let himself into his house and limped down the hall to the kitchen. He grabbed a cold soda and a pack of frozen peas to put on his hip. On second thought, he took a bag of frozen corn, too, for his knee. He made his way slowly to the bedroom. Taking a couple of the painkillers they'd given him a script for at the hospital, he resigned himself to a sleepless night.

But tomorrow would be another day. And he had his first solid lead in the Babineux case.

SAM HOBBLED INTO the squad room the next morning. It didn't take long for Colin to call him in. Moreover, he wasn't surprised to learn that the most likely match for the vehicle that had nearly run him down belonged to Joel Sinclair. While he had an incomplete plate and he was off on one letter, Camden Falls was a small town, and there was no such thing as coincidence, he reminded himself.

He thought about going to the Sinclair Gallery himself. Admittedly, he would've enjoyed advising Joel Sinclair that he had to come into the station for questioning, but his hip was too damn sore.

He sent a uniform instead, and took some satisfaction in knowing that for Sinclair, being escorted out of his workplace by a uniformed police officer would be an embarrassment. Sam knew it was malicious, a bit of payback for the way Sinclair had been goading him. Small of him, maybe, but he wasn't feeling his most gracious with the pain he was experiencing.

Sam smiled thinly when he saw Sinclair being brought into the squad room. He didn't look too happy about the situation.

Motioning for the uniform to follow with Sinclair to an interview room, Sam rose and limped forward.

"What happened to you?" Joel asked when they were alone.

Sam raised his eyebrows, but refrained from answering.

"Not my problem," Joel said and shrugged.

"Isn't it?" Ignoring what appeared to be genuine bafflement on Sinclair's face, Sam read him his rights. "Do you understand your rights?"

"I didn't do anything," he grumbled.

Sam could see that Sinclair was trying to maintain his tough exterior, but anxiety was leaking through. Although both Sam's hip and knee were throbbing, he didn't want to sit. He wanted to maintain a dominant position. Instead, to ease the pain, he leaned against a counter at the back of the room. "I beg to differ. Are you the owner of a beige MDX?" He recited the license plate.

"Yeah. So what?"

"Your vehicle was seen last night outside a property leased by the gallery, and it was involved in a hit-and-run." Sam resisted rubbing his aching hip. "So, let's try this again. Do you understand your rights?"

Joel glowered at him.

Sam crossed his arms and waited.

"Yes, I do," Joel finally mumbled.

"You have the right to legal counsel."

"I don't need legal counsel since I didn't do anything."

"For the record, you refuse legal counsel?"

Joel nodded.

"Was that a *yes*?"

"Yes! Can we get this over with?"

"That all depends on you and your cooperation."

"If you think I had anything to do with a hit-and-run…" Sinclair's eyes widened, and his gaze shifted to Sam's hip. "*You* were hit by a car? You think *I* did it?"

The shock and outrage didn't seem contrived, either.

"I didn't do it," Joel insisted. "I went out with a few friends after work. Since I knew I'd be drinking, I left my vehicle in the gallery's parking lot. I got a ride home. Never drove my SUV." He leaned back in the chair and looked smug.

That was an unexpected twist. It was simple enough to verify if he was with others, as he claimed. "For the record, you state that you didn't drive your Acura MDX yesterday evening?"

"Didn't I just say that?"

Sam didn't want to jump to conclusions about Joel's belligerence. It could mean he was innocent but just as easily that he wasn't. People re-acted to police interrogation in different ways.

"Was there any damage to it this morning?"

"Not that I noticed."

"Do you have an issue with me verifying that?"

Joel hesitated for an instant, but then shook his head. "No, I don't."

"Does anyone else use your vehicle or have keys to it?"

"My grandmother. Chelsea might still have a key." He sneered at Sam. "She did when we were dating. I don't think I asked for it back."

Jackass, Sam thought and glared at him. Did he really think he could deflect the blame on Chelsea? Or a nearly eighty-year-old woman?

Joel's antagonism dissipated and he raked his fingers through his hair. "Look, I didn't use my vehicle last night. I went out with some friends to watch the Bruins game. Whenever we go out and drink, we have a designated driver. It wasn't me last night, so I left the SUV at the gallery. For what it's worth, the guys can alibi me. So can the bartender, the owner and several of the regular patrons of MacCabe's Pub."

Sounded as if he had a solid alibi. If his claim checked out, it wasn't him.

But what were the odds of a car the same

make and model as Sinclair's, with the part of the plate he'd been able to get nearly matching his, driving away from the gallery's warehouse, and in such a hurry?

Sam didn't have grounds to detain Sinclair any longer. "Okay. We're done here. I'll need the names and contact information for the people you were with last night."

"Sure."

When Sinclair rose, Sam's manners and professionalism dictated that he say something. "Thank you for your cooperation."

"Yeah. No problem," Joel murmured, as he walked out of the interview room ahead of Sam.

Although not quite back to square one, Sam wasn't much further ahead with the investigation.

CHELSEA WAS WITH a couple from Sacramento, California, when Joel stormed into the showroom. Tina had told her that he'd left with a police officer while Chelsea was out at lunch.

She'd thought maybe there'd been some news about the Babineux. But seeing the temper roll off Joel in waves, she realized that whatever had happened obviously hadn't been good news.

Chelsea eased away from the couple when

it was reasonably polite for her to do so and rushed to Joel's office. "What's wrong?" she asked after closing the door behind her.

The fulminating look he gave her nearly had her backing out again.

"I was taken to the police station for *questioning*," he said through gritted teeth.

"They think you stole the Babineux?" Chelsea was dismayed. They couldn't possibly believe he had anything to do with it.

"Your *boyfriend* got hit by a car last night and he thought I did it."

"What?" Everything after the part about Sam getting hit was just noise as far as Chelsea was concerned. "You did *what*? Is he okay? What happened?" It didn't even occur to her to argue that Sam wasn't her boyfriend. "Is he in the hospital?"

"No, he's not. He's the one who questioned me about it. He seems okay. He must've just got clipped. He's limping some."

Relieved to know that Sam was well enough to be at work, she felt her heart rate settle. Marginally. She gave Joel a questioning look.

"What, now *you're* thinking I had something to do with it?" he asked, the anger smoldering.

"Did you?" The words were barely a whisper, but she had to know. Joel had been acting strange the last couple of months and she'd sensed his hostility toward Sam on more than one occasion. She *had* to know, and she trusted him not to lie to her. Even if he tried, she'd be able to tell.

The look on his face was infused with disappointment. "Seriously, Chels? You know me and you *seriously* think I'd do something like that?"

She didn't. Not really. "An accident maybe...?"

"If I'd hit someone—*anyone*—I'd stay. This was a hit-and-run." He shook his head sadly. "No, Chelsea. I didn't have anything to do with it."

For a moment, she saw the man she'd cared about, and she regretted causing him pain.

"And thanks for the concern about me," he added sarcastically, and the moment was gone.

"I'm sorry, Joel. Since you're back here, I trust they satisfied themselves that it wasn't you."

"Only because I have an airtight alibi. I was with Dave and the guys watching the game at MacCabe's. I didn't have my vehicle with me."

She nodded. "I'm glad you're cleared."

The sadness in his eyes returned, reminding her again of the sweetness and affection they'd once shared. Although she could recall and hold those times dear, her interest now lay elsewhere—as much as that might hurt Joel if he still believed they could reconcile. Despite the distance between her and Sam right now, she couldn't deny her feelings for him.

Despite Joel's assertions that Sam was fine, Chelsea had to confirm for herself that he truly was. She needed to go to him. "Look, I'm sorry, but I have to leave early. If Mr. Hadley returns, could you please let him know for me?"

"Sure. Chels," he called after her as she reached the door. "He really is okay."

There was the gentleness again. Her eyes filled with tears and she nodded. "Thank you."

Chelsea didn't bother calling Sam. She didn't want to give him the opportunity to put her off. She *had* to see him and not just to assure herself that he was fine.

That irrepressible need made her reexamine her feelings for him. Never having been truly in love before, she didn't have any comparison, but that in itself told her something.

Trying to put a name to it, the only thing she kept coming up with was that she was falling in love with Sam.

Marla was behind the reception counter when Chelsea walked into the police station.

"It's nice to see you again," she greeted Chelsea.

"You, too. Is Sam available?"

"Let me check."

Chelsea watched Marla punch in some numbers on a keypad, then murmur into her headset. "He'll be out in a minute," she said.

Chelsea wandered around the lobby, pausing by one of the commemorative pictures of an officer who'd lost his life in the call of duty. Thinking of Sam getting hit by a car and how much more serious it could have been had her blood running cold. Hearing a door open, she swung around and saw Sam. She felt a sudden tightness in her chest.

Thank God, he was alive!

The urge to run to him and throw herself in his arms was intense. If the look in his eyes meant anything, he wasn't unaffected, either.

She couldn't resist and rushed over to him.

When he lurched a bit as she wrapped her arms around him, she was immediately contrite for not having considered his injury.

She quickly backed away and reached out to steady him. "I'm sorry. I am sooo sorry."

Bracing an arm on the door frame, Sam smiled weakly, a smile that was more of a grimace. "It's okay. Worth it," he said, taking a couple of deep breaths.

Obviously having witnessed what had just

happened, Marla hurried around her desk to open the door. She couldn't conceal a grin. "Um, Chelsea, why don't you help Sam back here?"

"Yeah. Sure. Thanks." That was when she noticed he was wearing loose-fitting khakis. She knew he wouldn't dress so casually for work without good reason. The injury must have been worse than Joel had led her to believe, and she felt bad again about throwing herself at him with such force.

Slipping an arm around Sam's waist, she helped him through the doorway. She glanced at Marla, who was back at her desk, and smiled at her gratefully.

"Is there somewhere we could speak? In private? That would be more comfortable for you?" she asked Sam.

He led her to the coffee room. No one else was there, so he closed the door behind them. As soon as he turned back, Chelsea hugged him again, but more carefully this time. When he put his arms around her and held on, she felt that tightness in her chest once more.

Emboldened by his reaction, she cradled his face in both hands and feathered kisses on his cheeks, forehead and lips.

"I'm so sorry you're hurt. Are you okay?

You're limping. Does it hurt much? Is anything broken? What happened?"

Sam took a small step back and laughed. "Whoa! Slow down. Other than a very sore hip and a not-quite-as-sore knee, I'm fine. Can we sit, though? It does hurt more when I put weight on my leg."

"Oh, of course."

"Would you like a coffee?"

"Water, please." Her throat was parched. When he started awkwardly toward the fridge, she leaped up. "What was I thinking? You sit down. I'll get it. Coffee for you?"

He nodded and gratefully made his way to the table in the center of the room. Chelsea joined him soon after with their drinks. Ignoring her water, she reached for his hand. "How did it happen? Do you really think Joel had anything to do with it?"

"No, I don't believe Joel did it." He summarized the events of the evening before. "Joel's alibi held. But I haven't dismissed the idea that it was his car. The make, model and plate are too similar to those of the car that hit me."

"He said he didn't have his car with him last night. Could someone have stolen it?"

"And returned it by morning to the exact place Joel had left it? I doubt it. Even if that was the case, it would've been too coincidental for someone to randomly steal his car and drive it to a warehouse leased by the gallery."

Chelsea had realized that, too, as soon as the question was out of her mouth. "But then how could it have been his car? Did he lend it to someone?"

"He said no. He did say his grandmother has a key to it."

Chelsea chuckled, then compressed her lips. "You think *Mrs. Sinclair* took Joel's car, drove to the warehouse for some reason, and then hit you and left the scene?" Chelsea shook her head. "That's not possible."

"I don't think so, either," Sam said. "Joel also said you used to have a key to it."

Chelsea straightened her back and stared at him. "Joel suggested *I* did it?"

"No. He said you used to have a key. Do you still?"

"Of course not!" The horror that Sam might think she'd do something like that washed over her. Then she thought about it. Had she ever returned the key to Joel? She couldn't remember. She'd used his car only once or twice, when hers was in for repairs. And that time she'd lent her car to Paige, so Paige and Jason could visit her parents at Christmas. But even if she still *had* the key…

Tears welled in her eyes. "You think I could do that? Hit you and leave you there?"

Sam rose awkwardly and held out a hand to Chelsea. "Come here, please."

She rose, although she still felt hurt. He drew her into his arms, cradling her to his chest, and kissed the top of her head. "I needed that," he murmured into her hair. "To answer your question, no, not for an instant did I think that. Nor do I believe you had anything to do with the theft of the Babineux." His arms tightened around her. "Police protocol be damned, I missed you and I want to see you. Be with you."

The simple words, said with unconcealed emotion, caused a pleasant warmth to spread through her. She snuggled closer, shut her eyes and absorbed the sheer bliss of being in his arms. Yes, she was falling in love with Sam. *Had* fallen in love with him.

When the door opened behind them, they sprang apart like two guilty teenagers. Well, *sprang* might not have been the right word to describe Sam's awkward retreat.

A tall man with medium-length brown hair and a rugged face stood in the doorway. "Am I interrupting?" he asked with a half smile.

Chelsea shifted her gaze from the new arrival to Sam, and caught him rubbing his forehead. "Colin, I'd like to introduce you to Chelsea Owens. Chelsea, this is my captain, Colin Mitchell."

"Pleasure to meet you, Ms. Owens. A real pleasure," he added, slanting Sam a quick look.

"You, too, sir. Uh, Captain," she responded, feeling the heat on her neck making its way up to her cheeks.

"Colin's fine," he assured her. "I'll grab a coffee and leave you two to…your discussion," he said, shooting Sam a knowing half smile.

The moment Colin closed the door behind him, Chelsea covered her face with her hands. "Oh, gosh. Your captain? How embarrassing! I'm sorry I put you in that predicament in front of your boss."

Sam touched her shoulder gently. "I'd bet it's not the first time Colin's seen people embrace. Besides, if I remember correctly, I initiated that hug."

"I know…but I came here. To your workplace and—" Her emotions were in turmoil. She was concerned about his injury. She was excited about her feelings for him and the fact that he hadn't pushed her away. All the emotions were threatening to overwhelm her.

He nudged her closer to him. "Chelsea. Shh. It's not a problem." He rested his head on hers again. "I needed this more than I realized." He drew back and raised her chin. "I missed you and I want to start seeing you again. Are you okay with that?"

Tears blurred her vision and clogged her throat. Not ashamed to let him see how she felt, without averting her gaze, she nodded.

"I'm glad," he said softly before lowering his head to brush his lips across hers.

That kiss was unlike any that Chelsea had exchanged with Sam before.

It left her a little breathless…and more stirred by a kiss than she'd ever been.

She couldn't help but think of the future.

A future with Sam.

CHAPTER SEVENTEEN

CHELSEA COULDN'T GET Sam off her mind as she drove away from the police station.

He cared about her!

And she was on cloud nine about that, but the rest of it didn't make sense.

None of what had been going on since All That Glitters and Shines was broken into made sense. There was no point in going back to the gallery now, she decided, as it was almost five. A light snow was falling, reminding her that it was nearly time to put up her Christmas tree and decorations.

She *loved* Christmas.

And she hoped that this year she'd be sharing it with Sam.

Although she'd promised Paige she'd be at her house on Christmas Eve to celebrate with their friends and neighbors, and she'd spend Christmas Day with her parents, she still loved to make her own apartment as festive as possible.

"Hey, Mindy. How was your day?" she asked when her cat padded over to greet her at the door. "How about an early dinner, huh?" she asked as she pulled off her boots and hung up her coat.

She picked up Mindy and rubbed her ears, eliciting a satisfied purr. Carrying the cat to the kitchen, she plopped her down in front of her dish, filling it with kibble. Next, Chelsea fixed herself a large salad and poured Sprite over ice.

Finished with her dinner, Mindy leaped onto the kitchen chair next to Chelsea's. Shooting a hind leg up in the air, she began to bathe herself.

While Chelsea ate, she kept turning her discussion with Sam over and over in her mind. She had to agree that the odds of a car just like Joel's stopping at the warehouse seemed too coincidental. Who else, other than Mrs. Sinclair, could have keys to Joel's car? She knew he occasionally lent his car to one of his friends, but that wasn't plausible, either. If Joel had done that, he would've told Sam, when Sam had asked him. Besides, she was acquainted with most of his friends, and none of them would have any reason to be in the industrial part of town.

But then the only explanation would be that

Joel was lying and he'd gotten his friends to lie, too, on his behalf.

That was implausible.

No, none of it made sense.

When Chelsea finished eating, she rinsed her dishes and put them in the dishwasher. She turned on the television and tried distracting herself, first with the news, then a sitcom. But her thoughts kept returning to Joel's car, the warehouse and what any of it might have to do with the theft of the Babineux.

The warehouse was integral to whatever was going on. That much she was sure of. Why else would someone have tried to run Sam down in front of the building?

It was almost eight o'clock when Chelsea decided she couldn't sit around idly or she'd go out of her mind. She'd take a drive to the warehouse. She had no idea what she'd do once she got there since she no longer had the keys, but she was too restless to stay home.

She gave Mindy an apologetic rub and promised she'd be home within the hour.

The snow had stopped and the roads were damp but clear. She still didn't know what she planned to do as she turned onto the deserted street and drove by the warehouse to park a half a block away. To be on the safe side…

Climbing out of her Honda, she leaned against the fender and contemplated her options. She glanced over at the building and noticed a dim light. Was it possible that someone was inside? There weren't any other cars on the street, but that didn't mean someone couldn't have parked at the back near the loading dock and accessed the building from there.

The adrenaline rush made her heart knock against her rib cage. She thought about getting back in her car and driving away. She had no business being here. And what if the person who'd hit Sam came back? Or was inside? Then *she* could be in danger.

Art theft was one thing. But someone nearly running Sam down had her protective instincts kicking into high gear.

If she peeked inside, she might be able to see who it was—or at least get a description. Chances were it would be the person who'd hit Sam. The thought of Sam's injury trumped any worries about her own safety.

Still, she'd exercise reasonable caution. She'd take a quick look through one of the windows, being careful not to be seen.

That was all she'd do.

Chelsea stowed her large handbag in the trunk and locked it. She didn't want it to encumber her if she had to hide or run. She also left the door to her car unlocked and pocketed her keys.

Just in case…

She looked both ways before she hurried past the entrance. The window was high, but holding on to the frame and standing on her tiptoes, she could peer inside.

Although the light was dim, it was sufficient for her to see the space. With a clear view of the interior, she noticed the large crates immediately.

The work space she'd seen before was still there but empty.

No discernible movement. No indication of anyone being inside. She glanced toward the back room. She couldn't see any light, so it was improbable that someone was inside.

She turned her attention to the three crates in the middle of the room.

They weren't the same ones she'd seen before, as Mr. Hadley had inventoried those, and most of the pieces were now on display at the gallery. There'd been nothing remarkable or out of the ordinary about any of them. With the additional procedures they'd put in place since the Babineux fiasco, she trusted they were the originals.

These crates must have been a new shipment. She hadn't heard of another one coming in. Then again, there wasn't anything unusual about that, either. This time of the year, they normally stocked up for Christmas gift buying. It was one of their busiest seasons.

Since she still hadn't seen any movement, she began to suspect there was no one inside.

Despite her gloves, her fingers were getting numb hanging on to the windowsill in the cold, and she nearly lost her purchase. Dropping down to the soles of her feet, she considered her options again. Admittedly, they were limited. But the light got her thinking. Sam had described the incident when he was hit in a manner that implied he'd startled whoever had been inside. Seeing Sam, that person had fled, hitting Sam in the process. Was it possible the person hadn't finished whatever he'd come to do last night?

If he'd been frightened, he might not have remembered to turn the light off. And if he hadn't thought of that…how about the door?

Was there any chance that he'd left in such a hurry he'd neglected to turn off the lights, set the security alarm and lock the door?

And if he'd been too scared to come back, maybe the warehouse was still unlocked.

There was only one way to find out.

She inched over to the door, feeling very much like a burglar. With that thought came guilt. So, not a burglar. Better to think of herself as a *spy*.

Peering about surreptitiously, she closed her hand around the doorknob.

She drew in a deep breath and twisted it. It turned, and with the slightest force the door swung open. She almost squealed with nerves and excitement. Doing a quick fist pump, she took one last look up and down the street before she slipped inside the building.

Just as she had the time before, she closed the door behind her and locked it. Remembering the security system, she checked the panel. The light was green; no intrusion alarm had registered. The person obviously hadn't set the alarm system.

Chelsea tiptoed across the room toward the crates. Realizing that she was actually *tiptoeing* caused a moment's misgiving about the rightness of what she was doing. But then she reminded herself that her motivations were honorable and on the side of the law. She worked for the gallery, this was gallery property and why *shouldn't* she be here, if everything was aboveboard?

Her cautionary measures were to protect her, if in fact there were bad guys to worry about.

Yes. What she was doing was noble and good. Absolutely, she assured herself.

The workstation was her priority.

The countertop was completely empty. Pulling a tissue out of her pocket, she used it to open a couple of drawers and cupboards.

As Sam had said, there were no art supplies. The only items were for packaging.

Next, she moved over to the crates and examined them. The tools she needed to open the crates—a screwdriver, hammer and chisel—were in one of the drawers of the worktable. But she couldn't open the crates while holding tissues. And if she looked inside the crates with bare hands, she'd leave fingerprints.

She could explain all of that to Sam, but if she was already viewed by some as a suspect in the theft of the Babineux, and if the contents of these crates—whatever *that* was—pertained to the theft, would fingerprints incriminate her? She sighed.

In for a penny, in for a pound, clichéd as that was.

She opened the first crate.

Dropping back on her heels, she scrutinized

the painting. It was a duplicate of a piece they had on display at the gallery.

She let out a huge breath.

Forgery was the only explanation. And if so, it supported what they suspected had happened with the Babineux.

Someone was copying the works of art. Even in the very dim light, if *this* was the forgery, not the one hanging in the gallery—something she couldn't be sure of—it appeared that it was a darn good job.

She turned toward the back room, which had been set up as a private exhibit space the first time she'd been in the warehouse. She narrowed her eyes. Maybe her initial thought about the space had been correct. It wasn't intended for their regular customers. Rather it was used to show the original works to potential black-market buyers, with the forgeries displayed at the gallery.

She scrambled to her feet.

If that was what happened to the Babineux, how many other forgeries had she sold to un-witting customers who might not have taken the precautionary measures Mr. Anderson had? People who didn't have their acquisitions ap-praised and authenticated themselves?

If that was the case, someone at the gallery

had to be involved. It couldn't be an accident or a one-time occurrence. It was calculated and... nefarious.

Looking down at the painting she'd uncrated, she was staring at proof.

Could it be Mr. Hadley or Mrs. Sinclair?

Or Joel? After all, it was his car that Sam believed he'd been hit by. Which meant she'd dated a *criminal* for over two years! How likely was that?

Tina wouldn't have done it. Deborah? No, she couldn't see Deborah doing it, either.

Who then?

Could it be that whatever was going on here *wasn't* related to the Babineux theft, and she was overreacting again? She knew that sometimes paintings were replicated without ill intent. Old paintings required precise climate control. Perhaps this was a new sideline of the gallery's, replacing masterpieces for their owners to display without concern about damage, while they locked away the originals in climate-controlled safes.

That made sense, except for why she wouldn't have known about it. But it was a more plausible explanation than having discovered a major counterfeit operation associated with the Sinclair Gallery.

And if something illegal *was* going on?

There were two more crates she hadn't opened. One was small…holding a little sculpture perhaps? The other was large enough to contain another painting.

She checked her watch. She'd been inside the warehouse for nearly half an hour. What difference would another fifteen minutes make? She wanted to have a look at the contents of the other two crates.

Opening the smaller one first, she was shocked to discover jewelry boxes. Flipping a couple of them open, she found necklaces, earrings and a heavy silver bracelet. She put everything back and resealed the crate. This one obviously didn't belong to the gallery; it had to belong to All That Glitters and Shines. She knew Mrs. Sinclair let the Rochesters use the warehouse to store their surplus stock when required.

She moved to the final crate and opened it.

Perplexed, she stared at the painting. It wasn't one she'd seen at the gallery, that was for sure. It was a seascape in the style of one of the old masters. But it seemed familiar. Jogged a memory.

The painting depicted a group of men in a boat on a rough sea. Most of the men were preoccupied with keeping the craft afloat, but one gazed out of the canvas right at her.

The style.

The composition.

It looked remarkably like a Rembrandt.

But that was impossible, she chided herself, because Rembrandt didn't paint seascapes.

She'd take a picture and do an internet search when she got home to see if she could identify the painting.

She wondered where she had put her hand-bag—then remembered she'd locked it in the trunk of her car. And her iPhone was in her bag.

Lowering her head, she rubbed her temple with her fingers.

Stupid. Stupid.

Should she risk running to her car and get-ting her phone?

The longer she stayed, the more nervous she became, and the greater the likelihood that she'd be discovered.

No, she didn't want to risk it.

Then another idea occurred to her.

She hurried back to the workstation and took a chisel and some of the brown wrapping paper from one of the drawers. She could, at least, take a small scraping from the painting. She'd be able to have the scraping tested, determine when the painting had been done, and consequently conclude whether it was an original or a replica.

Carefully removing a very small scraping from the lower corner, she folded it inside the wrapping paper and stuck it in her pocket. As quickly as she could, she recrated the painting and, to the best of her recollection, left everything as she'd found it.

There was nothing she could do about locking the door, since she didn't have a key, but at least she closed it securely behind her.

It was after ten when she got home to her apartment. Mindy showed her displeasure about Chelsea's long absence in no uncertain terms. Chelsea had to coax her out from under her bed, lavish her with attention and bribe her with a few of her favorite treats. Finally satisfied that Mindy had forgiven her, she grabbed a bottle of water and her iPhone and sank down on the sofa.

She did a quick search on her phone. "How about that?" she murmured. Rembrandt *had* painted a seascape, but only *one*. And that one—*The Tempest on the Ocean*—was among the priceless stolen pieces.

She was horrified and glad at the same time

that she'd taken a scraping from the painting. She'd done it as unobtrusively as she could—but imagine if she'd damaged the work of a great master, worth tens of *millions* of dollars! If, in fact, it was the original... On the other hand, it seemed unlikely that she'd happened upon a painting that had eluded the FBI for over a quarter of a century. Still, the scraping would determine when the seascape had been painted and whether it *could* truly be *The Tempest on the Ocean.*

Remembering that she'd left the door to the warehouse unlocked, she almost decided to race back and take the painting... But how ridiculous to think it was the original, especially when the other painting she'd seen was evidence that works of art were being replicated. *The Tempest on the Ocean* had to be a replica, too. No question.

If she went back and took it, *she'd* be stealing.

No, it was best to leave things as they were. Too late to call Sam, anyway. If she did call him, he'd never believe that she might have found one of the missing paintings from the Thompson Museum. Particularly considering how things had turned out the last time she'd told him what she'd seen in the warehouse.

She'd tell him in the morning.

And face his anger about having entered the warehouse again without permission.

But if there was even the *slightest* chance that she'd found the original *The Tempest on the Ocean*, Chelsea couldn't ignore the enormity of it.

She sprang up, prompting an irritated meow from Mindy, who'd been curled up asleep beside her.

She put the folded piece of wrapping paper with the scraping in the bottom of her jewelry box for safe keeping.

She'd studied the Thompson Museum heist in college. Thirteen priceless works of art had been stolen from the museum in '90s, Rembrandt's *The Tempest on the Ocean* being one of them. The other stolen pieces included four—no five—works by Old Masters.

All priceless!

The FBI had been searching for them ever since, with no luck.

She took a deep breath.

Sam would think she'd lost her mind. If the FBI hadn't been able to find any of the missing works, how was it possible that she really *had* been looking at *The Tempest on the Ocean*?

She paced the length of her living room and back again.

Think. Think!

She retrieved her laptop, sat down and checked her facts.

Might as well go right to the source, she thought, and clicked on the link taking her to a page on the Thompson Museum website.

Yes, the incident had occurred during the early-morning hours. Two thieves, dressed as police officers, had entered the museum and walked off with the artwork.

They got in because the security guard on the door had let them in.

Then, the two men had lured the guard away from his desk and the only panic alarm button on the premises. The first guard was told to summon the other guard on duty to the security desk, which he did. The thieves then handcuffed both guards and took them into the basement.

A little over an hour. That was all it had taken from start to finish.

Later that morning, the security guard who showed up to relieve the two night guards discovered that the museum had been robbed.

At that point, the Cambridge police and FBI were called in.

Rembrandt's *The Tempest on the Ocean,*

painted in the early 1600s, was among the stolen works, as she'd correctly recalled.

To date, none of the paintings had been recovered, despite the museum and authorities continuing to actively investigate all leads.

How could it be that no one had come forward in all these years? The stolen paintings had to be in a private collection, with highly selective viewing.

And if she *had* found one of them… *Oh, my God!*

Best to sleep on it and she'd talk to Sam in the morning. That was the only rational thing to do.

He'd help her decide what to do next.

CHAPTER EIGHTEEN

DURING A MOSTLY sleepless night, Chelsea convinced herself that she hadn't been wrong about what she'd seen at the warehouse. The only question was whether the painting was the original or a replica.

She had to tell Sam.

"I need to see you!" she exclaimed as soon as he answered his cell phone when she called him from the gallery.

"That's a terrific way to start off my morning. Miss me?" he asked in a teasing tone of voice.

"Yes. No. I mean, yes, I miss you, but that's not why I have to see you." He could fluster her so easily.

"Okay, then why?"

"I'd rather tell you in person. Can I come see you during my lunch break?"

"Sorry, but I have a meeting late morning. Then I'll be in the field for the afternoon. How about after work?"

Chelsea supposed she didn't have much choice and had to trust that all would remain as she'd found it at the warehouse. "Okay. Would you like to come to my place for dinner?"

"Dinner? At your place? How could I say no?"

She smiled. "Great! How's seven?"

"Perfect. I'll see you then."

The instant she hung up the phone, she collapsed back in her chair. What had she been thinking? Her mouth had been faster than her brain. The words had tumbled out before she realized what she was saying.

Well, she couldn't take them back. And she had to admit, she *wanted* to do something special for him.

She'd work hard, skip lunch and leave early. That way, she'd maximize her time to...to throw something together.

Despite working nonstop and missing lunch, by the time she'd finished everything she had to do that day, it was after four. That gave her less than three hours before Sam showed up on her doorstep expecting to be fed. As she lived mostly on fast food and frozen meals, there was nothing in her fridge that would suffice. She had two choices.

She could pick up takeout on the way home,

or she could call Paige and see what she rec-
ommended for a quick, no-fail meal.

She tried Paige first.

Chelsea tapped her pen on the desktop as she
waited for Paige to answer her phone. When
she finally did, Chelsea relaxed marginally. "I
hope I'm not taking you away from something
urgent," she said. "I need your help."

"What I'm doing can wait. What's up?"

"I invited Sam to dinner."

"You're seeing him again?"

"Oh, yes. Yes. I'm sorry I forgot to tell you,
but it just happened." And he'd been hit by a
car, but she didn't have time to get into that
now.

"So, about dinner…"

Chelsea heard a quiet snicker. "Knowing
you and your aversion to cooking, that tells
me things are good and you're really serious
about him."

Chelsea twirled the pen in her hand. "Yes,
and yes." She was in love with him, but that discussion would have to wait, too. "Um, there's
something I need to discuss with him."

"Oh?" Chelsea could hear the smile in
Paige's voice. "It's sounding more interesting
by the minute."

"No, no. Never mind about that for now. I'll

fill you in when I see you. Right now, I need a recipe. Some kind of dish I can manage."

"How about if I come over tomorrow and help you prepare a meal you can simply put together and heat up?"

"That would be great. There's just one problem."

"What's that?"

"Sam's coming over tonight."

"Oh?"

"Yeah." Chelsea felt the dejection creeping in. She'd been impulsive, as usual, and was bound to disappoint him.

"I'm sorry, Chels, but I can't do it this afternoon. Jason has a school recital. Daniel and I promised we'd be there, and we can't let him down."

"Of course. I understand." She bolstered herself with the thought that hands-on assistance wasn't what she'd expected when she called.

"Chels, hold on a sec, please."

Chelsea heard murmuring while she waited.

"I'm sorry, but I have to go. I'll help you prepare a dish next time. For tonight, why don't you pick up takeout on your way home? I'm sure Sam won't mind. It's about spending time with him, isn't it?"

"Yes. You're right. Thanks, Paige."

"Good luck, and I look forward to hearing how it went."

Chelsea packed up her briefcase while she contemplated her options for takeout. The Italian restaurant where she got her pizzas was convenient, so she settled on some sort of pasta dish. She'd stop by the grocery store on her drive home and pick up garlic bread, a salad and dessert to go with it. If she was lucky, she'd have time to straighten up her apartment, shower and change.

She glanced up when someone tapped on her closed door. "Come in," she called.

Tina pushed the door open and stuck her head in. "Chelsea, I'm sorry to bother you, but Mrs. Dixon is here and she refuses to deal with anyone except you. She has her eye on the Hampton sculpture. I tried to tell her you were busy, but she wouldn't take no for an answer."

Chelsea got out of her chair. "Not to worry. I'll see her." She considered how chatty Mrs. Dixon, a sweet but lonely widow, could get and hoped it wouldn't take too long.

"Not long" turned into an hour. By the time Chelsea rushed back into her office, she knew she'd be cutting it close. She made a call to the Italian restaurant, then grabbed her briefcase and handbag and dashed out of her office.

SAM WAS PUNCTUAL. The knock on Chelsea's door came precisely at seven.

Had he been standing outside waiting for the seconds to tick down? She smiled as she straightened a setting on her dining-room table, lit the candles she'd placed there, then hurried to the door to let him in.

Sam was holding a bottle of wine and a bouquet of flowers.

"Hi. You look…" His gaze swept over Chelsea, causing a warm sensation in her belly. "You look wonderful!"

She was glad she'd chosen primping over straightening up her apartment.

"Great dress, too."

The short, electric-blue jersey dress with the cowl neckline seemed to have done the trick, she thought with satisfaction.

He handed her the bottle and the flowers. Then he placed his hands lightly on her waist and tugged her toward him. She saw the sparkle in his eyes before her lids drifted closed as he touched his lips to hers.

The kiss was gentle. Soft.

But it sent shivers up her spine. When he stepped back, she missed his warmth. "Um. Hi" was the best she could manage. "Thank you for these," she added, lowering her nose to the flowers and inhaling their spicy, sweet scent. "They're beautiful. I'd take your coat, but I don't have a free hand," she said with a wide smile.

"That's okay." He gestured toward the closet and she nodded. "Something smells terrific," he said as he hung up his coat. Chelsea felt a flush on her cheeks, and was glad he wasn't watching her. "Um, why don't we start with some wine first?"

"Sounds good. And who's this?" he asked as Mindy sauntered toward them, pretending indifference.

"That's Mindy. She's a cross between a cat and probably a Great Dane, if you go by her size."

Sam squatted down as Mindy came closer. "You're a big gal, aren't you?"

Mindy rubbed against Sam's hand as he scratched her and then wove between his legs.

Chelsea noticed the trail of gray-and-white fur Mindy left on Sam's black pants. "I'm sorry. I should have warned you. She's a shedder." She glanced around, wondering where she'd left the fur brush.

Sam straightened, brushed at his pant legs. "It's not a problem," he said with an easy smile.

Relieved that Sam was so relaxed about it,

Chelsea watched Mindy continue to thread her way through Sam's legs. It normally took Mindy a while to warm up to people—if at all. "Looks like you've got Mindy's approval, and that's no small accomplishment."

Sam bent down to give the cat another scratch. "Really? She seems friendly."

"Ha! Spoken by someone who doesn't know this cat!" She motioned with the hand holding the bottle, inviting him to follow her. "Mindy generally likes to keep to herself. It's unusual for her to be so outgoing with strangers."

"Maybe she's selective and a good judge of character," he said as he walked down the hall with her.

Chelsea laughed. "Maybe. You don't have a pet?" she asked.

"I wish I could have a dog, but with the time I spend at work and my unpredictable schedule, it's not possible."

As Chelsea stepped into the kitchen, she remembered the pasta she'd put in the oven to keep warm. "Would you mind pouring the wine?" she asked as she arranged the flowers in a vase, then moved over to the stove to yank open the door. Delicious aromas wafted out, and she was relieved to see that neither the pasta nor the garlic bread had burned.

"What are we having?" he asked, filling the two glasses she'd placed on the counter.

Chelsea wished she'd put the salad in a glass bowl rather than just sticking it in the fridge in its plastic take-out container. "Caesar salad to start," she replied, trying to block his view of the container. "Pasta with garlic bread."

He sniffed the air. "Wonderful! I love lasagna."

"It's not lasagna," she said, managing to empty the salad into a bowl and disposing of the container without the sharp-eyed detective noticing. "It's fettuccine alfredo."

He was about to take a sip of his wine, but paused. "You make fettuccine alfredo in the oven?"

She held back a laugh. Might as well come clean, she decided. "No. I don't make it in the oven." She accepted the glass he held out for her, then took a slow sip. Lowering her head, she glanced up through her eyelashes. "Truth be told, I didn't make it at all. I was keeping it and the bread warm until you got here." She gestured toward the salad bowl. "Oh, and keeping the salad cool. I didn't make that, either."

She didn't know if she should laugh or be embarrassed when he nearly choked on his wine.

He waved his free hand until he could swallow and was able to speak again. "Sorry, sorry. I didn't mean to do that."

He looked endearing and she decided to go with the laughter. She took another sip and gave him a flirtatious look over the top of her glass. "We all have our strengths. Cooking happens *not* to be one of mine."

"Lucky for us, it is one of mine!"

She gaped at him, considering the muscular build, the all-around tough-guy appearance. *"You cook?"* she asked, her brows raised.

"Uh-huh. And quite well, I've been told. I enjoy it. Sort of a hobby."

A grin spread across her face. "Well, what do you know? How perfect is that?" she added under her breath.

"Excuse me?"

"Oh, nothing." She set her glass on the counter and turned back to the oven. "Would you take the salad out to the dining room while I finish *preparing*—" she said with playful emphasis "—our dinner."

"Sure. But I need a minute first."

She glanced over her shoulder, just as he moved closer, cupped the back of her head and gave her a kiss. "Sorry. I couldn't resist," he said before grabbing the salad bowl and walking out of the kitchen.

"How about that..." she breathed. A man who looked the way he did, could affect her with a simple kiss and knew how to cook. A keeper, she thought as she arranged the pasta in a serving bowl, the bread on a platter, and went to join him.

Mindy was winding around his legs again when she entered the dining room.

"Not friendly, you said?"

"What can I say, she likes you." As they sat down and she watched him stroke Mindy's back, her heart started to thud. *Darn it all.* She was falling deeper and deeper in love with him. Belatedly, she realized he'd said something she'd missed entirely while she'd been in her own little world. "Sorry, what did you say?"

"I asked what you wanted to discuss," Sam said after he took his first taste of the salad. "Great salad, by the way, and the pasta smells wonderful. Well worth the effort," he added with a grin.

"Thanks. I slaved over a hot oven for...oh, all of about ten minutes!" She returned the grin. Then her smile dimmed as she remembered why she'd invited him over in the first place. "I want to talk to you about the warehouse."

"I thought that's what it might be."

"Sam," she said earnestly. "Please listen. And trust me on this. I know art."

She proceeded to tell him everything as they finished their salads and started on the fettuccine.

Halfway through his main course, he rose and began pacing.

When she'd finished, he turned back to her. "What were you *thinking*, going to the warehouse?" he demanded.

Chelsea felt her heart sink. "That's it? That's what you have to say about what I just told you? If I'm right," she rushed on, before he had a chance to respond, "and this is a counterfeit or black-market operation, the paintings involved could be worth *millions* of dollars. And what about *The Tempest on the Ocean*? What if it *is* the original? Do you have any idea how significant a find that would be?"

CHAPTER NINETEEN

SAM DIDN'T KNOW if he should be more incredulous over Chelsea's belief that she'd found one of the stolen Thompson Museum masterpieces or the fact that she'd gone back to the warehouse on her own after he'd nearly been run over there! The thought of her being injured sent an electric jolt through his system. "Chelsea, why did you go back to the warehouse? Without even telling me?"

"But—"

"No *buts*. First, I could charge you with interfering with a police investigation."

Her mouth dropped open. "The...the warehouse is rented by the gallery and I work for the gallery..." she stammered.

"Oh, really? And were you there on gallery business?" he challenged her.

She gulped audibly, and Sam regretted his vehemence.

But with the disbelief and anger had come an overwhelming fear of what might have happened to her. His hip was healing, although it wasn't 100 percent yet, and the ache drove home the risk she could have faced.

He spun away from her, the sudden movement causing a sharp stab of pain. He dragged his fingers through his hair. Wrestling his temper into submission, he turned to her again. "Chelsea, you shouldn't have gone in there. Not only is it a matter of interfering with a police investigation, but if you're correct about what you saw—" He held up one hand to silence her when she was about to object. "*If* you're correct," he repeated, "you could have compromised important evidence. Since you were already there, you should've called me right away…and not touched anything." He took a deep breath, then addressed the part that worried him the most. "If I scared someone off yesterday before he had an opportunity to secure the warehouse again…he'd be worried about the safety of what's inside. If he didn't go back the night he'd hit me, probably because he expected police presence, I'd say chances are good that he planned to do it last night." From the expression on her face, he could tell he didn't have to state the obvious—what could have happened to her, if she'd been caught in the warehouse.

Chelsea exhaled heavily. "I'm sorry. I wasn't thinking. Then...well, the excitement of it all..." She stared down at her hands and frowned.

He was tempted to take her in his arms and kiss that frown right off her face.

He shook his head. What was *he* thinking?

Sitting down, he waited until she looked at him again. The shimmer of tears in her eyes left an ache in his heart.

"I'm sorry. I...I do stupid, reckless things sometimes."

He reached for her hand. "I apologize, too, for being hard on you. What's done is done. Now, are you sure it was jewelry in one of the crates?" Sam asked.

Chelsea rolled her eyes in response.

"Okay. Sorry." He hadn't really doubted her. It just got him thinking again about the possible connection between the jewelry store robbery and what was going on at the gallery. He leaned back. "Let's put aside the prospect of a stolen Rembrandt for the moment." That was the part of her story he found the hardest to believe. "Let's say you did see a duplicate painting. I read that eccentric collectors of art sometimes keep the originals under lock and key in rooms with rigorously controlled temperatures to preserve them, and they hang replicas on their walls."

"Well, yes…"

"They'd have to entrust the valuable original to someone for the reproduction of the work. Someone highly reputable. Wouldn't the Sinclair Gallery fit that bill?"

Chelsea released a long breath. "Yes, I suppose." She picked up her glass but didn't drink. "I suddenly feel very foolish. That thought had occurred to me as well, because everything you said is true. Mrs. Sinclair and Mr. Hadley are both highly regarded, distinguished professionals in the field, and I could see how they'd be called upon in such circumstances. Also, as I've said before, I don't believe they'd jeopardize their reputations by being involved in something illegal." She finally took a drink.

Sam reached for the bottle and topped up their glasses.

Looking at her, he could almost see that she had a headache brewing, and he hated hearing the defeat in her voice. Unfortunately, she wasn't helping her own cause. The longer she spoke, the more skeptical he became. What she'd suggested about a painting stolen from the Thompson Museum—and where it might be—was too outrageous.

As those thoughts went through his mind, she suddenly sprang up from her seat.

"I'll be right back." At Sam's questioning look, she added, "I have something that will help, I think." Not waiting for a response, she hurried out of the room.

She returned a couple of minutes later, holding a folded piece of wrapping paper. Sitting down, she handed it to Sam.

"What's this?"

"It's something that can prove if I'm right about the Rembrandt. About seeing *The Tempest on the Ocean*." She shook her head. "I should've told you about it sooner."

She'd been so excited about what she had to say, it was understandable that she'd neglected to tell him everything. Sam glanced down at the folded paper. "What is it?"

"It's important. I can't believe I didn't tell you."

He was enchanted by her, and she had his full attention. "Chelsea?"

"Okay. Okay. Sorry, again. I took a scraping from the painting. The one I think is the Rembrandt. The paint can be tested to determine its age. I'll take the sample to one of the labs we use tomorrow. If the results show that the paint's from the early 1600s, that'll help, won't it?"

Sam stared at her unblinking. Yeah, that could be crucial evidence, although he didn't want to think about the implications of Chelsea potentially having damaged a priceless work of art—if by chance it was the Rembrandt. Or how she'd obtained the sample. On the other hand, he knew he needed something solid to be able to get a search warrant. If the paint sample fell in the right time frame, that would add weight. "Yeah, it would help, but let *me* get it tested. If it proves to be of the right vintage, at least we'll preserve the chain of evidence from this point forward." He didn't know how he'd explain where he'd gotten the sample of paint to begin with, never mind dealing with the possible repercussions. He'd worry about that later. For now, he wanted to focus on Chelsea.

"I'll get the paint tested tomorrow, but for now? Can we put all this aside?" He slipped the folded paper in his jacket pocket and took her hand in his. Running his thumb gently across her knuckles, he met her eyes. "For now, why don't we concentrate on us?"

THE FLICKERING CANDLELIGHT, the gentle touch on her hand and the words, in Sam's deep, persuasive voice, made it easy for Chelsea to put everything else out of her mind. They spoke about family, his and hers.

"I have three siblings. Two brothers and a sister," Sam explained. "There's only eight years between my youngest brother and my older sister. We were close as kids and still have a very tight bond."

"Oh, I envy you that," Chelsea said with true longing. "After I was born, my mother couldn't have any more children. Don't get me wrong. My parents are terrific. They gave me a wonderful upbringing. They're fantastic role models, but it's not the same. I was always a little jealous of my friends who had brothers or sisters."

"Siblings can have their drawbacks, too," he said with a chuckle. "I've got two brothers, relatively the same height and weight as me. While we all lived at home, I could never find my favorite clothes or shoes when I wanted them."

Chelsea thought of the time she'd lent her dress and boots to Paige for her first big date with Daniel. And how often she'd rifled through Paige's closet to borrow a sweater or skirt. She would've loved to share a wardrobe with a sister. Just one of the benefits siblings had, in her opinion. "That doesn't sound so bad to me," she countered. "You can talk all you want about the drawbacks, but I only have to look at your face to know none of that really matters." She felt the twinge of regret she always did when she thought about it. "My parents are great, but I've always wanted a big family."

He glanced away briefly and his smile was melancholy when he looked back at her. "I bet you will have one. You strike me as the type of person who knows what she wants and goes for it."

Chelsea grinned. "Yeah, I guess I like to think of myself that way."

And the more she thought about it, the more she wanted Sam. She knew he couldn't have kids of his own—he'd told her that—but she hoped if and when the time came, he would be open to alternatives, such as adoption.

For the moment, she let herself get lost in his cool blue eyes.

"COLIN, I NEED a few minutes of your time," Sam said when his captain entered the squad room the next morning.

"Okay." Colin gestured to his office with the Starbucks cup he held.

Sam followed him in and dropped into the visitor's chair.

"Does this have to do with the Babineux theft?"

"Correct."

Colin shrugged. "That darn case continues to elude us and has been taking up most of your time. The last thing either of us wants on our hands is a Thompson Museum heist lite."

"Funny you should mention the Thompson heist," Sam said with a humorless laugh.

Colin raised his brows. "I get the feeling I'm not going to like what you have to tell me."

"Probably not."

"What is it?"

Sam filled Colin in on what Chelsea had shared with him the evening before.

"Let's put aside for the moment what she was doing in the warehouse and how she got in there."

Sam nodded. "Appreciate that."

"How credible is she?"

Sam's instinct was to defend her, but he had to be honest with Colin. There was too much riding on it. "She has an active imagination, however, she wouldn't make this up. I'm not sure what it all means, but why would there be a carton of expensive-looking jewelry in the gallery's warehouse at the same time as those forgeries—assuming that's what they are—if there wasn't a connection?"

"Good point. What about the painting, the Rembrandt that was stolen from the Thompson Museum?"

Sam compressed his lips as he considered how best to handle that question. He had to admit that he still remained skeptical of Chelsea's claim that she'd found one of the stolen paintings that had eluded the FBI for so long. "Seems unlikely that it's the original. Considering everything else Chelsea said and the fact that a very convincing forgery was substituted for the original Babineux, I suspect the painting she saw is a replica of *The Tempest on the Ocean*. But…we have a way to prove which it is."

"How?"

"She took a paint sample."

"What?"

"You heard me. She took a scraping from the painting, and I have it."

"Well, let's get it tested," Colin said. "I'll contact the FBI."

Colin made the call and spoke to Special Agent Ferguson, who had the file for the Thompson heist. Sam listened in on the conversation and shrugged at Colin's exasperated expression when the special agent all but laughed at Colin for suspecting they knew the whereabouts of one of the stolen paintings.

Still, he provided Colin with the name and contact information for a qualified and trusted lab in Boston to have the paint sample tested.

It seemed that Sam would be driving into Boston that day, despite the coming snowstorm. The sooner he could get going, the better the chances that he'd be back before the worst of it hit Camden Falls.

Sam called Chelsea as he headed to his vehicle, and told her he had the go-ahead to get the paint sample tested.

"Would you like the names of the companies we use?" she offered.

"Thanks, but it won't be necessary. I've got a contact in Boston," he stated as he got into his car and started the engine. He could tell that Chelsea was curious about whom he'd be using and how he'd gotten the name, but he wasn't prepared to let her know they'd spoken to the FBI. "I have to go, but I'll call you later."

"You're going *today*? They're saying this storm will dump at least ten inches on us."

He smiled. "Yeah, I heard that, too. Which is why I need to get going."

Chelsea's concern was evident in her voice. "If you're sure you have to go today, please be careful driving."

"I will. I'll call when I can." He paused. "Chelsea, I had a nice time with you last night. Thanks again," he added before he hung up.

The drive to Boston wasn't too bad, although it took him nearly twice as long as it would have without the inclement weather. He had no trouble finding the company, and the man he was to see, William Johnson, who appeared to be waiting for him.

"Detective Eldridge." The short, slight man with thinning hair held his hand out to Sam. "Special Agent Ferguson called and asked that I make this a priority."

"I appreciate it, Mr. Johnson."

"Bill, please. Can you tell me anything further about the sample I'll be testing?" he asked as they walked into a bright, spacious laboratory. "Agent Ferguson didn't give me any details."

Sam understood why. In no way did they want to influence the results of the test. If they mentioned the possibility that Bill might be testing a scraping of the stolen Rembrandt, there was always the chance—slim though it might be—that the prospect of such a discovery could influence the results. "No, I'm sorry, but I don't have any details to share with you, either. We need to know, as precisely as possible, the age of the paint."

Bill nodded and switched on the task light over a workstation. "Agent Ferguson said the same thing. I should be able to tell you a year, give or take five, with ninety percent accuracy."

"That should do it."

Sam took a seat in one of the hard plastic chairs lined up along a wall and disinterestedly flipped through a magazine he'd picked up at random from a pile on a small table. He was amused by the sounds Bill made as he ran his tests, his tone becoming more gleeful as he progressed.

"Detective?" Bill finally called to Sam as he swiveled around on his stool. Sam rose and walked over to him. "I've run several tests and repeated a couple of them, just to be certain."

To keep Bill from having to crane his neck to look up at him, Sam wheeled a stool from the adjoining workstation closer and sat on it. "What have you got?"

"It's rare that I get to run tests on samples this old, and guessing why the FBI might be interested in testing a paint sample, I have some thoughts on what we're dealing with."

"What are the results?" Sam asked, in an attempt to keep him focused.

"I think you'll be pleased. In my professional opinion, the paint sample you gave me dates around the early 1600s, likely of Dutch origin. If I were to speculate—"

Sam rose and held up a hand, not wanting to confirm or deny Bill's speculation. If they truly were onto something as significant as finding one of the paintings stolen from the Thompson Museum, he didn't want conjecture or innuendo floating around. He certainly didn't want it hitting the media. "Thank you for your immediate attention to this. I'd appreciate having the sample back. Please send your report directly to me." He exchanged his business card for the now properly sealed paint sample. He could tell Bill was disappointed to let go of it. "Please keep our discussion and your test results strictly confidential."

"Understood, but what about Agent Ferguson?"

"I'll inform him," Sam said, and wondered how that conversation would go, in light of the information he now had.

CHAPTER TWENTY

IN THE HOUR Sam had spent in the lab, the storm had intensified. He considered the wisdom of driving to Camden Falls versus getting a hotel room in Boston for the night, but with the results of the test, he didn't want to put off getting back into the Sinclair Gallery's warehouse. He contacted Colin and updated him.

"I'm as sure as I can be about the results, considering I'm not a scientist and didn't run the tests myself."

"I have a difficult time believing what it means," Colin said.

"I know. Me, too. I can tell you Bill Johnson seemed competent and he was skeptical enough that he repeated a couple of the more crucial tests."

"Do you have the report?"

"No. He was working on it when I left and said he'd send it to me as soon as possible. I'll pull over at the next gas station and check my cell phone."

"Okay. Forward it to me as soon as you can."

"Will do. I'll call Ferguson next. Let him know what we have. I expect he'll want in on this now," Sam added with some regret. "Can you start on the warrant?"

"You bet."

Sam had a brief conversation with Ferguson. In view of the storm and because the forecast now said it wouldn't let up for several more hours, Ferguson gave Sam the go-ahead to search the warehouse without him once the warrant came through, if he wasn't there yet.

For the first time since Sam had set out that morning, he was glad of the miserable weather. He was a team player as much as the next guy, but he wanted to be the one to search the warehouse before the FBI began leading the investigation. Stopping at the next gas station, he checked his emails.

Bill had been true to his word.

The report was in his inbox.

It was clear and concise, and exactly what they needed. He sent a thank-you note to Bill and forwarded the report to Colin, along with an update on his ETA. He sent a copy to Ferguson, too.

As Sam inched along I-93, he debated calling Chelsea. It was an active investigation, on a much larger scale than they'd anticipated. Police procedure was not to share information. But Chelsea had brought the matter to him, she knew where he'd gone, and she'd be impatient to hear the results.

Most of all, he wanted to call her—just to hear her voice.

"Are you okay?" was the first thing she asked, which made him smile.

"I'm fine. How can I not be, moving a few feet an hour?" he assured her, only half-joking.

"I'm sorry it's such a bad drive, but I'm glad you're going slow in this weather."

"Ha! At this rate, I'll see you in March!"

Chelsea laughed. "Then you have time to tell me what happened."

He inhaled deeply. "Chelsea, you have to keep what I'm about to tell you strictly confidential. You can't tell *anyone*. No forgetting or innocently dropping a hint. I need you to promise me that."

"Sam…" He could hear the exasperation in her voice.

"It's not intended as an insult, but I have to emphasize the point, because I'm breaking protocol here."

"Okay. I promise," she conceded.

"Thanks. Now, if you're not sitting down,

you might want to. The paint sample has been dated around the early 1600s—"

Her squeal on the other end of the line made him flinch.

"I knew it. I knew it!" she exclaimed. "It *is The Tempest on the Ocean*!"

"Before you get too excited..." Too late for that, he thought when she squealed again. "Let's take it one step at a time."

"How can it *not* be the Rembrandt?"

"First, is there any possibility that the original might've been copied at the time it was first painted? Are you aware of any paintings by the great masters having been duplicated in their day?"

"No, but hypothetically speaking, if it happened, I imagine that would make the replica priceless, too."

Yes, that made sense to him. It was quite likely that a replica done back in the 1600s would be valuable.

"So, what now?" she asked, her voice imbued with excitement.

"We've notified the FBI. On the strength of the testing, we're getting a search warrant for the warehouse. I'll execute it once I'm back in Camden Falls."

"Can I come with you? Like sort of as an expert consultant?"

He had to smile at that. "No, I'm sorry, that's not possible." Seeing the long row of brake lights up ahead, glaring through the steadily falling snow, he smacked his steering wheel. It wasn't looking good, especially when he noticed the flashing lights of a police vehicle off on the shoulder around the next curve, probably because of an accident. This was bound to delay him further.

"If the warrant comes through before I'm back—" which seemed more likely now "—then someone else will execute it," he said grudgingly. "Either way, I'm sorry, but it's not possible for you to attend."

They spoke a few minutes longer, and Chelsea made him promise to drive carefully before they hung up.

SAM PULLED INTO the parking lot of the police station shortly before nine that evening. It had taken him the better part of the day to go from Camden Falls to Boston, get the sample tested and drive back, most of that time spent behind the wheel.

The drive hadn't been an easy one, and he was exhausted from the concentration it had required. He couldn't wait to get out of the car and stretch his legs. He hadn't spent this much time sitting behind the wheel in ages, and his injured hip and knee were both throbbing.

Standing in the station's parking lot, he turned his face up, welcoming the cool caress of snowflakes on his skin. It beat the heck out of the hissing, sluggish heater in his police-issue vehicle.

Colin had texted him about half an hour earlier to let him know he had the search warrant. Since he'd been just outside Camden Falls, Colin had agreed to wait for him before exercising it.

Sam felt he could drink a whole pot of coffee, but he'd settle for a strong cup, black, to keep him going.

"Hey, Kim," he greeted the evening receptionist. "Colin's in, right?"

"Oh, yeah. I think the carpet in his office is threadbare from all the pacing he's done, waiting for you."

Sam smiled at her. "Thanks."

"Sam?" she called after him.

He stopped and turned. "Yeah?"

"Heck of a storm out there today. I'm glad you made it back safely."

That was one of the things he'd come to

value, living in Camden Falls. People genu-
inely *cared* about each other. "Thanks for that.
I appreciate the concern."

He walked as fast as he could, considering his injuries, through the squad room and
straight to Colin's office.

"You're back!" Colin exclaimed when he saw
him standing in the doorway, and pushed out of
his chair. "You sure you're up to this?"

"Darn right I am."

"Let's get it done, then. It's not every day we
get to make a bust to recover a priceless work
of art the FBI's been searching for over a quarter of a century!"

They left the station soon after, Sam with a
take-out cup of coffee in his hands. Colin took
the wheel behind his sure-footed SUV. They'd
agreed Sam had done enough driving in the
miserable weather for one day.

"You know where the warehouse is?" Sam
asked.

"Oh, yeah." Colin glanced over and grinned.
"I had to do something to occupy myself while
you took your sweet time getting your butt back
here."

Sam laughed. "Write me up for slacking off
on the job."

Colin patted him on the back. "I'll do that. Right after this bust."

When they were halfway there, Colin called the division. "Go ahead and contact him now."

"What was that all about?" Sam asked when he'd hung up.

"The desk sergeant is notifying Hadley."

"You wanted him to know, but not so much in advance that someone could've gotten there before us," Sam deduced.

"That's right."

When they pulled up in front of the warehouse, they saw a vehicle already there, blanketed in a thin layer of snow, the engine running.

Sam recognized it as a law enforcement vehicle. "What's that all about?" he asked Colin.

His boss looked over at him as he parked his SUV behind the other car. "With your additional delay because of the accident, Ferguson managed to get here before us, after all. When he called me, I told him to meet us here."

Sam tried not to sulk about it, since this was going to be the biggest bust of his career, but he understood that the FBI had a right to be there.

The road hadn't been plowed in the last couple of hours, nor had the sidewalk been cleared. The accumulation of snow was at least six inches since the plow had last gone by. Their footsteps left deep troughs as they trudged from their vehicles to the warehouse door. Sam tried to ignore the screaming pain in his hip and knee.

They went through proper procedure, and as they were about to enter, Hadley arrived in his Audi.

Sam made the introductions.

"Can you tell me why we're here?" Hadley asked. He looked perplexed and a little annoyed, but Sam didn't detect any nerves or apprehension.

"We have reason to suspect that there might be stolen property in the warehouse."

"That's just not possible!"

Hadley's outrage seemed genuine, but he didn't hesitate when Ferguson asked him to unlock the door.

The alarm system let out its audible warning until Hadley disarmed it. That and the locked door told Sam someone had been in the space since Chelsea.

Using a flashlight, he located the light switches and flipped them on.

"What the heck?" Sam couldn't hold back the exclamation, and his words echoed through the warehouse.

Colin dropped a hand on his shoulder. To placate or to warn him? Sam didn't know.

This had nothing to do with Chelsea's overactive imagination; the authenticated paint sample attested to the fact.

He slowly turned around.

Nothing.

Not a thing in the entire warehouse, other than the workstation and the enclosed room at the back.

Not a crate. Not a painting.

The warehouse was empty.

SAM HAD HAD a long day, but it was far from over.

He rode back to the station with Colin, Ferguson following behind in his own vehicle.

"They must've moved everything out sometime last night or during the day. Either because they'd planned to do it all along, or because they'd been tipped off," Sam said, once they were all in Colin's office.

"Let's consider the latter first. Who knew about what you did today?" Colin asked.

"The scientist in Boston who did the testing."

"Yeah, but he didn't know where you got the sample, or what we suspected," Colin responded.

Sam jerked a shoulder. "No, he didn't know where I got it, although he had some thoughts about what it meant. I didn't let him speculate, but I bet he wouldn't have been far off."

"Regardless, we trust him," Ferguson interjected. "He's done work for us before."

"The fine art community is small, according to what I've learned," Sam responded. "It's hard to say who he might know and what he might have said."

"We trust him," Ferguson repeated.

"Is there any chance the results he gave Sam aren't correct?" Colin asked Ferguson.

"I don't think so. What purpose would that serve? If he was playing games, wouldn't it be more likely that he'd tell Sam there's nothing remarkable about the sample? Just common current-day paint?"

Colin nodded. "Yeah. Did anyone else know?" he asked Sam.

"Chelsea Owens knew where I'd gone."

"Reasonable, since she'd given you the paint sample," Colin said.

He might as well face the fire, Sam thought. "She also knew the outcome."

Colin shot a quick glance at Ferguson, then glared at Sam. "You *told* her?"

Sam nodded.

"What were you thinking?" Colin's tone was quiet. Emphatic. Sam knew that meant he was angry. "Putting that aside for now," Colin went on, "because it doesn't make sense that she'd tell you what she'd seen, give you the paint sample and either be personally involved or tip someone off—was there anyone else?"

Sam started to shake his head, then thought back. "When I called Chelsea, she was at the gallery. I have no way of knowing whether anyone overheard her end of the conversation. The possibilities include Joel Sinclair, the owner's grandson, and Adam Rochester, the jewelry store owners' nephew. I've seen him on a couple of occasions visiting Joel. There's also an admin person, another sales associate and the curator."

"Could Sinclair have heard anything? You're still convinced it was his car that hit you?"

"It's possible he did, and yes, I am. We don't have enough to bring Sinclair in for questioning again, do we?"

Colin shook his head. "Since he's alibied for when you were hit and there was no discernible damage to his vehicle, no. And not for this."

"Any chance Owens is screwing with us?" Ferguson asked. "Maybe she has an ax to grind with the gallery or its owners?"

"No way," Sam retorted. "Not a chance. Her aspiration is to be the next curator. She's invested in that place. She wouldn't do anything to compromise that."

Colin glanced at Sam again. "Is it possible she's been told it won't happen? That the grandson will take over and this is retribution?"

"No" was Sam's immediate denial. "She's too much of an open book. She would've told me if that was the case…" He considered the couple of weeks he'd put things on hold between them because of the Babineux investigation. No. She still would've told him in the last few days, since they'd started seeing each other again. Except they'd had a lot of other things on their minds—his injury. Her visit to the warehouse.

"Sam, talk to me."

He couldn't believe it of Chelsea. "Even if she was told she had no chance at the job, she wouldn't do something like this. We might not be able to bring Sinclair in, but that doesn't mean I can't have another chat with him," he said. And with Chelsea. Colin didn't need to know that, but it would have to wait until tomorrow.

For now, Sam had to sit through the remainder of the painful debrief with Colin and Ferguson, and then they had to formulate a strategy.

By the time they finished, Chelsea had called him and sent several texts. Responding to her would have to wait until tomorrow, too.

He had to get some much-needed sleep.

THE MORNING DAWNED bright and sunny. The plows were still at work catching up from the day before to clear the side streets, but the major roads were bare, with large piles of snow on the shoulders.

The instant Sam walked into the gallery, Chelsea hurried over to him. She took his hand and pulled him to a corner of the showroom. "What happened?" she asked in a hushed whisper. "I tried calling you at home last night and on your cell. I didn't know what to think."

"I had a meeting with Colin that ran quite late," he replied. "When I got home, I went straight to bed."

Her eyes were a stormy green. "I was worried about you. I knew you made it back to town, and then when I couldn't reach you…"

"I'm sorry," he said ineffectually, but he was touched by her concern. No one outside his immediate family had worried about him like that in a long time. It was a nice feeling.

"Well, did you find it? Did you find the Rembrandt?" she asked, still whispering.

Sam's gaze shifted over her shoulder. Joel was walking out of the office area.

"Excuse me," Sam said to Chelsea and waved to Joel.

"Detective," Joel greeted him as Sam approached.

"Could I have a few minutes of your time?" Sam asked.

"For?"

"I'd like to ask you a couple of questions."

"You're not going to grill me about your accident again, are you?"

"No," Sam assured him.

Joel nodded and led Sam to his office. Ten minutes later, Sam walked back out. He had no significant new information, but he'd managed to irritate Joel. As much as he would've been happy to pin the emptying out of the warehouse on Joel, his answers and body language led Sam to conclude that it hadn't been him. The one thing of interest to Sam was that Joel claimed the last time he'd tried to go to the warehouse, his key hadn't worked. That was months ago, and he'd forgotten about it, he said, since he hadn't had any reason to go there recently.

Sam was beginning to suspect that if there *had* been something in the warehouse or if something illegal was going on there, Joel had no knowledge of it. If it was an inside job, that left the curator, Nadine Sinclair, Tina Stevens, the administrative assistant, and the other sales associate, Deborah Grant.

And Chelsea.

When Sam returned to the showroom, Chelsea was occupied with a middle-aged woman. She sent him an exasperated look behind the woman's back.

Miming to her that he'd call later, he waved goodbye and left.

He'd just reached his own vehicle, when he decided to have another look at Sinclair's SUV. Sam had begun to wonder if he might have been wrong about the particulars of the vehicle that had hit him. He was aware that Colin had already had it checked for dents or any other sign of impact and there hadn't been one. Understandable, since Sam had taken the brunt of the force.

But since he was here, anyway, he might as well check it out.

He pulled up the collar of his coat. He'd left his gloves in his vehicle, so he shoved his hands into his pockets and walked around the block to the gallery's back lot, where the staff generally parked. As he rounded the corner he caught a movement. Stepping back hurriedly, he peered around the edge of the building. The back of Joel's MDX was open and the movement he'd glimpsed had come from behind the vehicle.

Sam waited until the person, bundled up in a heavy winter coat and ski hat—not unlike those worn by the person who'd hit him—closed the back door. Then he locked the vehicle and stepped around it.

The person turned toward Sam and, for the first time, Sam could see his face.

CHAPTER TWENTY-ONE

ADAM ROCHESTER POCKETED a set of keys as he walked from Joel's MDX toward the back entrance of All That Glitters and Shines.

Sam managed to duck behind the wall without being seen. He was tempted to go back into the gallery and ask Sinclair a few more questions. On second thought, he decided to have a chat with Chelsea first.

That meant he'd have to tell her they'd found the warehouse empty. So be it. He needed some answers about Adam.

Instead of going back inside, he got into his car and called her from his cell. "Chelsea, I'm sorry I left without more of a goodbye, but you were busy," he said, trying to explain his earlier behavior when she answered. "Do you have time for a coffee?"

"Yes. If you can wait a couple of minutes."

"Sure. I'll be outside."

While he waited, Sam had someone at the station run Adam Rochester for him. Chelsea's "couple of minutes" stretched into fifteen by the time she appeared. At least the wait had given him the opportunity to receive and review the report on Rochester.

Sam drove them to The Coffee Shoppe. They'd barely sat down when she leaned in and started quizzing him.

He clasped her hands in his. "There was nothing in the warehouse."

"What?" The single word sounded more like a squeak.

"The warehouse was empty."

She tugged her hands away. "I saw what I saw, Sam. I wasn't imagining it," she stated emphatically.

"I know. You got the paint sample to prove it."

"Then how could it be?"

She looked so deflated, so sad, he wanted to gather her in his arms. But right now, he needed her help to fill in some of the details about Adam, Joel and their relationship. "First, I'd like to ask you about the box of jewelry you saw at the warehouse. Okay?"

She nodded rapidly. "Yes. Was that at least still there?"

He hated to disappoint her again. "No, it wasn't. But can you describe what you saw?"

She closed her eyes. When she opened them again, she gave him a detailed description.

"Have you seen any items like that in All That Glitters and Shines? Anything that you think would resemble them?"

"I wouldn't know." She shrugged. "I'm not big on expensive jewelry, so I don't really look at the display cases when I drop in. I'm mostly there to visit Mr. and Mrs. Rochester."

Sam nodded. "You told me that Adam's lived with his aunt and uncle for most of his life."

"Yes, that's correct."

"Tell me again about his mother, and how that came about, please."

"Adam's father, who was quite a bit younger than Mr. Rochester, was in the military and was deployed overseas a number of times. His mother didn't handle being on her own with a young child well. She had a drug and alcohol problem, but when Adam's father was killed in the line of duty, it pushed her over the edge. I was told that both the drinking and the drugs got worse. Mr. Rochester was already more of a father figure in Adam's life than his brother had been. The Rochesters tried to help her, but one day she simply disappeared and Adam began living with them."

Sam thought back to what he'd learned about

Adam's mother. She'd been institutionalized but she'd been out for a while, with no fixed address. "Do they know where she is?"

"Not that I'm aware of. I gather that she'd contact the Rochesters occasionally, asking for money. First, they'd give her some, but the requests became more frequent, and they suspected she used the money for drugs and alcohol, so they stopped giving her any. Eventually, she stopped asking."

"You don't think she's had any contact with Adam?"

Her big green eyes turned sad. "I don't think so. Adam's recollections of her are vague at best. In my opinion, he loves her—or at least the memory of her—but I doubt that either Adam or the Rochesters have had any contact with her, or tried to find her."

"It must have been tough on Adam."

"Yes, I'm sure it was. When his mother's addiction got worse, frankly I think the Rochesters feared for Adam's safety and well-being. Not only because of his mother's behavior, but the people she associated with. When she went to jail for possession with the intent of trafficking—that's how she tried to make money to support her habit—thankfully Adam was no longer living with her. The Rochesters saw that as the final straw and obtained custody of Adam. He was already living with them, but they wanted to make it permanent and legal."

"How old was Adam at the time?"

"I don't know. Maybe ten or twelve, but that's just a guess, because that was also about the time Adam and Joel became friends."

"And the mother? Do you know what happened to her after she got out of jail?"

"I have no idea. It's not something Adam talks about. I only know bits and pieces because he confided in Joel, and Joel shared some of it with me."

"Have Adam and Joel always been close?" Sam realized he'd covered some of this with her before, but he wanted to get the full picture.

She sighed. "What I understand from Joel is that they used to be closer. They started to drift apart a few years ago."

"Did you ever hear why?"

"No. They had some sort of falling-out. I know you don't think much of Joel, but he is loyal. He never told me what their argument was about, even when we were dating."

"They still seem to be on good terms. I've seen them together several times."

"Oh, yes. Just not as close as they used to be."

"Are they close enough at this point for Adam to borrow Joel's vehicle?"

Chelsea's brows drew together. "You think Adam's the one who hit you in Joel's MDX?" She shook her head slowly. "I don't believe he would've done it. But, yes, Joel would lend him his car, if he needed it. For example, if Adam's car was acting up or if he needed to run an errand for his aunt and uncle and required more room. I have to say again, if Joel had lent his car to Adam the night you got hit, he would've told you."

"Okay. Would Adam have access to the gallery's warehouse and would he have any reason to be there?"

"I don't… Oh, are you thinking because there was jewelry there, too, Adam's involved in whatever is going on?"

Sam smiled indulgently. "Chelsea, please let me ask the questions for now, and you answer them, all right?"

She returned the smile. "Sorry. I would've said no, since to the best of my knowledge, any use the Rochesters made of the warehouse was always through Joel, but you got me thinking. If Adam borrowed Joel's SUV, and Joel gave Adam his whole key chain, he would have access to the warehouse. But he wouldn't know the code to disarm the security system. No one at the gallery would give him that."

Joel had only to give him the key once, Sam thought, since Adam could have then made a copy. But Joel had said his key wasn't working, so who would have rekeyed the lock? Adam? Yet Hadley's key had worked for Chelsea. And it had certainly been fine both times when Sam had been at the warehouse with him... As for the security system, if Adam had been inside the building with Joel, he could've seen Joel enter the code to disarm it. People often didn't realize how easily security measures could be breached by bad guys because of people's carelessness. It happened all the time.

Sam watched Chelsea's expressive face. She was no doubt turning everything they'd discussed over in her head. "I need you to promise not to discuss this with anyone, okay?"

"Yes, I understand and I promise," she replied without hesitation, but he could see that wherever her thoughts had led her, she was more than likely concerned for her friends, the Rochesters.

He hoped that her loyalty and concern for them wouldn't trump her promise of confidentiality to him. "Are we good?" he asked.

She nodded. "Yeah. This is all so strange and unbelievable."

"What we're dealing with here isn't commonplace for me, either. It's not every day that I have a lead on a stolen painting worth millions of dollars."

"*Tens* of millions," Chelsea corrected him. She glanced out the window and Sam also watched the steadily falling snow for a few minutes. When she turned back to him, she smiled, then bit her lower lip. "If we're finished with that topic, I have another question. I know Christmas is still a couple weeks away, but I was thinking… Paige and Daniel are holding a Christmas Eve get-together."

Her expression was hopeful, so unguarded, he felt his heart tumble for her all over again.

"I thought…"

She again had her lower lip caught between her teeth, and he found it impossible to look away.

"Would you… Would you go with me?"

Had he caused that nervous hesitancy in her, when she'd always seemed so sure of herself? The idea that he might have was like a punch straight to his gut. His family would understand if he joined them just for Christmas day. Heck, his siblings were all over the place at Christmas with their significant others. Spending Christmas with Chelsea had a special appeal. "Yeah. I'd like that. Thanks for asking."

Her face glowed like a bright ray of sunshine.

A few simple words could do that for her. What kind of a fool was he to deny himself her company for several weeks?

"If you're free one evening, you could also help me decorate my apartment," she suggested hopefully.

He hadn't done much in the way of Christmas decoration for the last few years. Not since Nicolas had died. His heart hadn't been in it. But with Chelsea…it would be fun. "I'd like that, too," he repeated.

As he watched, her smile wavered.

"What's wrong?" He didn't want to see her good mood fade.

"I was just thinking that Mr. Weatherly moved from the building after he married Laura."

"That makes sense," Sam said cautiously, not clear on what the issue was.

"Yes. Don't get me wrong. I'm happy for them. But all my friends in the building seem to be leaving. We had such a close-knit group. Now, Paige is gone. Mr. Weatherly's gone. And the Bennetts aren't getting any younger. Their daughter's been urging them to move in with

her family in Providence. Or, if they prefer, relocate to a seniors' assisted-living residence."
Chelsea's lower lip trembled. "They've been my
family for as long as I've been in Camden Falls.
Now it seems they're all moving on."

For the first time since Katherine had left
him, Sam thought of a family of his own, and
he pictured Chelsea in the leading role. The realization staggered him. He wanted to comfort
her. Reassure her. But the thought of family…
marriage…and the impossibility of his having
children, when he knew how much she loved
and wanted them, gave him pause.

He checked his watch. "Chelsea, I'm sorry,
but I have to get back to work."

The abrupt change in his demeanor obviously wasn't lost on her, if her long, sad look
was any indication. "Oh, I should get back,
too," she finally murmured. "So, we're on for
Christmas Eve?" she asked uncertainly.

He realized she was giving him an out, in
case he'd changed his mind. Much as he wanted
to take it and make some excuse, he wasn't that
big a coward. Nor was he that inconsiderate.
He'd told her he'd go, and he knew it meant a
lot to her. "Yes." Admittedly, it meant a lot to
him, too.

Despite his reservations and misgivings—or

perhaps because of them—when he helped her out of his car in front of the gallery, he drew her close and kissed her gently. Instead of joyful, it felt sad and left him longing.

She looked up at him with troubled eyes. "I don't understand."

He had no words of reassurance, but he brushed a hand across her cheek. "I'll see you soon."

CHAPTER TWENTY-TWO

SAM PARKED HALF a block down and on the other side of the street behind All That Glitters and Shines. From there, he could see both the front and back entrances of the two businesses. The storefronts were decked out for Christmas, which reminded him that he'd promised Chelsea he'd help her decorate her apartment. He sipped his cooling coffee as he watched the Rochesters enter their store at half past nine. He knew it opened at ten. Chelsea and Hadley were already at the gallery. He'd purposely arrived at eight thirty, half an hour after he expected Chelsea and Hadley to be inside, not wanting to risk Chelsea noticing his police-issue vehicle.

He saw the administrative assistant, Tina, arrive, followed by Joel with the other sales associate. What was her name? Deborah Grant? Right. She and Joel had arrived together, and in Joel's SUV. He watched them approach the entrance, shoulders touching, sharing a joke and laughing. He wondered if Chelsea knew that Joel had apparently moved on.

If Deborah and Joel were having a relationship, would *she* have access to his car? To the warehouse? Something else to consider.

At quarter to eleven, he got what he'd been waiting for. Adam hopped out of the passenger side of a navy blue Nissan and waved as the car drove off. Sam glanced around to see if anyone was watching—not that it would matter, but he preferred to know. Seeing no one, he climbed out of his car.

"Adam," he called before the other man had made it to the back door of the jewelry store. "I'd like a word with you."

Shock and apprehension registered on Adam's face. "What for?" he asked.

Sam hadn't bothered with gloves, and the wind was decidedly chilly. He shoved his hands into his coat pockets. "I'd like to ask you a few questions."

"Can we do it some other time?" Adam avoided eye contact. "I'm already late for work."

"This won't take long." He kept his voice casual. "Police business."

Adam shivered. From cold or nerves, Sam didn't know. "It would be good to get out of the cold. We can do this at the police station or in-side the store. Your choice."

With his head lowered, Adam shot an anx-ious glance at the store. Being nervous didn't make him guilty. Adam Rochester had struck him as the skittish sort from the first time they'd met. "Is there an office in the store that we can use?" Sam suggested.

"No. I mean, yes, but I'd prefer not to do it there." Adam pulled his hands out of his pock-ets and spread them. Sam noticed that they were trembling. "I don't want to upset my aunt and uncle."

Sam watched him carefully. "Why would they be upset?"

"It's not that I did anything wrong!"

Sam held his gaze without responding. Yes, nervousness might not be an indication of guilt—but immediately assuming that the questions had to do with something he'd done rather than the robbery at the store could be.

"I don't want them worrying about why I'm talking to you," he went on.

"We can take this to the station, as I said."

Adam's face paled, but then he nodded. "Yeah. All right."

"Do you want to let them know you'll be late?"

Adam's mouth worked furiously without making a sound for a few moments. "No. That's okay. I was running behind this morning, anyway. They won't mind if I'm a little later."

Sam interpreted that to mean the Rochesters were accustomed to their nephew not being on time. He wondered if they had any inkling of what he'd learned from the police report about Adam. Adam had started following in his mother's footsteps. He had a drug habit, and had minor possession-related misdemeanor charges from other jurisdictions on his record.

Sam motioned toward his cruiser and noted the jerky gait, the nervous shifting of Adam's eyes, as he opened the back door for him.

"Do I have to sit back there?" he asked, pointing.

"If you want to go to the station, yes."

"Okay. Okay, yeah." Sam placed his hand on Adam's head to guide him as he got in, as was procedure to keep people from bumping their heads on the door frame.

By the time they got to the station—a short fifteen-minute drive later—Adam seemed to have shrunk in on himself.

The report hadn't been wrong about Adam's drug use, and Sam might have underestimated the degree of his drug addiction.

As Sam watched Adam guzzle the water he'd handed him once they were inside the interview room, he fleetingly felt sorry for the kid. Having lived under the influence of a mother like the one he'd had, it would've taken extraordinary strength of character to rise above his formative years, despite the love and care he'd received from the Rochesters.

Sam poured more water into Adam's glass. Adam obviously hadn't had a fix that morning.

Heck, the guy had probably developed his dependency in the womb, since the report on his mother implied she'd been using before she became pregnant. Depending on how severe Adam's addiction had been at birth, Sam hoped he'd been properly diagnosed and treated before being released from the hospital. If not, the kid wouldn't have had a chance from the start.

Pushing his sympathy aside, Sam sat down opposite Adam.

Twenty minutes later, he had everything he needed. Sam had a uniform take Adam to a holding cell and went to see Colin.

"How did it go?" Colin asked.

"No question that Adam has a drug habit that needs to be fed and that costs money. Unlike his mother, he didn't choose trafficking to support his habit. He's got his own moral code of sorts, and he's retained enough of a conscience that he knew he was in trouble and why. He didn't want to be responsible for turning other teens onto drugs."

"That's something, at least. If he was into trafficking, he probably would've messed up by now and we would've had him."

"Probably. Through his friend, Joel, he's met many influential people in the art world. When one of those people made an offhand comment about forgeries and insurance fraud, it got him thinking. His aunt and uncle's store gave him access to jewelry that was easy to fence. But another chance conversation opened up a much larger opportunity for him with the gallery. One he couldn't resist. He had a new partner and almost limitless potential. He'd convinced himself that if he could acquire enough money, he could use it to seek treatment for his addiction and get clean. He said he wanted to do it for his aunt and uncle. The intention was there, but the strength of character wasn't."

Colin's lips formed a straight, hard line and he shook his head. "So, you were right about a connection between the jewelry store robbery and the theft of the Babineux. Is he the person who hit you?"

"Yes. Adam used Joel's SUV—at times he

borrowed it, at others he'd simply taken it without Joel's knowledge when he knew Joel wouldn't be using it. It's an old vehicle with a regular key, and he had it copied. Joel, of course, didn't realize Adam had done that, which is why it didn't come up in my earlier conversation with him. Adam just as easily got the key to the warehouse copied a couple of years ago. Joel lent him his entire key chain when he'd let Adam store some supplies for the jewelry store in the warehouse. Unwise, but he'd given him the security code, too."

Colin raised his eyebrows. "He's been at it that long?"

"No. I believe he was trying to beat his addiction back then. He said he copied the keys because he thought they might come in handy at some point. I believe he was thinking about what he could do for money, but hadn't acted on it yet."

"And he confessed to hitting you with Sinclair's car?"

"He tried to deny it at first, but ultimately he broke down and confessed to that, too. He claims it was unintentional. An accident when he panicked and tried to get away as quickly as possible. I believe him."

Colin nodded. "Does Joel Sinclair have a role in what's been going on?"

Sam shook his head. "I don't think so. At least not directly. He also hasn't had access to the warehouse since Adam had the lock changed at his partner's behest. Apparently, their *business* was flourishing, and they decided they needed to find alternate premises. Secure and not associated with the gallery. In the meantime, as protection against Joel getting in and discovering what they'd been doing, the lock was rekeyed.

"I'll interview Joel again, but there are a couple of other steps we'll need to take first. My interpretation is that Joel learned of Adam's drug problem a few years ago, when he could no longer hide it from him because of how close they were at the time. Joel tried to get his friend to quit. When that didn't work, it drove a wedge between them."

"So, the drug-addicted nephew of the jewelry store owners somehow managed to mastermind an operation that involved not only forging and selling jewelry but also fine art? And somehow he happened upon the stolen Rembrandt worth millions of dollars?" Colin leaned back in his chair and crossed his arms. "I find that hard to believe, if that's what you're telling me."

Sam made a snorting sound and smiled wryly. "No, that's not what I'm telling you.

Adam started with the jewelry end of it, but the art forgery? It's far beyond him. He's not the mastermind. He's been a pawn. We have a bigger fish to catch."

"CHELSEA, COULD YOU do me a favor?" Mr. Hadley asked.

There was another storm threatening and traffic at the gallery was slow, so Chelsea had been absorbed in trying to understand the financials again. She glanced up from her computer screen. "Sure."

"I have some paperwork that Nadine has to sign. Unfortunately, she had one of her migraines overnight. Although she's feeling better this morning, she still has a headache and she didn't get much sleep, so she'd prefer not to come to the gallery." He handed her a file folder. "Since Joel's booked solid with meetings today, would you mind taking these documents to her and getting her signature?"

"No problem."

Chelsea shut down her computer, put on her boots and coat and headed out.

Mrs. Sinclair opened the door as Chelsea arrived. She was dressed in velvet lounge pants and a matching top. Even though her hair was as impeccably styled as usual and her face was made-up, both were lacking luster and polish.

Placing a hand on Mrs. Sinclair's elbow, Chelsea helped her into the living room. "I'm sorry you're not feeling well," she said once they were seated.

"I'm much better, thank you. It's just the vestiges of a darn migraine. But this, also, will pass. If it's not too much trouble, could you make us some tea?"

"I'm happy to do it." Chelsea gave her the file folder. "You can start looking at those, if you wish. I'll be back in a few minutes."

When Chelsea returned with the pot of tea, two mugs, sugar and milk, all on a tray, Mrs. Sinclair had nearly finished reading the documents. Chelsea fixed her a cup and poured herself one, too.

"What is the—"

Whatever Mrs. Sinclair was going to ask went unsaid at the sound of the doorbell.

"Would you mind getting that for me, dear?" she asked instead.

Chelsea nodded and rose.

The shock of seeing Sam standing at Mrs. Sinclair's door with a man and woman she'd never seen before but would've recognized as law enforcement from a mile away caused a hard knot to form in her stomach. "What are you doing here?" she finally managed to ask.

If his furrowed brow and downturned lips were any indication, Sam was surprised to see her, too, but not in a happy way. "What are *you* doing here?"

"I'm here to have Mrs. Sinclair sign some papers. What about you?" she challenged, feeling disconcerted.

The man standing behind Sam stepped forward. "Do we have a problem?" he asked in an officious voice.

"Special Agent Ferguson, this is Chelsea Owens. Chelsea, Agent Ferguson is with the FBI. So is Special Agent Angela Wilson."

Chelsea felt her heart thud heavily. The FBI? What were *they* doing here? With wide eyes, she stared at Sam and tried to ignore the agents. Resting her hand—suddenly cold and clammy—on Sam's forearm, she asked, "Am I in trouble?"

Sam's expression softened, and he touched her hand and squeezed it before subtly moving it off his arm. "No, Chelsea. We're here to see Nadine Sinclair."

"Is everything okay, Chelsea?" Mrs. Sinclair called from the living room.

Sam glanced at Ferguson.

"We'd appreciate it if you'd ask her to come to the door," he said to Chelsea.

She looked back at Sam, trying to read anything in his eyes that might hint at what was going on.

Sam's nod was nearly imperceptible. "Do as he asked, please," he said quietly.

Walking back into the living room, Chelsea said to Mrs. Sinclair, "There are some people at the door to see you."

"Who are they?" she inquired, her tone imperious. "I'm not expecting anyone."

"I think you'd better go see for yourself," Chelsea responded and nearly flinched at Mrs. Sinclair's furious look. Her headache must be getting worse, Chelsea rationalized, as she guided her to the front door.

"Yes, may I help you?" Mrs. Sinclair asked, as her gaze skipped from one face to the next, resting on Sam.

Ferguson stepped forward again, introduced himself and his partner, and showed her his badge.

It wasn't bafflement or annoyance that Chelsea read on Mrs. Sinclair's features, but something darker. She also saw resignation.

"We have a warrant to search your home," Ferguson continued, handing her the paper.

"Detective Eldridge will stay with you while we execute it."

What are they doing? Chelsea wondered. She tried to attract Sam's attention, but he was focused on the FBI agents. "There has to be a mistake here!" she interjected, frowning at Sam. "Mrs. Sinclair is not well today. Can we take this into the living room? You can explain what it's all about, and we'll sort it out." With an arm around Mrs. Sinclair's shoulders, Chelsea started to lead her away.

Sam grasped Chelsea's elbow firmly and held her back. "Chelsea, let the agents do their job."

"Mrs. Sinclair has a right to know what this is about," she stated with conviction. "She—"

"Just a minute!" Mrs. Sinclair cut them off. "Don't talk around me as if I wasn't here or, worse yet, as if I was daft. I *do* have a right to know."

Ferguson nodded. "Yes, you do. We have a warrant to search your home for a painting called *The Tempest on the Ocean*, and for other possible stolen paintings."

Chelsea couldn't believe what she was hearing, but Mrs. Sinclair shook off her comforting hand. "This is ridiculous! I want to call my lawyer."

"By all means," Ferguson responded. "We'll wait."

Chelsea watched Mrs. Sinclair shoot the FBI agents a haughty look as she walked back to her office, accompanied by Agent Wilson, to make the call. Alone with Sam and Agent Ferguson, Chelsea shifted confused eyes from one man to the other. "You really believe Mrs. Sinclair has the Rembrandt?"

"Yes, we do," Sam responded.

"But...but..."

Sam turned to Ferguson, who nodded. "Might as well. She'll know soon enough."

"Chelsea," Sam began. "I interviewed Adam Rochester this morning. He's been working for Mrs. Sinclair to make money to support a drug habit. He's been the one using the warehouse for illicit purposes, but under Mrs. Sinclair's direction."

"I don't understand. Why would Mrs. Sinclair, who's so highly regarded in the art world, loving art as much as she does, be involved in something like this?"

"We don't have the answer to that right now," Ferguson interjected. "But we hope to find out."

Dazed, Chelsea nodded.

When Mrs. Sinclair and Agent Wilson returned, they sat the old lady down in the living room. She and Sam waited with her while the special agents executed the warrant.

The special agents were moving around upstairs, and Chelsea could occasionally hear furniture being shifted. When they made their way back down the stairs, she noticed the slight shake of Ferguson's head directed at Sam. She assumed that meant they hadn't found anything.

Chelsea wanted to jump up and yell that she could have *told* them Mrs. Sinclair was innocent. For Mrs. Sinclair's sake, Chelsea hoped they wouldn't find anything anywhere in the house. That it would turn out Adam had lied to Sam, and Mrs. Sinclair was innocent of the alleged acts. Whenever she glanced at the older woman, both her expression and demeanor were enigmatic.

Finished searching the first floor as well, the special agents had just taken the stairs to the basement when the front door burst open.

Sam rose immediately and hurried to the door. Chelsea could see it was Joel, and Sam was blocking his path.

Next to her, Mrs. Sinclair sighed. "Oh, dear God." For the first time since they'd begun the search of her home, she showed emotion and dropped her head into her hands.

While Sam and Joel had a heated conversation, Chelsea inched closer to Mrs. Sinclair. "What's going on? Has Joel done something?" she asked, incapable of believing that this kind old lady had.

Mrs. Sinclair shook her head. "No, he hasn't. My lawyer must have called him. My lawyer's on his way, too, to help sort all this out."

"Sort *what* out, Mrs. Sinclair? Do you know anything about the Rembrandt?"

Before Mrs. Sinclair could respond, Joel rushed into the room, followed by a frowning Sam. He sat down on the other side of his grandmother and took her hands in his. He obviously knew not to ask questions under Sam's intense scrutiny, so he simply confirmed that the lawyer would be arriving soon.

Chelsea got up and went to stand beside Sam. She had countless questions swirling in her mind, but she knew Sam couldn't answer them, so she stood silently next to him.

Hearing someone coming up the basement stairs at a quick pace, they all turned to the stairwell. Ferguson's face was grim when he entered the living room. Wilson followed him, an equally stern expression on her face.

"Who's this?" Ferguson asked Sam, looking pointedly at Joel.

They had a brief exchange, and Joel confirmed that it had been his grandmother's lawyer who'd called him.

Ferguson stepped closer to address Mrs. Sinclair. "We need you to provide us with access to the locked room downstairs."

Chelsea saw Joel's shocked look, but his grandmother didn't seem to notice. Her complexion had gone sallow, except for two bright pink splotches high on her cheeks. She nodded at Ferguson and rose. When she faltered, Joel sprang to his feet to steady her and help her move forward.

Ferguson held up his hand. "Only Mrs. Sinclair comes downstairs. Detective, if you can join us, Agent Wilson will stay here with Mr. Sinclair and Ms. Owens."

Chelsea sat in an armchair, while Joel remained on the sofa. Neither of them dared say anything in the presence of Agent Wilson, but Chelsea could see the concern and confusion in Joel's eyes.

A few minutes later, Sam escorted Mrs. Sinclair back into the living room.

She looked a decade older than she had earlier that morning. With hunched shoulders and trembling hands, she sat next to Joel but avoided making eye contact with him, as much as he tried.

When the doorbell sounded, Agent Wilson indicated for Joel to go ahead and open the door while she stood in the hallway so she could see both the front entry and the living room, where Chelsea and Mrs. Sinclair remained seated. A moment later Joel led a short, portly man in a steel-gray suit into the room. Since he hurried over to Mrs. Sinclair, Chelsea assumed he was the lawyer.

Agent Wilson moved back to the entry leading to the hall to allow the lawyer and his client an opportunity to speak privately. But even where Chelsea sat, not too far away, she couldn't hear what they were saying. She couldn't miss, however, that the lawyer was getting agitated, as was Joel, who sat closer and was likely within hearing range. At one point, the lawyer demanded to see the search warrant. After scrutinizing it, he handed it back to Agent Wilson.

For the life of her, Chelsea couldn't figure out what was going on.

It felt as if an eternity had passed before Sam came back up the stairs. The lawyer shot to his feet, but Sam silenced him with a gesture.

Instead, he turned to Chelsea. "Please come downstairs with me."

Chelsea looked at Mrs. Sinclair, then at Joel and even the lawyer. Mrs. Sinclair's head hung, her eyes closed and hands clenched. Joel's expression was pained and the lawyer's stoic. Wilson's face was inscrutable. Chelsea wasn't getting any indication of what was going on from any of them.

When she joined Sam, his countenance was gentle and maybe a little amused. She appreciated the light touch of his hand on her lower back as he escorted her to the stairs. "You're going to be making history here," he whispered as they started down the steps.

CHAPTER TWENTY-THREE

CHELSEA HAD BEEN in Mrs. Sinclair's basement before, but she'd always assumed it was a partial basement. What she hadn't known was that at the back of the small storage space under the stairs was a door. A door with some sort of electronic detection plate.

"It's a retinal scan access panel," Sam explained.

Retinal scan? Chelsea had seen those in movies. More recently, she knew, they'd started using them at airports for the "Trusted Traveler" program.

The doorway was short, to fit under the stairway. Sam had to duck to enter, although she could walk through upright…barely.

Sam stepped out of her way and she gasped when she saw the inside of the room.

No. Not a room. *Vault* was a better word for it.

The goose bumps on her arms weren't just because of what she saw. The cool air skimmed her exposed skin. The room was climate-controlled. She didn't have to check the control panel on the wall to know that the temperature would be between sixty-eight and seventy-two degrees Fahrenheit and humidity between 45 and 55 percent, ideal for preserving fine art.

There were no windows or any other points of access or egress. Just the low door through which they had entered. The walls were a warm white, the floor marble, to prevent the collection of dust, and polished to a bright sheen. But it was the paintings on the walls that made her legs go rubbery.

She groped for Sam's hand. "You do know what we're looking at, don't you?" she said breathlessly, disbelievingly. Reverently.

He squeezed her hand. "Even a neophyte like me would know. And if I didn't—" He jerked his head toward Ferguson, already examining and photographing the paintings. "His actions would be a definite giveaway."

Chelsea let out a laugh as her gaze rested on *The Tempest on the Ocean*, hung in the most prominent location. But the Rembrandt wasn't the only priceless work of art in the room.

Sam cautioned her not to touch anything in the room to avoid leaving fingerprints. Not to interrupt the special agent. But just *being* there!

For this momentous occasion. To be able to see these masterpieces, some of which hadn't been seen in public for over a quarter of a century!

She felt a little light-headed and was grateful for Sam's continued grasp of her hand.

As Sam had said, she was part of history.

Her eyes stung and she focused on breathing to keep from hyperventilating.

She took a few steps closer to *The Tempest on the Ocean* to better admire it. She could hardly believe she'd actually *touched* it when it was in the warehouse.

"Ms. Owens?"

Chelsea nearly jumped at the sound of Ferguson calling her name. "We've ID'd two more paintings that belonged to the Thompson Museum." Yes, Chelsea could see them now. Another work by Rembrandt, and one by Manet, which Mrs. Sinclair had a replica of on display in her living room.

Chelsea's heart raced and she felt light-headed again.

"Ms. Owens, can you identify any of the other pieces in this room?"

Taking a slow walk around, she studied all the paintings. There were a couple of pieces that had been at the gallery for a time before they'd sold. Her assumption was that, like the

Babineux, the originals had been swapped for duplicates, and the forgeries were what had gone to the purchasers.

She was glad that Sam held her hand the entire time. They stayed three feet back from the walls, as Ferguson had instructed, but she was allowed to take as long as she wanted.

In total, including *The Tempest on the Ocean*, five of the paintings missing from the Thompson Museum were there. She knew them by sight. She identified as many of the other works as she could, but several of them stumped her.

As it occurred to her that she could never have her fill of admiring the paintings, another thought struck her. She took a slow turn around the room. All this beautiful art…locked away in this vault. Not to be shared, but for the pleasure of Mrs. Sinclair only. It made her feel unbearably sad. With a heavy heart, she thanked the special agent.

"No, thank *you* for your assistance, Ms. Owens," Ferguson said.

With a final look around the room, trying to permanently commit it all to memory, Chelsea walked out with Sam.

"This is so wrong," she murmured to him.

"I agree. She never should have stolen those paintings."

Chelsea stopped in the hallway and gazed up at him. "Yes, of course, that's wrong, but it's not what I meant. It's such a shame—so *selfish*—to have those beautiful paintings locked away all these years so that no one other than Mrs. Sinclair can appreciate them."

Sam nodded thoughtfully. "I see your point."

As they mounted the steps, she realized that they hadn't really needed her assistance downstairs. It must have been something Sam had arranged. She was eternally grateful to him for having pulled whatever strings he had for her to be in that room. He might not have appreciated art or loved it the way she did. But for him to understand how much this had meant to her? Well, if that wasn't a sure sign of love, she didn't know what was.

Of love?

She looked at him with shrewd eyes. Was it possible that he *loved* her?

As they reentered the living room, Chelsea's gaze was drawn to Mrs. Sinclair. Joel sat next to his grandmother, his arm around her.

All the years that Chelsea had liked and respected Mrs. Sinclair couldn't be negated by the discovery of what she'd been involved in… likely the entire time she'd known her. Chelsea touched Sam's arm. "What will happen to her?"

"She'll be interrogated, with her lawyer present, and charged. I expect she'll be released on bail, but it's in the hands of the FBI now." His eyes searched Chelsea's face. "It's serious, though. She'll do time."

Sympathy warred with outrage in Chelsea's heart.

Sympathy won out.

Feeling the sting of tears, she walked over to the sofa and crouched down in front of Mrs. Sinclair. She hadn't known what she intended to do and found herself apologizing to the old woman. After all, she was responsible in a way for what had just taken place.

Mrs. Sinclair's eyes met hers. "It isn't your fault, my dear. It was a middle-aged woman's folly and an old woman's greed that led me here."

Not understanding what Mrs. Sinclair meant, other than that she didn't hold Chelsea responsible, she shifted her gaze to Joel. Had he known what his grandmother was involved in? Had he been part of it? Could that have caused the preoccupation that she'd sensed in him that had contributed to the breakdown of their relationship?

The pain and horror etched on his face suggested that he hadn't known.

"Ms. Owens," someone called.

She glanced toward the sound of the voice and saw a tall, handsome, dark-skinned man, wearing a sharp suit, standing next to Special Agent Wilson. She'd been so focused on Mrs. Sinclair that she hadn't noticed the stranger when she'd returned to the room.

A quick look at Sam told her he didn't know who the man was, either.

Chelsea went to stand beside Sam, wanting to take strength and comfort from him.

The stranger joined them and introduced himself. "I'm Alan Lancaster, a representative of the Thompson Museum."

"We contacted Alan, once we knew we were onto something," Special Agent Wilson explained.

"It's a great pleasure to meet you both," Alan said. "I understand you're responsible for our being here today," he added, turning intense coal-black eyes on Chelsea.

She thought again about what would happen to Mrs. Sinclair—whether she deserved it or not—and her own part in it. She found it difficult to feel good about what was going on. "I suppose," she acknowledged in a subdued voice.

"I'm glad I got here before you left so I had

a chance to meet you," Alan said. "I need to go downstairs to verify which of the paintings stolen from the Thompson Museum are here. We'll have our experts authenticate them, but based on the information I've been given, there's no doubt in my mind that we have some of our treasures back. I look forward to seeing you both again," he concluded before heading toward the basement.

It was the middle of the afternoon before Chelsea went home. Sam had explained that he had to meet with Colin, the FBI special agents and Alan Lancaster at the police station, and then deal with report writing.

Chelsea felt terrible for Mrs. Sinclair and for Joel, but she still couldn't believe what she'd been part of. For more than a quarter of a century those paintings had been missing, eluding the FBI and the museum's security personnel, and *she'd* been the one to start the process of their recovery!

The thought of those paintings being back on the walls of the Thompson Museum, replacing the empty frames that had been in their place for more than twenty-five years—as a symbol of hope, awaiting the paintings' return—made her giddy with excitement.

"Thank you," she whispered to Sam when he

walked her to her car. "You have no idea how much it meant to me to see those paintings."

"I might not appreciate art, but I do have a pretty good idea what it means to you," he said, almost echoing her thoughts from earlier that day. He traced a fingertip gently along her cheek and touched his lips to hers.

"Thank you," she repeated in a whisper.

"You're welcome. I'll come and see you as soon as I can."

SAM ARRIVED AT Chelsea's apartment shortly after nine. The moment he stepped inside, she threw herself into his arms.

"How could this have happened?" she asked. "I've been sitting here, trying to make sense of it." She shook her head. "I can't. I can't get my mind around it. I can't even believe that all this is real. That it's not just a foolish dream and I'll wake up any minute!"

"I can assure you, it's not." He dropped a kiss on her temple. "We've got a confession from Nadine Sinclair."

"A confession? To what? Did she… Was she…"

Sam laughed. "Chels, if you want me to answer a question, you have to at least finish it."

She liked the familiar way he said her name. It implied intimacy and gave her hope. She took three deep breaths. "Okay, let me take your coat and make some coffee first."

While she hung up Sam's coat, Mindy strolled over to him. He picked up the cat, stroking her head as he followed Chelsea into the kitchen.

Chelsea did her best to contain her curiosity until the coffee was made and they were sitting in the living room, Mindy curled up on Sam's lap. Taking another deep breath, she willed herself to slow down and ask the questions one at a time. She started with the most burning and improbable question first. "Was Mrs. Sinclair involved in the Thompson heist?" She'd done the math in her head, and knew that Mrs. Sinclair would have been fifty-one when the theft had occurred.

Sam ran a finger across Chelsea's forehead.

"What are you doing?" she asked.

"Trying to smooth the worry lines."

"I can't help it. I'm upset about what's happening to Mrs. Sinclair. How did she get the paintings? *Was* she involved in the heist? What did she confess to?"

"I'm going to go out on a limb here," he said. "You have to promise not to say anything about any of this to anyone."

Chelsea rolled her eyes, but it was more

about form than irritation. "Here we go again. Yes, I promise."

"The Thompson Museum heist remains the biggest robbery of its kind to date, has stumped the FBI for decades and was perpetrated by a grandmother." Sam laughed, not with humor but with astonishment.

Chelsea leaned forward and grabbed his hand. "So, Mrs. Sinclair did do it? She *stole* the art from the museum?"

"Not on her own, no. But she was instrumental in it. She was in her early fifties at the time. Recently widowed after her husband, son and daughter-in-law died when the small plane they were taking for a ski trip crashed. She was already looking after Joel, as she was his only remaining family."

Chelsea nodded. Neither Mrs. Sinclair nor Joel liked to talk about the accident—understandably—but she knew about it, because Joel had shared the sad story with her.

"According to her, she came into some insurance money, but not enough to support a young boy and put him through college. She'd been working part-time at the Thompson Museum in their public relations department. After the accident, she accepted a full-time job as head of public relations and fund-raising. That allowed her to gain insight into the inner workings of the museum…including some of its vulnerabilities."

"She has a degree in fine art, and she'd always had a passion for art," Chelsea murmured. "Joel said that in her youth, she'd dreamed of being an artist."

Sam nodded. "Through one of the museum events she organized, she met a wealthy Saudi prince. He was very urbane, Americanized, as she described it. I expect she was still a very beautiful woman, and he wooed her…that was her word for it. She arranged for a private tour in exchange for a sizable donation to the museum. The prince, reportedly, had an extensive private collection in his home in the United Arab Emirates, but he developed a fascination with some of the works at the museum. When he asked if it would be possible to purchase those pieces, Mrs. Sinclair remembered that she'd laughed at his audacity. He was very accustomed to having anything he wanted. In retrospect, she believes that her response fueled his desire for the pieces he coveted. By then, she was completely enthralled by the prince. They started seeing each other, and he lavished her with attention and gifts."

"This all sounds like a fairy tale. Joel never

mentioned anything about his grandmother dating a prince. In fact, he'd always wondered why she never married again." Chelsea felt sad. "I thought it was because Joel's grandfather was her one great love."

"Obviously, that wasn't the case. I don't think Joel knew about it. He was young and likely still struggling with the grief over the loss of his family. Anyway, Mrs. Sinclair came up with the plan. The prince provided two of his trusted men to execute it. They were part of his personal security team. Americans, but handpicked to ensure loyalty and discretion. And extremely well paid for their services. When they had the paintings, the prince let her choose four pieces as a reward. Those are the other ones we saw in her basement. Once he had what he wanted, he broke off the relationship."

"He used her!" Chelsea exclaimed, indignant on Mrs. Sinclair's behalf.

"That's her take on it. She had her art but, of course, couldn't share it with anyone. As much as she regretted her actions afterward, she couldn't go to the authorities because she was fully culpable. She could no longer work at the museum for fear of inadvertently revealing her role in what had happened. To further ensure her silence, the prince gave her a large sum of money, which she used to leave Cambridge and open her gallery here."

"So why the forged paintings? How do they figure into all of this, and what's Adam Rochester's role in it?"

"She had these priceless works of art, but she couldn't share them with anyone nor could she sell them. The Manet was her favorite. She liked it so much that she wasn't satisfied with seeing it only occasionally when she indulged herself by spending time in her private vault. She commissioned a replica. Through her connections, she found an artist who's highly skilled and was known not to be too scrupulous about the assignments he accepted, if he was well paid. He replicated the painting for her. He worked from high resolution photographs."

"That's how it started?"

Sam nodded.

"How on earth did she and Adam get together, and why involve the gallery?"

"When the gallery began to flounder and not turn the profit it had in its earlier years, she was having trouble supporting herself, the large house she had, and the lifestyle and charitable giving she'd grown accustomed to while the prince's money lasted. I gather that having a lot of money had become integral to her sense of self-worth. She had in her possession stolen art worth tens of millions of dollars that she couldn't sell, even if she wanted to. The pieces she'd acquired through legal means she couldn't bear to part with, either.

"When Joel confided in her about Adam's drug problem, and his concern that he couldn't get him to seek help, Mrs. Sinclair offered to see what she could do. It was through her discussions with Adam that she discovered how severe his addiction was, and that he'd been stealing and selling items from his uncle's store to support his habit. But he always ensured that his aunt and uncle recouped the amounts from their insurance company. Adam didn't want to see them hurt. He also realized that he couldn't keep doing what he was because, sooner rather than later, the insurance company would catch on."

"And what about the forgeries?"

"It was Mrs. Sinclair who came up with the idea of selling originals on the black market and the forgeries through the gallery, thereby doubling the take on the paintings. She preyed on Adam's addiction to ensnare him, to force him to help her. The artist she'd used to replicate the Manet was more than willing to join in. He was also able to replicate some of the jewelry from All That Glitters and Shines, so the replicas could be sold in the store and the originals fenced."

"But art can't be fenced the way jewelry can, am I right?" Chelsea asked.

"Yes, you are. Which explains why the private show space was created in the warehouse. That's where they'd show the original pieces to black-market buyers."

"But how could they get away with that?"

"Until the Babineux, they'd gone for more moderately priced pieces. Ones for which insurance companies wouldn't require authentication."

"Why didn't they stay with that if it was working?" Chelsea still couldn't believe she wasn't in the middle of a bad nightmare.

"Mrs. Sinclair needed money and so did Adam. She wasn't willing to part with her works of art. In fact, if I read her correctly, her collection had become an obsession and she wanted to add to it. As for Adam, his addiction drove him. Out of desperation, Mrs. Sinclair reached out to the prince to see if he'd give her more money, but he categorically refused. More than twenty years had passed since she'd last spoken to him. He saw her as ancient history and no longer of interest. To him, she was an old woman with no value. When she threatened to go to the police, despite her own role in the Thompson heist—telling him she'd claim that she'd been coerced—he still refused to give her cash. But to ensure her ongoing silence, he offered her one of the Thompson paintings that he personally had grown tired of."

"The Tempest on the Ocean?"

"That's right."

"Why was it shipped to the warehouse, instead of her home?"

"Good question. She wanted to have it replicated, so she could have the original in her vault but the replica on her walls for others to admire."

"And I found the painting before it had been transferred to her private collection."

"So it seems. And after it had been replicated."

"What happened to everything else I'd seen in the warehouse?"

"That first night you entered, Adam was there. He'd recognized your car and had seen you inside, too, through the window."

"The footprints I saw in the snow were his?"

"Correct. Mrs. Sinclair instructed him and the artist, who was using the space to replicate the works, to empty the warehouse. I caught

Adam when he was there to move everything out of the warehouse, which is why he needed Joel's SUV. The crates wouldn't fit in his car. But I interrupted him and he was spooked. He was afraid to come back the same evening, worried about possible surveillance, but he did return in the middle of the following night."

"After I left?"

"Yes. A couple of hours later."

Chelsea nodded slowly, trying to absorb everything she'd heard.

"Occasionally they received legitimate shipments there, so Adam rekeyed the warehouse at Mrs. Sinclair's behest, to prevent Joel from accidently discovering what they were doing."

"But Mr. Hadley had the new key, too. Is he part of all this?"

Sam shook his head. "No, he isn't. Mrs. Sinclair had to give him a key for those times when the warehouse had to be accessed for legitimate purposes. She trusted he wouldn't use it unless she asked him to. And they could ensure that there was nothing amiss anytime she needed him to go there. When I asked how they would have handled it if Joel had confronted them about the lock having been rekeyed, she admitted that they hadn't thought that through, but would have come up with something, if the need arose. Fortunately for them, he hadn't and they were looking for a new place from which to operate."

"They could have gotten away with what they were doing, but ultimately greed got the better of them."

"Perhaps," Sam acknowledged.

"Now what? I mean, what about the rest of the stolen pieces, the ones that are still in the prince's possession?"

"The FBI is working on it. They'll have to jump through some international hoops, but my bet is they'll get the paintings back."

"And the prince? What about him?"

Sam shrugged. "I doubt they'll be able to extradite him, since he's part of the royal family. He'll never be able to set foot on US soil again, but there likely won't be major consequences for him."

"And how does any of this connect with the robbery at All That Glitters and Shines?"

"Good question. I'd originally thought that the break-in was intended to test police-response times for a more significant robbery. That's what got me looking at the gallery to begin with. But that's not what was going on at all. The morning of the robbery, Adam had been out all night. He was low on money and needed a fix. He simply wanted to steal a few pieces of jewelry that he could quickly fence, which is why he didn't take any of the most valuable pieces. He also figured his uncle would recover the cost from the insurance company."

Chelsea's eyes widened. "Adam hurt his uncle?"

Sam nodded. "He said he didn't intend to. When he found his uncle there, Adam claims he panicked. Quite likely, as he hadn't used for a while. He said hitting his uncle was an accident, and when he realized what he'd done, he tripped the panic alarm. He said he wanted to make sure his uncle would get medical help fast. My opinion is that it wasn't accidental, but it wasn't premeditated, either. It was impulsive, and it was rage and disgust at himself for hurting his uncle that then drove him to cause such extensive damage in the store."

Chelsea shook her head. "I can't believe all this. I never would have thought it possible of Adam *or* Mrs. Sinclair."

Sam looked sheepish. "I briefly wondered if you could've been responsible for the jewelry store robbery, because of the way you burst onto the crime scene. There are many documented cases of perpetrators returning to the scene, and…well…it seemed so unusual for you to storm into the store the way you did…"

Chelsea couldn't hold back a smile. "I'm glad you only wondered about that for a brief time. But Adam came to the store, too!"

"Yes, he did," Sam acknowledged. "But we contacted him at his uncle's behest."

"It's all very distressing," Chelsea murmured. Her heart broke for Mrs. Sinclair, in particular. Had she done what she did for the love of a man or had it been about greed all along? Love must have been the original motivation, Chelsea decided, and how sad for Mrs. Sinclair to discover that her love was unrequited.

"Well, it's over," he said, obviously trying to draw her out of her melancholy mood.

She forced a smile. "I know. Believe me, I'm glad. And relieved."

"Then what's wrong? Talk to me," he encouraged, when she remained silent.

"I feel sorry for Mrs. Sinclair." She raised one hand before he could respond. "I know what she did was illegal, but I can't help feeling sorry for her. She's seventy-eight. The thought of her going to jail at that age… She's always been kind and considerate to me. She gave me an opportunity at the gallery when I had no experience."

"You have a soft heart, Chelsea." He leaned closer and brushed his lips gently across hers.

"There's a line between right and wrong. When someone steps over it, there have to be consequences."

"Wouldn't it be enough for her to give the paintings back? Perhaps make a donation to the museum?" Chelsea scratched at the handle of her coffee mug. "Yeah. I know that won't do it," she said grudgingly.

"There's something else bothering you. I can see it. Do you want to talk about it?"

"I suppose I'm feeling lost. Rudderless, so to speak." She smiled weakly. "You know how I've been working toward being the next curator of the gallery?"

He nodded.

"That's how I've always lived my life. I set a goal and work toward it. It's always been important to me to be goal-oriented." She sighed heavily. "I loved the Sinclair Gallery. From the day I started there, I dreamed of being its curator. I've worked hard to prove myself. Mr. Hadley was supportive and encouraging. With less than two years to his retirement, I was sure I'd be ready and the gallery would be mine to run." She lifted her hands, let them drop into her lap again. "Now? I have no idea what'll happen to the gallery. Joel called me after he left Mrs. Sinclair's house. He's heartbroken about his grandmother." She angled her head. "He isn't involved, is he? I don't think he knew what his grandmother was doing."

"I can't say for certain. The FBI will be investigating him, but his grandmother claims he had nothing to do with any of it. That's how it looks to me, as well."

"That's something, at least." She nodded. It wasn't a categorical no, but it gave her hope.

"You're worried about Joel, too?"

Chelsea nearly smiled as she sensed a bit of jealousy. "Well, yes. I'm concerned about him as a friend, but it's also the gallery I'm worried about. We might all be out of a job."

"You believe the harm to its reputation will be insurmountable?"

Now she smiled. "Actually, I think just the opposite. If it's cleverly done, the connection to the Thompson heist could be turned to the gallery's advantage. The whole mystery and intrigue surrounding the theft could be capitalized on to draw people in."

He took her hand. Linked his fingers with hers. "Then why are you worried?"

"Joel talked to me about it because he didn't know who else to turn to. He'll probably sell the gallery. If he can't sell it, he'll close it. He's never been a fan of art. All he really cared about was his grandmother and his inheritance. Now that I know the gallery has been a money-losing enterprise, I understand why he was so concerned about Mrs. Sinclair's finances and the deteriorating condition of her home. The gallery was depleting her resources and the value of what would eventually come to him." She fidgeted with the hem of her sweater. "We also talked about what happened between us. I now understand his change in demeanor and his preoccupation near the end of our relationship. He might not have known what his grandmother was involved in, but he sensed there was something going on. He was worried about her, but also hurt that she'd shut him out, when they'd always been close.

"He won't reopen the gallery. He'll try to get what he can out of it, but he won't reopen it," she repeated sadly. "So not only did my chance to become curator go…" She made a *pfft* noise and snapped her fingers. "I'll be out of a job, too. There aren't a lot of art galleries in Camden Falls," she said with a harsh laugh. "My options are to find another career…or move to Boston." The thought of that—and leaving

Sam—caused a sharp pain in her chest. She *loved* Sam.

He wasn't unaffected by her, either, she mused. She could see it from the look on his face.

Chelsea dropped her head back against the cushions and closed her eyes. "How could Joel not want to own the gallery?" She shifted her head toward Sam, and she didn't hide the intensity of her feelings. "What a dream that would be! Not just to *manage* the gallery, but to own it! To decide what to buy and when. How to display the works to maximum effect. To plan showings and events. Oh, my gosh, what a thrill that would be! So much more than just managing it. To have complete and unfettered control." The passion with which she'd started to speak diminished, and she ended on a quiet sigh. "I'm out of a job. The gallery I love so much will close."

Chelsea jolted at the sudden, forceful knock at her door. Mindy was startled awake, too. She leaped off Sam's lap, but not before digging her claws into his thighs, judging by the hiss he let out and the grimace on his face.

Chelsea glanced at her watch. It was after ten. She couldn't imagine who would be at her door that late in the evening. Suddenly fearful that there might be something wrong with Mr. or Mrs. Bennett, she rushed to the door and flung it open.

Relieved that it wasn't one of her neighbors, she wondered why the representative from the museum, whom she'd met briefly at Mrs. Sinclair's home, was at her door.

Sam stepped up beside her and she reached for his hand. "Mr. Lancaster, what can I do for you?"

"May I come in?"

Sam squeezed her hand reassuringly.

"Yes, please." She opened the door farther. With no idea what he wanted—and part of her feeling anxious that she was in some sort of trouble—her manners still overrode all else. "May I take your coat?"

"Thank you, but that won't be necessary. I won't be staying long," he assured her. "Ms. Owens, as I said earlier, you're responsible for what happened today," he added. "For the Thompson Museum recovering five of the stolen pieces, including *The Tempest on the Ocean*, and with a very viable lead to recover the rest."

"Well, um…"

Sam gave her a not-too-gentle nudge. She glanced up at him and caught his encouraging grin.

"I don't have the words to tell you how much I appreciated being there today. Thank you."

"We're the ones who can't thank *you* enough."

"Oh, no, it's not—"

Before she could finish her sentence, Sam rested a hand on her shoulder. "Let the man finish," he whispered in her ear.

Alan must have noticed the interplay, because he grinned at her. He reached into the inside pocket of his coat and withdrew a pale gray envelope with the Thompson Museum logo on the top left corner and her name in the center.

"I had to speak to the Thompson Museum's curator as final authorization before I released this to you. Here you go," he said, offering her the envelope.

She turned a questioning look at Sam as she accepted it. He was grinning, too. Not knowing what to expect, she felt her stomach clench. "What's this?" she asked in a barely audible voice.

"Open it and find out," Alan told her.

With shaking fingers, Chelsea broke the seal

on the envelope and reached in to pull out its contents. She unfolded the sheet of paper.

"Oh, my God!" she exclaimed, and was glad that Sam was beside her so she could lean on him. He wrapped an arm around her waist to steady her. The check that had been folded inside fluttered as she held it in her hand. Wide-eyed, she looked at Alan. "I…I don't understand…"

"The museum has been offering a reward for the return of the stolen masterpieces for more years than I've worked there. You were instrumental in their return. That's your reward."

"But…but…" Her voice cracked, and she cleared her throat in embarrassment. "But this is *two million* dollars!"

"Yes, it is. That's forty percent of the reward. If we're able to recover the remaining pieces from the Saudi prince, it will be my great pleasure to present you with the remainder of the five-million-dollar reward."

Chelsea gaped at him.

"Well, I've completed my final task for the day." Alan held his hand out to Chelsea. When she placed hers in his, he covered it with his other hand. "Sincere and heartfelt thanks not only from me and the management of the museum, but from art lovers the world over."

After Chelsea closed the door behind Alan, she leaned against it and stared at Sam. "Can you believe this?" She narrowed her eyes. "You don't look surprised. You *knew* about it?"

He nodded and kissed her parted lips. "I knew about the reward, but I also knew that they'd have to authenticate the paintings. It might not be my field of expertise, but I thought they did it rather quickly."

"Yes, that's true."

Chelsea glanced again at the check in her hand. She couldn't believe what was happening. At a loss for words, she threw herself into Sam's arms for the second time that evening.

He held her tight for a long moment, then cupping her face with his hands, he smiled down at her. "Chelsea, you are the most remarkable woman I have known in my life." He brushed his lips over hers. "We met under less than normal circumstances, but I'm so happy we did meet." He kissed her again. "I never thought I'd say these words again. Chelsea… I love you."

Chelsea blinked rapidly so she could see his face through the tears that swam in her eyes.

She placed her palms on his cheeks and finally said the words that she'd known in her heart for some time. "Oh, Sam, I love you, too!"

EPILOGUE

LARGE FLAKES OF SNOW drifted gently down as Sam lifted the three large bags from the trunk of his car. He held Chelsea's gloved hand as they walked past the white picket fence and up the driveway to Paige and Daniel's house. It was Christmas Eve, and they were spending it with Paige and Daniel, Jason and Emily at the Kinsleys' home, along with all of Paige and Chelsea's friends.

Jason opened the door for them, and his eyes rounded when he saw the bags of gifts.

"Hey, squirt!" Chelsea greeted him with a hug.

"Hi, Aunt Chelsea. Hello, Sam. Is there anything in those for me?" he asked, pointing to the bags.

Chelsea tugged gently on his hair. "There might be. Have you been good this year?"

"Aw, c'mon, Aunt Chels!"

"All right. I'll take that as a yes," she said as they brushed the snow off their coats and boots before stepping into the vestibule.

Scout darted out of the living room, followed by Paige.

"Chelsea!" Paige exclaimed and rushed over to embrace her, then rested her hands on Chelsea's shoulders. "You look wonderful."

"Is that so hard to believe?" she teased as she reached down to scratch Scout's ears.

Paige laughed. "Well, with everything you've been through these past weeks, I thought you might be a little tired. So, how does it feel to be the new owner of the Sinclair Gallery?"

"Excuse me, but it's now the *Chelsea* Gallery," she said with mock haughtiness, then grinned. "Quite spectacular, although it doesn't seem real yet."

"I think it's great news that the second half of the reward money came through so quickly after the recovery of the remaining works of art, and you were able to close the deal before Christmas. What a wonderful way to start the new year. As a gallery owner!" Paige's voice softened. "I also think it's wonderful and generous of you to pay Charles Hadley the salary he would've earned over the next two years so he could retire early and move back to England to be with his nephew."

"Honestly, it wasn't that much and not entirely altruistic, since it gives me a completely free hand in restructuring the gallery."

"Say what you will, I know you did it more for him than for yourself." Paige took another appraising glance at Chelsea. "Not only do you *not* look tired, you look very happy." She turned to Sam and gave him a hug, too. "And speaking of which, I'll bet you're the reason for it. Thank you for joining our celebration this evening."

Entering the living room, Chelsea realized that they were the last to arrive. Laura and Harrison Weatherly were sitting by the fire, baby Emily nestled in Laura's lap. Emily was in an elf onesie, complete with an elf hat. And the staid and conservative Mr. Weatherly was cooing to the baby. Chelsea had to blink to make sure she wasn't imagining it.

Jason ran over to sit on the floor next to Mrs. Bennett's chair and resumed playing a card game with her. Daniel was setting the table, and Paige excused herself to go back into the kitchen to finish preparations.

Chelsea knew that the next day Paige and Daniel and the kids would be visiting their parents—just like she and Sam had agreed to split the day between their respective families. But tonight was about friendship.

This was her family, Chelsea thought, as much as her mother and father were. Not of blood, but of love. That brought to mind her discussion with Sam about his determination not to pass on the recessive gene he carried for spinal muscular atrophy. She was glad she'd had the chance to assure him that to her, adopting children—who would be theirs because of love rather than blood—would be perfect.

Sam's fingers were linked with hers, and she curled hers around his more tightly. It reminded her of when she'd first met him and how she'd wondered what it would feel like to do exactly what she was doing now. It felt perfect!

Dinner was served soon afterward, and it was a boisterous and joyous affair. As had become tradition, Daniel and Paige announced that Jason's most recent checkup revealed that he remained cancer-free. Everyone cheered and clinked their glasses together. And two years to the day after Harrison and Laura had announced that they were engaged, they jubilantly proclaimed that they were adopting a child from Guam.

Chelsea couldn't have been happier for her friends. She and Sam gave each other a meaningful look, reaffirming their belief in adoption.

After dinner, everyone gathered in the living

room around the fireplace again and exchanged gifts. When all the gifts had been unwrapped and all the thanks had been given, Sam tapped his temple. "I can't believe it! I left one of my gifts in the car."

Chelsea had wondered why she hadn't received anything from him, but assumed he was saving his gift to her for Christmas morning. She'd given him a cashmere sweater and a new winter coat, but she still had another gift for him once they were alone.

"Excuse me, everyone, while I go outside to get it," Sam said and left the room.

He returned a few minutes later with a large rectangular object wrapped in bright foil paper. Based on its shape and size, it didn't take a genius to figure out that his gift had to be a painting. Chelsea felt a moment's unease worrying about Sam's taste—or lack thereof—in art, but repressed it quickly. If that was the biggest issue between them, a difference in taste and in their appreciation of art, she could consider herself fortunate.

All eyes were on her as Sam handed her the gift-wrapped package. Jason scrambled over, his interest obvious. "I know what it is, Aunt Chelsea! I know what it is!"

"Well, don't spoil it for me, squirt," she said

good-naturedly, giving him a gentle nudge. She fixed a smile on her face as she carefully peeled away the paper.

The only sounds were the strains of "All I Want for Christmas Is You" playing in the background and the wood crackling in the fireplace, as Chelsea removed another strip of paper. The colors she could see were muted and gray-toned, not the bright, cheerful colors she preferred.

She glanced up at Sam. The joy and excitement written all over his face nearly stopped her heart. She loved him so much, but why did he have to give her a *painting*, knowing their tastes ran in very different directions? And in front of her friends and neighbors? If that first glimpse of it was any indication and it turned out to be as depressing as she feared, how was she going to mask her reaction to it? The last thing she wanted to do was hurt or embarrass Sam.

She peeled off another strip of paper. What she saw was even gloomier. She'd just have to unwrap the whole darn thing and brave it out.

Removing another piece of the wrapping paper, what she saw struck a chord in her memory. Uncertain…even apprehensive, she locked eyes with Sam.

He grinned at her foolishly.

She might as well get it over with, she decided as she peeled away the last of the wrapping…and stared with disbelief at the painting.

Jason bounced on his toes. "Let's see it!"

"Sam…I don't understand?" Chelsea murmured.

"Here," Sam said, grabbing a dining-room chair and facing it toward the living room. "Why don't you put the painting here so everyone can see?"

Not knowing if she could or should say anything, she did as he suggested. When she'd positioned the canvas and moved out of the way, no one spoke, but Mrs. Bennett let out a snort.

Chelsea sent her a cautionary frown.

Mrs. Bennett seemed unapologetic. "I'm sorry, but my age entitles me to honesty. That's a rather depressing-looking painting, Sam. Why on earth would you have bought it for our Chelsea?"

"Mrs. Bennett!" Chelsea exclaimed, horrified. "This is…" she hesitated and made eye contact with Sam. "This is Rembrandt's *The Tempest on the Ocean*."

He had a huge grin on his face and took a step closer to the painting.

She continued to hold his gaze as she sat

back down on the sofa. "This…this isn't the original."

He chuckled, ignoring Mrs. Bennett's question and Chelsea's comment. "What do *you* think of it, Jason?" he asked.

"I don't know if Jason should critique other people's work," Paige interjected, obviously not wanting him to offend Sam by expressing his opinion.

"It's okay. I'm interested in his reaction…as an artist." Sam winked at Jason.

"How sweet," Paige commented. "Would anyone like more coffee?"

"Jason," Sam continued, "Why don't you come have a closer look?"

"Wait. What's that?" Jason asked, scooting up to the canvas and pointing to the bottom center. "Aunt Chelsea, come see!"

With unsteady legs, she rose and walked over to the chair, kneeling in front of it, next to Jason.

"See! Right there." Jason pointed again, nearly touching the painting.

Chelsea saw it, as well. Affixed to the painting, appearing to be held in the outstretched hand of the man on the canvas, was something shiny. The sudden pounding of her heart echoed in her ears and drowned out the music in the background.

She looked up at Sam.

"What? You don't like it?" he asked, still grinning.

When she touched the object, it dropped into her hand. She stared down at her palm and the diamond ring that sparkled there.

"I… don't understand," she said, swiping at the moisture on her cheeks with her free hand.

Sam knelt beside her. "It's an engagement ring." He picked up the ring. "Knowing how much your friends, *family* really, mean to you— and figuring you'd be less likely to turn me down in front of them—I thought this would be the most appropriate way to ask you to marry me. So…" He took her left hand in his. "Chelsea Owens, will you marry me?"

Chelsea looked at the loving and expectant faces of her friends. An unorthodox proposal, yes. Risky—and possibly embarrassing—if she did say no, but so very right for her. To share this moment with the people who meant the most to her, after her parents. How did she get this lucky? To have these wonderful people in her life, loving her and caring about her.

And to have such an incredible man love her and want to spend the rest of his life with her.

"Aunt Chels." Jason tugged on her sleeve. "I think Sam wants an answer."

Her laughter burst out as she looked back at Sam. "I'm sorry. I was trying to take it all in." While she deeply appreciated that he'd included her friends, she wanted her answer to be for him alone at first. She leaned in and spoke in his ear. "Oh, yes!"

Jason tugged her sleeve again. "We couldn't hear you!"

Chelsea looked down at Jason and ruffled his hair. "I said yes!" she declared so everyone could hear her this time.

To a chorus of cheers and congratulations, Sam swept Chelsea into his arms and kissed her. "I'm a very lucky man to have found you. I love you," he murmured.

"I love you, too," she whispered, returning his kiss. "And the painting? I know it's not the original."

He chuckled. "Definitely not. Not on the salary of one of Camden Falls's finest. The original *The Tempest on the Ocean* is now in its rightful place at the Thompson Museum, thanks to you. But the FBI recovered the replica that Mrs. Sinclair had commissioned, and this is it."

Chelsea turned her attention to the painting. A flawless reproduction in every way.

"With the investigation over, I was able to acquire it for you. I thought it might be an interesting addition for the Chelsea Gallery."

She was at a loss for words again, and her eyes misted. "Are you serious? Do you have any idea what displaying this painting could mean for my gallery?"

He shrugged. "Well, I remember you saying that if spun the right way, your gallery's connection to the Thompson heist could be of benefit. You also said when we were leaving Nadine Sinclair's private vault that it was a shame not to have beautiful pieces of art on display to be appreciated. You and I might have differing views on what is beautiful, but this painting could have languished in an FBI evidence storage room. No, it's not the original and it's not worth millions," he said, "but it's yours."

She briefly glanced to where Sam had ingeniously fastened her engagement ring. Turning back to Sam, she said, "It's not the original, but to me, it's priceless!" And in a softer voice, she added, "And so is what we've found. Together."

* * * * *

Get 2 Free Books,
Plus 2 Free Gifts—
just for trying the Reader Service!

Get 2 Free Books,
Plus 2 Free Gifts—
just for trying the
Reader Service!

YES! Please send me 2 FREE Love Inspired® Suspense novels and my 2 FREE mystery gifts (gifts are worth about $10 retail). After receiving them, if I don't wish to receive any more books, I can return the shipping statement marked "cancel." If I don't cancel, I will receive 4 brand-new novels every month and be billed just $5.24 each for the regular-print edition or $5.74 each for the larger-print edition in the U.S., or $5.74 each for the regular-print edition or $6.24 each for the larger-print edition in Canada. That's a savings of at least 13% off the cover price. It's quite a bargain! Shipping and handling is just 50¢ per book in the U.S. and 75¢ per book in Canada.* I understand that accepting the 2 free books and gifts places me under no obligation to buy anything. I can always return a shipment and cancel at any time. The free books and gifts are mine to keep no matter what I decide.

Please check one: ☐ Love Inspired Suspense Regular-Print   ☐ Love Inspired Suspense Larger-Print
                      (153/353 IDN GLW2)   (107/307 IDN GLW2)

Name   (PLEASE PRINT)

Address   Apt. #

City   State/Prov.   Zip/Postal Code

Signature (if under 18, a parent or guardian must sign)

Mail to the **Reader Service:**
IN U.S.A.: P.O. Box 1341, Buffalo, NY 14240-8531
IN CANADA: P.O. Box 603, Fort Erie, Ontario L2A 5X3

Want to try two free books from another line?
Call 1-800-873-8635 or visit www.ReaderService.com.

* Terms and prices subject to change without notice. Prices do not include applicable taxes. Sales tax applicable in N.Y. Canadian residents will be charged applicable taxes. Offer not valid in Quebec. This offer is limited to one order per household. Books received may not be as shown. Not valid for current subscribers to Love Inspired Suspense books. All orders subject to approval. Credit or debit balances in a customer's account(s) may be offset by any other outstanding balance owed by or to the customer. Please allow 4 to 6 weeks for delivery. Offer available while quantities last.

Your Privacy—The Reader Service is committed to protecting your privacy. Our Privacy Policy is available online at www.ReaderService.com or upon request from the Reader Service.

We make a portion of our mailing list available to reputable third parties that offer products we believe may interest you. If you prefer that we not exchange your name with third parties, or if you wish to clarify or modify your communication preferences, please visit us at www.ReaderService.com/consumerschoice or write to us at Reader Service Preference Service, P.O. Box 9062, Buffalo, NY 14240-9062. Include your complete name and address.

LIS17R2

Get 2 Free Books,
Plus 2 Free Gifts—
just for trying the
Reader Service!

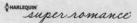

READERSERVICE.COM

Manage your account online!

- Review your order history
- Manage your payments
- Update your address

> *We've designed the*
> *Reader Service website*
> *just for you.*

Enjoy all the features!

- Discover new series available to you, and read excerpts from any series.
- Respond to mailings and special monthly offers.
- Browse the Bonus Bucks catalog and online-only exculsives.
- Share your feedback.

Visit us at:

ReaderService.com

RS16R